*Personal Leave*
*TOP SHELF*
*An imprint of Torquere Press Publishers*
*PO Box 2545*
*Round Rock, TX 78680*
*Copyright © 2006, Sean Michael*
*Cover illustration by Atta Vazzy*
*Published with permission*
*ISBN: 1-934166-37-5, 978-1-934166-37-6*
*www.torquerepress.com*

# Personal Leave
## By Sean Michael

## Chapter One

Rock unfolded himself out of Decker's fucking tiny Honda and shouldered his bag. He waved Decker and his wife off.

"Enjoy your downtime, Sarge," Decker called out.

"You, too."

Rock shook his head and chuckled. Damn, but the kids were getting younger every year. And he was getting so these training missions were a pain in the ass. He was spoiled was what he was, fed three of the best squares a day he'd ever eaten by the sexiest fucker alive who had an ass with his name stamped all over it.

He headed up the front walk, grinning as he heard Grim, Rigger's huge mutt, barking his fool head off. He was in for a tongue bath. Of course the dog wasn't the one he wanted it from.

He swung his bag around as he opened the door, letting Grim jump on that instead of him. "Go on, you act like I've been gone for months instead of two weeks." Chuckling, he scratched Grimmy behind the ears. "Silly mutt."

Grimmy barked and whined, pushing right into his hands. He could hear the music coming from the kitchen, hear the washing machine rattling along and a deep Southern drawl cussing something.

He wandered in, found long, long, long legs in skin-tight jeans sticking out from under the kitchen sink. His cock went hard at the sight -- two weeks was a long time when a man was missing the best blowjobs the world had to offer.

He crouched down next to the sink, hand reaching out to touch the flat belly. "Problems?"

The tight muscles jerked, a dull clunk and a "shit" floating out into the kitchen. Then Rig started sliding out, a little, blond mustache appearing before bright grey eyes. "Hey, Blue!"

He shook his head, grinning as he reached out to slide a finger along the lip fur -- that was new. "Hey, Rig. You got a welcome home for me?"

Those amazing, fucking lips wrapped around the tip of his finger, the suction immediate and just fine.

Rock groaned, muscles going tight. "Oh, fuck, yes." Christ, he'd missed this, missed Rig. He held those grey eyes, letting Rig know. Rig's teeth scraped along the pad of his finger, the nerves there lighting up and echoing in his prick. He growled a little, earning them Grimmy's attention. He pushed the dog away with his free hand. "Yours isn't the tongue I'm interested in, mutt."

Rig chuckled, bit the tip of his finger. "Ah, Grimmy isn't going to get the love?"

Rock snorted. "He got plenty of love when I came in. And I'll bet he got plenty of love from you while I was gone." As long as there wasn't any dog hair on the sheets.

"He did okay." Rig chuckled, eyes dragging over him, slow enough that he could almost feel it.

"You miss me?" he asked, flexing a little. If he was standing he'd be strutting.

"I might have spent a few nights with my hand, yeah." Rig licked his lips, bare belly going tight.

Rock watched that tongue sliding over Rig's lips, his focus sudden and sharp. "Just a few?" he asked, leaning in, his own tongue sliding where Rig's had been. He groaned at the scent and taste of pure Rig.

"Mmmhmm." Rig opened up, pushed right into his kiss like the man was starving, pure and simple.

He slid out of his crouch onto his knees, hands sliding over Rig's back and down to cup that fine ass. Heat and want hit him like a wave, making him groan into their kiss.

Rig pulled back a little, panting. "My hands are filthy, man. I've been working."

"Your mouth seems to be working just fine," he pointed out. Man didn't need his hands for sucking.

"You haven't gotten any less observant since you've been gone." Smartassed redneck.

Rock chuckled and shook his head and stood, groaning a little as he stretched up, hands over his head. Let Rig get a good long look at what he'd been missing for a couple of weeks and see how smartass he was feeling then.

Rig watched every move, teeth sunk into that bottom lip, thighs parting a little, cock filling in those tight jeans.

Yeah, that's the look he wanted. He let his own eyes range over that long body. "I'm about two seconds from tossing you over my shoulder."

"I can't wash my hands in here until I get the pipe reattached, Rocketman."

Rock rolled his eyes. He'd just spent two weeks rolling around in the mud and Rig was worried about a bit of dirt on his hands. "I don't give a shit." He reached down and hauled Rig up, taking that mouth, letting Rig know he meant it.

His own personal cowboy just pushed into him, rubbing and sliding, hands tugging his T-shirt right out of his waistband. Now that was what he'd been expecting. Wanting. He moaned into Rig's mouth, hands finding that ass again, rubbing them together.

The kiss went deep, sharp, Rig fucking stealing his breath and making his heart pound. Nobody on Earth kissed like that man. Rock gave back as good as he was getting, taking no prisoners. Rig's hands slid up under his shirt and he groaned, his own fingers sliding along the long spine.

"Mmmhmm. Wanting you." Rig nipped his bottom lip, hard enough to feel it down to his toes.

Rock growled a little, hands finding Rig's ass and tugging him close. "I've got what you want right here. Gonna give it to you." And then they were going to fuck in the shower and then in bed and then he was going to sleep for twelve fucking hours.

"Yeah, you do that." Rig chuckled and rubbed, legs wrapping right around him and squeezing tight.

He held onto Rig's ass, squeezing it, holding his lover's weight easily. He was tired from two weeks of training, but he wasn't *that* tired.

He found the spot on Rig's neck that made the man wild, sucking and licking it, careful not to leave a mark. That earned him a shitload of little moans, Rig's hips rolling, finding a sweet, solid rhythm against his belly.

"Skin," he muttered, following the line of Rig's collarbone; his own hands were a little busy for undoing zippers. He squeezed Rig's ass again.

"Mmmhmm." Rigger fished his cock out, fingers wrapping right around it and squeezing.

"Oh, fuck." He nodded, lips meeting Rig's, tongue pushing in as his prick pushed through Rig's fingers. His Rabbit knew where to touch, how to make him growl and jerk and shake. "You, too," he muttered, wanting to feel the silky heat of Rig's prick next to his own.

"Yeah." Rig leaned back, trusting his touch, unbuttoning those tight jeans. Rock fucking loved that, the way Rig knew he wouldn't be dropped, not by him.

He watched Rig's prick push through the open zipper and groaned. Hell, yeah, that's what he needed, the two of them hot and hard and sliding together. The smell of horny redneck hit him like a runaway train, made his balls draw up tight and right. Made him ache.

"Fuck. Soon." His whole body jerked as Rig wrapped a hand around both their pricks, the heat fucking amazing. His hips sawed, his hands tugging Rig tight against him.

"Uh-huh. Give it up." Rig stretched, rubbing good and hard, body tight as a board.

"For you," he groaned, hips bucking as he came hard, his spunk hot between them.

Rig hummed, kissing him and licking his lips, murmuring as that hand kept moving, made slick and wet. He pushed one hand into the back of Rig's jeans, squeezing the warm flesh. "Come on now. It's your turn and then I'll fuck you up against the tiles."

"Mmm... shower sex." Rig shivered, winked, those grey eyes happy and dancing.

He laughed, tickled and pleased as fuck to be home. "Shower sex. You notice I offered that before I asked for a blowjob."

"I noticed. You're good to me, Blue Eyes."

"Well, I guess that goes both ways." He started down the hall, carrying his Rabbit easily. "There is chocolate pie in the fridge, isn't there?"

"There is. Made it yesterday after Coleman called."

Rock hummed happily. Oh yeah, now he knew he was home.

He got them into the bathroom and set Rig down on his feet. Once his hands were free he cupped Rig's face and looked at it. Just looked. Yeah. Mouth to die for. Thin nose. Silly mustache that could go now he was home. Blond curls. And grey eyes that looked at him like he was a fucking god.

He brought their lips together, touching softly. Rig hummed, the kiss starting off easy and getting deep.

That 'stache tickled his lips, his nose and he growled a little. "That's gotta go, Rig."

"Hmm?" Rig hummed, licking at his lips, distracted.

He chuckled. He'd get it later. For now, this was more important. He chased Rig's tongue down and began to suck on it, fingers sliding to push the tight jeans down over Rig's hips. Those tight, almost white curls covered the base of Rig's cock, the scent of want and heat just exactly what he needed.

He slid his hand along Rig's prick. It was hot silk and fit in his hand better than his own. "Want you."

"I'm all yours, Blue. Fuck me."

"Hell, yes."

He pushed off his own jeans, helped Rig step the rest of the way out of his. Then he pushed Rig into the shower, turning it on so the water fell on them, hot and wet, flavoring their kiss. Rig made all these sweet, little noises, just pushed them into his lips as they slid together. He slid his hands over Rig's skin, the water making it slick, letting his fingers just slide. He found one of Rig's nipples, tugged on it, wanting more of those noises that belonged to him.

"Fuck. Want. Goddamn." Rig arched, hands reaching up to wrap around the showerhead.

Oh, fuck, just look at that. It stretched Rig out for him, and he touched every bit of Rig he could touch, mouth sliding on Rig's skin, sucking the water right off it.

"Jim. Rock. Fuck. I need." Rig was almost shaking with it, lips open, water pouring down.

"I've got what you need right here." He rubbed against Rig and then slid his hands up along Rig's arms, loosening those fingers from around the showerhead. "Turn around, Rabbit." He put Rig's hands on the tile.

Oh, look at that ass. Rock slid his fingers down Rig's spine, watching all the way down. He spread Rig's ass cheeks, the water dripping along Rig's crease, teasing. Groaning, he went to his knees and licked from the base of Rig's back down to his balls, those long legs parting for him, Rig just begging for it.

"Oh, sweet fuck. Rocketman."

"Uh-huh." He licked again, and pointed his tongue, breaching the tight, little hole.

Rig groaned, that ring of muscles squeezing his tongue, Rig's cry ringing out. Humming, he started fucking Rig's ass with his tongue, spreading and slicking Rig's hole, getting it ready for his cock.

The water kept pouring around them, hot and wet, the scent of Rig rising and fading as the water slid over his tongue.

"Rock. Rock. Fuck. Don't stop. I. Shit." Mmm. That's it. Just give it up.

He didn't plan to stop until he'd made Rig come and then he was going to fuck the tight, little hole until he was lost in it. He pushed his tongue in further, one hand sliding up between Rig's legs to cup those balls and move on Rig's hot prick.

"Blue..." Rig started moving faster, rocking between his tongue and his touch, the soft cries just ringing out.

He traced Rig's prick with his fingers, loving the heat of it, the softness of the skin. There were veins and bumps, the head round, tip leaking with more than just water from the shower. Circling Rig's cock, he let it slide along his palm, groaning at the way the head seemed to expand as it pushed out through his fingers.

"Gonna. Oh, sweet fuck. Gonna, Blue." Rig arched, hands scrabbling at the tiles.

Yeah, that was the fucking idea. He stabbed into Rig's ass, hand tightening around the sweet prick. Give it up.

Heat poured over his fingers, Rig's hips pumping gracelessly. Oh, yeah. Just fucking like that.

He kept fucking with his tongue until Rig stopped pushing into his hand and then he stood, mouth dragging up along Rig's spine, taking in the taste of water and of Rig's skin beneath that. He spread those cheeks with his fingers and nudged at the little hole, slick with his saliva, his Rabbit ready for him.

Rig didn't say a word, just arched and pushed back against his prick, took him right in. Rock groaned, sinking in deep. His head dropped to Rig's neck, one hand finding Rig's hip, the other sliding along Rig's arm to curl their fingers together.

He started to thrust, moving with long, slow, deliberate motions. He hadn't been buried in this heaven for over two weeks and that was at least fourteen days too long. Rig knew just what to give him, how to push back and short him out with that tight, little cowboy butt.

He'd planned on making this last, on bringing Rig back up and making Rig come again, but instead he was pounding into Rig, faster and faster, taking what he needed. He wasn't hearing any complaints, either, Rig riding and rocking, squeezing his cock tight. He nuzzled Rig's neck, hand tightening on Rig's hip as he changed his angle, searching for Rig's gland.

"Oh. Oh, fuck. Blue." Oh, right there. Just right fucking there.

"I know," he whispered, fingers tightening, hips pumping harder. Some other time he'd do this all day long, but not today, not when he hadn't had this in weeks. He growled a little, letting Rig know it wouldn't be long.

"Fucking made for this." Rig's fingers squeezed him, that ass tight as a fist.

Groaning, he slid his hand around to Rig's cock. "You needing again?" he asked. He could hold out long enough to make sure Rig was taken care of again.

Rig groaned, cock jerking a little, throbbing in his palm. "Damn..."

Rock moaned, hand working Rig's prick, thumb playing over the head, pressing into the slit just a little as it flew by. Oh yeah, Rig was needing again. Needing exactly what Rock had to give him. He could feel Rig's body trying to hold onto him each time he slid out, could feel it welcome him as he pushed back in again. Fuck, it was good.

His feet slid a little on the tub, the action slamming him in deeper and Rig's head slammed back, the cry sweet and sharp.

Fuck. Just fuck.

Faster. Harder. He pounded into Rig with everything he had, just gave it all up for his Rabbit. Squeezing hard on Rig's cock, he came, shooting deep into that fine fucking cowboy ass.

Rig groaned, leaned into the spray. "Oh, welcome home."

He chuckled, lips moving along the back of Rig's shoulder. He was just tasting and touching, enjoying that he could.

"Thank you for keeping the home fires burning," he teased, cock throbbing inside Rig's body.

"Jackass." Rig chuckled, laughing at his bad fucking joke.

He kissed Rig's skin, and then groaned as he pulled out of that sweet ass. Unless Rig had put in a new heater, they were about to run out of hot water and his Rig did not like the cold, not for a second.

The water clicked off just as the heat died, Rig chuckling low. "Perfect timing."

"I've still got it."

Rig swatted his ass. "You've got something."

Laughing, he grabbed Rig in his arms and hauled his skinny cowboy out of the tub. "Looks to me like I've got you." He planted a kiss on Rig, hand reaching for the towels.

"You do. You want a nap or food first?" Rig licked a line of water off his collarbone.

He groaned a little at the touch, his hand slowly sliding the towel on Rig's body.

When he'd gotten home he would have said fuck then nap, but now that he'd had his taste of Rig, he found he wasn't that tired. "What kind of food?" he asked.

"There's steaks for the grill, potatoes."

His stomach growled and he grinned at the sound. They'd been on fucking MREs the entire time he'd been gone. "Food first. You make that sauce I like for the steaks?"

"Nope. I'm going to make you eat it like shoe leather."

He popped that skinny ass and then went back to drying off Rig's skin. Rig complained like hell if he got cold. "Shoe leather'd be an improvement to the crap I've been chowing down on the last two weeks."

"Oh, now. I know you love those MREs. Lust after 'em, even." Rig kept licking, kept nuzzling.

Rock snorted, though it wasn't easy with that mouth on him. "When I could be eating chocolate pie? I don't think so."

His hands slid over Rig's shoulders, a groan pulled out of him as Rig's mouth continued. Shit, he was going to be angling for that blowjob in a minute if Rig wasn't careful.

"You already got two, Rocketman. You can't be wanting another go-round."

"Been two weeks without that mouth," he pointed out. And damn, his boys had learned what a bastard he could be when he didn't get his usual Rig special wake-up call.

"Are you saying I'm fourteen blow-jobs behind?"

Well, that hadn't been where he was headed, but Rock was not one to miss an opportunity. He just nodded, lips twitching.

"Don't make me kick your ass, Marine." Rig chuckled, head shaking, hand wrapping around his balls.

He stilled, hand sliding down along Rig's arm to the wrist. "Now, Rig... I happen to know you want those in full working order."

Rig's thumb slid over the sac, stroking him, giving him just a little pressure, a little tug.

He licked his lips, hand sliding behind Rig's head, thumb staying to stroke his jaw. Then he bent and licked Rig's lips.

"Oh..." Mmm. That was it, that soft, hungry little noise. Yeah. He still had it, could still derail Rig with a touch, a sound. 'Course it would take more than two weeks with the grunts to lose that.

His tongue pushed into Rig's mouth, the kiss moving deeper, that fucking mustache tickling.

"I changed my mind," he murmured, pulling back to look into Rig's face.

"Mmm?"

He chuckled. "Gonna wait on nap *and* food. You need a shave."

"Now, now. I trimmed it."

"I didn't say *trim*," he pointed out. Stepping back, but keeping an eye on Rig to make sure his Rabbit didn't make a break for the door, Rock turned on the hot water.

"You know, I shaved the beard..."

"You missed a spot." Rock opened the medicine cabinet and took out the shaving cream, the razor.

"You're prejudiced against it..." Rig took a step back toward the door.

Rock arched an eyebrow, shifting his weight, ready to pounce. "Prejudiced? Against your mustache? I just don't like it."

"Isn't that prejudiced?" Rig scooted a little further.

He reached out, hand wrapping around Rig's upper arm. "You think calling me prejudiced is gonna get you out of having that piece of fuzz shaved off? It's not."

"I could hope." Fuck, that look was hot.

He slid his free hand along Rig's lips, watching those grey eyes. "Nothing wrong with hoping. Long as you realize it's in vain."

Rig nipped his fingers, mustache tickling his skin.

He chuckled. "Now you're trying to distract me from my mission."

"Mmmhmm."

"It might work." Rig's mustache tickled his fingers again. "But probably not."

"Probably?" Rig started sucking, head bobbing, tongue stroking the tips of his fingers.

He bit his lip to hold back his groan. "Yeah," he managed, voice rumbling up from his belly. "You're sucking too high."

"Too high?" Teasing little fuck.

He let go of Rig's arm to swat his ass. "It's shaving time," he countered.

"You perv." Rig laughed, leaned in to kiss him, tongue pushing into his lips and trying to distract him again.

That mouth was something else, and the distraction would have worked if Rig's mustache hadn't been tickling his upper lip.

He cupped Rig's face and broke the kiss. "Still too high," he whispered.

"Mmmhmm." Rig slowly slid down, lips sliding down his stomach. "Better?"

"Oh, fuck." He nodded, swallowing as his prick filled, fast and hard, eager for Rig's mouth. His hands slid through Rig's hair, his eyelids heavy as he watched Rig.

"Worth fucking leaving Texas for, Blue." Rig's lips opened, took his cock in, and hummed.

His groan was heartfelt, his fingers tracing Rig's lips where they were wrapped around his prick. "You know it," he muttered. Fuck. Nothing felt like Rig's mouth. Nothing.

Rig's head started bobbing, tongue working his shaft, pressing hard against the veins.

"Rig." He shuddered. He could feel it all the way to his fucking toes. His hips started to push, working with Rig's movements.

"Mmmhmm." Those long fingers circled his balls, rolling and petting as that mouth took him in deep.

Shit, for this he'd let Rig keep the mustache a little longer. He licked his lips, watching his prick sliding into Rig's mouth again and again. His redneck knew exactly what he needed, what he wanted, and how to give it to him.

Two fucking weeks since he'd had this, since he'd felt Rig's mouth pull the pleasure right out of his spine.

The pleasure built, Rig's lips and tongue driving him higher and higher. Rig's nose was buried in his pubes, throat tight and swallowing around the tip of his cock, demanding he come. He tried to hold back -- he didn't want it to end, not yet, maybe not ever. But that mouth was inevitable and he wrapped his hands in Rig's hair, fucking Rig's mouth with long, hard strokes.

So open, so fucking hot. Rig just took him all in, let him in to the root. His orgasm built in the base of his spine, surged through him, and he roared as he came, cock shoving deep and pulsing in Rig's throat.

That damned mustache tickled as Rig cleaned him off, sucked him dry. He growled a little, jerking as Rig's mouth pulled out an aftershock of pleasure. He was licking his own lips when Rig's finally pulled off, and he tugged his Rabbit up, mouth meeting Rig's. Rig moaned, the kiss lazy and slow, sweet as anything.

He rumbled from deep in his belly, feeling about as good and lazy as a man could. His fingers slid over Rig's cheeks, into the short curls as he lost himself in Rig's mouth. Again.

"Mmmhmm." Rig started moving him, backing him toward the bedroom.

"This isn't the way to the kitchen," he pointed out, not really protesting.

"You haven't forgotten what the house looks like. I'm impressed."

He chuckled, letting Rig turn him into the bedroom, letting Rig back him right up to the bed. "Wanting something?"

"Mmm. A nap before I go finish the sink."

"A nap. You." Rock grinned suddenly and fell back into the bed, tugging Rig down with him. "You haven't been warm since I left, have you?"

"Hmm?" Oh, butter wouldn't melt in that mouth. Rig curled right in, moaning low.

It felt good, lying back in his own bed. It felt better, having Rig wrapped up around him. Those damned arms and legs octopussing right around him.

He rumbled softly and let his eyes close.

Yeah, he was home.

\*\*\*

"Hey, Momma. Yeah, he's home. Nope, doesn't look any worse for wear. Yeah, we're eating fine." Rig grinned at Rock as Momma chattered on and on, just jabbering away like she didn't talk to him once a week.

He plopped down on the sofa and stretched out, the rain hammering the house, Grimmy snoring like a freight train. Yep. Perfect Sunday. Well, except for the fact that Momma'd been talking for an hour and Rock was starting to rumble some. Impatient man.

Rock glared over from the easy chair, turning pages of his magazine without even looking at them. Those blue eyes weren't furious or anything, but they weren't happy. Rock looked pointedly at his watch.

He mouthed over, "I *know*. She's chatty."

Rock rolled his eyes and growled a little. The man went back to his magazine, but a moment later tossed it at the coffee table. Then Rock reached over, fingers tickling the sole of Rig's foot. Oh, shit. He snorted, foot jerking back, toes curling. The corner of Rock's mouth twitched and Rock reached for his other foot, one hand holding onto his toes before it was treated to the same tickling touch.

He laughed, apologizing to Momma even as he chuckled again. "Momma. Momma, I... I gotta..."

"You boys. Tell Jim I said hello."

"Goodbye, Momma," Rock called out, fingers sliding from his sole to his ankle, the touch just a little harder now.

"Uh-huh. Bye, Momma. Love you." He clicked the phone off, dropped it. "You ass. She knew something was up."

Rock's eyebrow went up. "Something *is* up. And you've been on the phone with her all fucking day."

"Not all day, butthead. Just a while." He shook his head, stretched. "Thanks for the rescue, though. She might've gone on 'til church started."

"I wasn't rescuing *you*," Rock pointed out, hand warm where it was wrapped around his ankle. He was given a wicked look and then his foot was tickled again.

"No tickling, Rock. Damn. No tickling." He started laughing, tugging at Rock's hand, toes curling. Bastard.

Rock just laughed, hand holding his foot still as the tickles continued. Those blue eyes twinkled at him.

"B...bitch." Rig twisted, reaching for the sofa arm and tugging himself across the couch. He caught Rock by surprise, and managed to drag his Blue halfway out of the easy-chair thanks to the grip on his foot. Rock's laughter got louder and he pressed his mouth to Rig's sole, blowing a long raspberry on it.

"Blue!" He hooted, fighting not to kick Rock in the teeth, laughing so hard it almost hurt.

Rock's own laughter kept those lips dragging over his skin and then his ankle was bitten and Rock was climbing up over him on the couch.

"Hello there, Marine." He leaned up, stretching to get a kiss.

"Hello there, yourself." Rock moved slowly, mouth finally closing over his in a kiss that stole his breath.

"Mmmhmm." Rig groaned, one leg wrapping around Rock's hip and dragging them closer together. Yummy.

One of Rock's hands settled on his hip, wrapping around it like Rock was staking his claim. The other one settled in the cushion next to his head, keeping the bulk of Rock's weight off him. The kiss got deeper, Rock's tongue pushing in.

Oh. Oh, fuck yeah. Hello. He wrapped his lips around Rock's tongue, sucking good and hard. Rock's hips picked up the rhythm, sliding against him. Those blue eyes just stared into his, every fiber of Rock right there with him. Oh, hell. Horny fucker. Rig was fucking made for this.

Rock's thumb stroked his cheek, hips starting to grind slow circles against his. A low rumble came up from Rock's belly, just kind of echoing in his mouth, vibrating against him, as Rock's hand tightened it's grip on his hip. Oh, now. He could handle that, yessir, balls to bones.

The hand on his hip shifted, Rock's fingers tugging his t-shirt out of his jeans, teasing and warm along his waist.

"Mmm." That almost tickled. Almost. Mostly it just felt good.

Rock's fingers danced along his skin, moved slowly up his chest. He knew just where they were headed. He could read it in Rock's eyes. It was enough to excite the living hell out of him, enough to make his nipples hard and tight, make him ache.

"I know what you want," Rock told him, voice rumbling and deep. Rock's fingers stopped right beside his nipple, stroking just beneath it.

"Do you? Are you sure?" He was damn near panting.

Rock put his head back and laughed and those blue eyes just twinkled. Then Rock's fingers slid away from his nipple without touching, tickled along his ribs instead. "Well now, I thought I was, but seeing as you've asked... maybe I don't."

"Tease." He bit his own bottom lip, fighting the urge to groan, to beg for it.

"You know, I do believe that's the first time *I* have been accused of that." He was given a wink and then Rock's fingers slid back up until his thumb was sitting right near Rig's nipple. The nail finally -- finally -- snicked across the hard, eager little bit of flesh.

"Blue!" His belly went tight, his eyes rolling.

"You see? I know what you like." The touch came again, slow and hard, going straight to his cock.

"Uh-huh. Uh-huh." Yeah. More.

Oh, his Blue looked smug, so fucking pleased with himself. Rock's thumb pressed against his nipple and rubbed before sliding over to the other one. Rock could look as smug as he fucking wanted, as long as that didn't stop.

Rig's eyes closed, focus on that hand, his nipple, his cock.

"Yeah, you like that a lot." Rock growled a little and suddenly he could feel his Blue's breath against his skin. A moment later Rock's lips closed around his nipple, tongue flicking across the tip as Rock sucked on him.

God, he could come from this, rubbing and moaning, Rock's mouth driving him out of his fucking *mind*.

Rock's rumble vibrated his nipple as a free hand slid down to cup his cock through his jeans, the heel of Rock's palm catching him right above his balls and pressing so he could feel it to his toes.

"Fuck, yes." Anything. He'd fucking give the sexy son of a bitch anything.

"Yeah." Rock's mouth slid across his chest to his other nipple, licking and sucking all the way. That hand kept rubbing, making him harder and harder.

He was rocking and rubbing, fire sliding along his nerves and just setting him aflame. Goddamn. Rock's hand slid up over his erection and then popped the top button of his jeans, Rock moving so fucking slow. Like they had all damned day to do this.

"Want you. So fucking bad, Blue." Okay, that wasn't begging. It wasn't.

It was asking real nice.

"Yeah, I can see that." The big fingers grabbed his zipper and started to drag it down. Still moving slowly, tongue moving to torture the sweet spot on his neck.

Mean bastard.

Big, evil, beautiful, horny, sexy mean bastard.

Finally, his jeans were open far enough and that big, hot hand slid in to wrap around his prick. A hum sounded against his neck. Oh, hell yes. Rig arched, hips moving and fucking Rock's hand almost immediately.

"Slut," muttered Rock, voice growly and fond.

"Uh-huh. Uh-huh. Your point?"

"I think you're the one with the point, Rig." Rock's hand squeezed tight around him, thumb pushing against his slit every time the head of his cock pushed through.

"I am. Fuck, you make me feel good. So fucking hot. Don't stop."

"Stop? No, I'm not planning to stop. Not any time soon."

Rock's mouth covered his, the kiss deep and hard, Rock's hand never stopping, never slowing. Rig fucking melted, wrapping around Rock and humping with all he had, hips jerking. He wasn't given a moment to think or to breathe or to do anything but feel and fly. Rock was solid and hard and hot above him, demanding his pleasure.

He just dissolved as he shot, groaning and jerking and just giving it up. Rock groaned, tongue lapping at his lips as the hand around his prick slowed, but didn't stop. Sweet aftershocks moved through him, lighting briefly inside him.

"Fucking love that smell."

He just moaned. Like he could form words. Lord. Rock's hand came up, fingers spreading his own come on his lips. Then Rock leaned back in and licked them clean again.

Oh, fuck. That was hot. Sexy. Just goddamn. "Blue..."

"Yeah, right here." Rock's hips settled down against his, prick hard as fuck behind Rock's jeans.

He nodded, trying to make his fingers work, to get Rock's jeans open, maybe off. Something.

Rock chuckled, hips not helping as they rubbed that jeans-covered cock against his bare skin. "Someone's fuck-addled."

"Hmm..." Fuck-addled. Bastard. Hot, beautiful bastard.

Rock grinned at Rig, reaching down to undo Rock's button and pull down the zipper. "You think you can take it from there?"

"Come fuck my mouth." He could take it, all the way to the root.

Rock growled, those blue eyes going from warm and amused to hot and needy, just like that. Rock pushed the jeans right down and moved to straddle his shoulders. "Fucking love that mouth."

"Uh-huh." He wrapped his hands around Rock's thighs, lips open and hungry and ready to be fucked.

"Which one of us wants it more?" Rock asked, voice low and husky. His Blue slid that fat prick along his lips, painting them with pre-come.

"Does it matter, so long as we both want it?" He let his tongue drag, slide over Rock's slit.

Rock groaned, hips jerking, cock pushing against his face before Rock had a chance to line it up properly and tease just the head of it between his lips. "I want it, Rabbit."

He nodded, tongue starting to fuck the slit, pushing in enough to burn.

Rock's eyes rolled back a little, the low groan turning into a growl. "Yeah, Rig. Oh, fuck, yeah."

Rock pushed his prick in a little deeper, started to fuck his mouth with shallow, shallow thrusts. Yeah. Just like that, Rocketman. Take what you want. Fuck, this felt good, felt fucking sexy.

"Best mouth ever, Rig." Rock's voice was almost a growl, the thrusts slowly getting deeper, pushing that fat prick right to his throat.

Rig pulled harder, working Rock like the world's biggest damn Popsicle. Rock's prick leaked into his mouth, the flavor familiar and right.

Fingers slid against his check, soft and warm, like the eyes that gazed down at him. "Soon," muttered Rock, warning or promise, or maybe both.

He grinned, fingers sliding back to tap against that tight, tight hole. Soon worked for him. Rock roared and pushed deeper, cock throbbing in his mouth. Another jerk and push and Rock was coming, shooting down his throat. Oh, fuck yes. Just like that, Blue. He swallowed, tongue stroking as he cleaned that heavy cock.

Rock kept moving, sliding that heat along his tongue, before slowly pulling out. The hard body settled down half on top of him, arm heavy over his waist. "Mmm... now, isn't that better than jawing on the phone?"

"Uh-huh." What was the question?

Rock chuckled, breath hot and heavy on his neck, fingers sliding on his skin. "Yeah, this is how to spend a Sunday."

"Hell, yes." This and possibly a nice burger and a beer.

Or two beers.

"That mean the lawn is safe from you today?" Rock asked, corner of his mouth twitching.

"Mmm. Maybe. If I decide to grill out, I'll have to mow first."

Rock's hand tightened on his hip, tugging him into the hard body. "I'll buy you pizza."

"Mmm. Good plan." Excellent plan. Fucking amazing plan.

"Good. I can spend the afternoon fucking you into a stupor." Rock's hand slid off his hip and up to flick at one of his nipples.

"Oh..." He shivered and might have nodded a little. "I'm a fan of pizza."

"I'm a fan of fucking," muttered Rock, mouth meeting his, fingers tugging on his nipple.

"You and..." Oh. Oh, fuck. Sweet.

"Oh, speechless. It's a good look on you." Rock chuckled, licking his jaw, sucking on his earlobe. The touches and kisses were lazy, but held intent behind them, and Rock's prick had already firmed back up, pressing against him.

"You. Oh. Damn." He hummed, sort of stretching out under the kisses.

"No. Me. You. Fuck." Bastard. Teasing bastard. Teasing, hot, sexy bastard.

Rig nodded, body reaching for those big, clever hands.

"Need to lose this." This was his t-shirt, Rock's hands grabbing the bottom of it which was rucked somewhere up under his arms. Rock pushed it over his head and then slid warm fingers over him, tracing his ribs, his abs, teasing his sides.

"Mmm... You've got the best fucking hands, Rocketman."

"Yeah?" One slid over his hip, the other pushed his jeans right down to his knees and slid back up to up his balls, rolled them. "Thought it was my prick you liked..."

"Shit. I like, Blue. I just like." Was just fucking made for all of it.

"Good answer." Rock grinned and tugged on his balls a bit, just enough to let him know Rock was there.

"Yeah? You... you approve?" He spread wider, let Rock have more.

Rock licked Rig's lips, tongue pointed. "This mouth? I most definitely approve of what comes out of it. And what comes in it." Those big hands cupped and weighed his balls, palm rubbing them as a finger slid on behind them.

He grinned and ran his tongue along Rock's, the flavor there enough to make his cock jerk. "Shit, Marine. We're *all* approving of each other."

"Good." Rock grunted, the tip his finger pushing into Rig's body. "I'd hate to think you weren't enjoying yourself." The finger inside him pushed deeper, Rock's palms pressing against his balls.

"I do. Am. What-the-fuck-ever. More." Christ, that felt good. Better than good. Like cold beer on a hot day good.

Rock's eyes twinkled down at him, that shit-eating grin telling him that Rock knew it.

Two thick fingers pressed against his mouth, most of Rock's weight on him now, solid and good. "Suck."

Like he took orders worth a damn. Still, he had that whole oral thing going on and it was Rock and yeah. Sucking.

Once he was sucking on them, Rock's fingers slid and pushed in his mouth, fucking it like Rock was gonna be fucking his ass in a couple minutes. Low sounds were rumbling up out of Rock's chest, the thick prick sliding against his hip, that one finger on Rock's other hand teasing inside him.

Rig closed his eyes, working those fingers like he would Rock's prick. He licked and pulled, tongue flicking Rock's fingertips.

"Fuck..." The word was deep and low, full of fucking need.

It lasted another moment and then Rock yanked those fingers away, mouth closing hard on his. Rig damn near came, just from that. Their fucking kiss went from zero to sixty in nothing flat, his whole focus on Rock's mouth on his. Fuck, yes. Just like that. He almost didn't notice the single finger inside him being replaced with the two he'd been sucking on, Rock's tongue tangling with his, making him fucking fly.

He noticed it when those fingers hit his gland, though. Fuck, yes, he did. Bucking like he was breaking a colt, Rig's eyes rolled up and he humped, needing it hard and deep and now.

Rock kept up the assault with fingers and tongue, finally breaking off the kiss to grin down at him. "You wait for me now, Rig. Want you to come on my cock."

His head tossed on his shoulders, hand wrapping around the base of his prick. "Fuck, Blue. Fucking need you."

"I know it." Rock kissed him again and then eased those fingers out of him. "Nice and wide, Rabbit. Show me how much you want it."

He just nodded, one leg propping up on the sofa back, the other splayed out wide.

"That's it." Rock's eyes swept over him like a fucking touch, and then that fat prick was right where he needed it. Rock pushed in and in, filling him right up like nothing, like nobody, ever.

"Fuck, yes." He sort of shorted out, reaching out to grab Rock's arms, bracing himself to push down on that fat fucking cock.

Rock just grunted, going deeper and deeper, holding still for a moment, and then fucking him like he needed it, hard and fast. Over and over, Rock's cock spread him open, the pace hard and good. Rig just let himself go, riding hard; low, rough sounds poured out of him in waves. One of Rock's hands settled near his head, supporting Rock as that fat prick just slammed into him. The other slid between them and grabbed hold of his cock, jacking him in time.

"Fuck. Fuck, Blue. Gonna." He wasn't going to last. Couldn't. Needed. Fuck.

"Yeah. Fucking show me." Then Rock's mouth was on his again, tongue pushing in, a Marine invasion.

Spunk sprayed right out of him, his fucking cock aching as he shot.

Rock's hips kept moving, pushing, sliding past his fucking gland and making one aftershock follow another through his body. Then Rock stilled, heat pushing deep inside him.

"Mmm." His cock tried to jerk a little, appreciating that feeling.

Rock let himself down slowly, that weight so solid and good on him. "You've got to admit -- this beats mowing the fucking lawn."

"Not fucking the grass."

Rock laughed. "I should hope not. Your ass doesn't need any green stains."

"No. I'm pretty sure green asses need medical attention."

Rock's nose wrinkled. "Yeah, last one I saw did. Nas-ty."

He was given a wink and Rock shifted just enough to put most of his weight on the couch. "Naptime."

"You sure?" He snuggled in, one arm around Rock's waist. "I want cheesecake with the pizza."

"You blow me again later and I'll even go get the beer."

"Mmm. You got a deal." Later. Maybe in the shower. Mmm. Shower sex.

Yum.

"Good." Rock grunted and shifted a bit more, settling against him, one large hand on his hip.

Soon the familiar almost-snores sounded, Rock's breath hot against his skin. He wasn't sleepy. He wasn't, but Rock was warm and he was comfortable and Rig figured he could just... rest for a minute.

Yeah, that was it. Rest his eyes.

# Chapter Two

Grimmy was barking up a storm when he pulled up, big paws landing on the storm door. Man, Grimmy hated it if he was outside and unreachable.

"Chill out, pup. I'll be right there." Silly mutt.

Rig grinned, shook his head, and grabbed the beer and the bag of chicken.

Rock's voice growled out over Grimmy's barks. "He's missing you. You're late."

"Stopped and got supper. Grab him, would you? My hands are full." Late and tired and just a touch grumpy.

Rock grabbed Grim's collar and tugged him away from the door. "Come on, beast. You make him drop my supper and I'm going to have to beat you."

"No beating my dog." He chuckled and muscled into the kitchen, plopping the beer on the counter.

"They work you hard today?" Rock grabbed a couple of beers and opened one, handing the other over.

"You know it." Rig chugged one back, throat working. Long fucking day.

Rock grabbed the bag of chicken. "Smells good. Let's eat in the living room."

"Works for me." He got a handful of ass, squeezing a second. "How're you?"

"Mmm... better now." Rock pushed back into his hand and gave him a smile. "Come on, let's eat and then you can have your wicked way with me."

"Works for me." He plopped down on the sofa, legs spreading out as he sprawled.

Rock sat in his chair, those blue eyes on him. "Looking good, Rig."

He grinned, the words making him pleased as hell. "Yeah? You liking me?"

"Uh-huh." Rock watched a moment longer, just smiling and looking. Then he blinked and Rock opened the bag of chicken. "There biscuits in here?"

"Of course." Chicken came with biscuits.

Rock chuckled and grabbed two, along with a piece of chicken. He grabbed a biscuit himself, humming over the heat and butter and honey.

Rock wolfed down a couple of pieces of chicken and three biscuits before coming up for air, grinning over at him as a third piece of chicken was snagged. "This is almost as good as yours."

"It's a hell of a lot easier to make, though." Rig slid over, stretching out on the sofa. "And doesn't heat the house up."

Rock finished another piece of chicken and wiped his hands on a napkin. "There's nothing wrong with a little heat in the house." Nodding at the sofa, Rock added, "You leave some room for me there?"

"There's always room. Which end you want?"

"The one with your head." Rock got up and stretched, popped his neck a couple of times, and came over to sit with him.

He rolled up, then settled back in Rock's lap. "Hey, Marine." Man, Rock smelled good.

"Hey." Rock's hand landed on his head, fingers sliding through his hair. Legs spreading, Rock settled a little deeper into the couch.

"Oh. That feels good." He rubbed against Rock's bulge, humming a little.

"Oh, it sure does." Rock hummed, fingers massaging his forehead, his cheeks.

Rig nodded, melting, balls to bones. Oh, man. It was good to be him.

"I've got a three-day next weekend." The massage kept going, Rock's fingers catching on his five o'clock shadow.

"You and me both. I pulled that double last week."

"Fucking A." Smiling down at him, Rock rubbed a thumb along his lower lip. "Fucking A."

Rig just smiled, lips wrapping around that thumb and sucking, nice and easy. Mmm. Honey. The bulge against his cheek grew a little harder, those blue eyes smiling down at him.

"We could call it an early night..."

"We could. I'm all about you and me and a bed." Hell, a nice, long fuck and a hard sleep? Sounded like heaven.

"You wanna shower first? Been awhile since I drank the water off your skin."

"Mmm. I'm a fan." He rolled up and they did their thing -- he fed Grim and tossed the leftovers, Rock locked up and shit. Normal stuff. Good stuff.

They met in the hall on their way to the bathroom, Rock already half undressed and tossing his clothes in the general direction of the washer. Rig chuckled and got his t-shirt off, jeans unbuttoned. He'd get it all later.

Much later.

Maybe tomorrow.

Rock went for the sink as soon as they were in the bathroom, started brushing his teeth, those blue eyes just watching him in the mirror. It would take a stronger man than him to avoid the urge to grab that ass, so he didn't. Rock jerked, and then flexed the muscles in his hands, clenching and unclenching those firm butt cheeks.

"Fine fucking man." Rig bent, lips brushing the small of Rock's back.

Rock groaned, legs spreading just a little. He spat and rinsed, turned the water off.

Rig licked a lazy circle, then moved down, loving on his old man. Those legs spread a little wider, Rock's hands landing on the counter for balance. Rig wrapped his hands around Rock's thighs, thumbs rubbing the soft, soft skin on the insides.

"Fuck, Rig..." Rock's groan was low, slowly filling the room.

"Yeah. Yeah, Rocketman." He licked a slow line along Rock's crack.

"Shit, Rig. Don't fucking stop." That raw note in Rock's voice was worth crawling over glass naked for.

No. No, he wasn't going to stop. Rig settled in, tongue dragging along Rock's crease, pressing against that tiny, tight ring of muscles. Groans and moans and sweet rumbles filled the small room, Rock's thighs trembling, that little hole opening and closing for him. He just petted away, hands sliding over Rock's legs.

"Shit, Rig. Hot. Fuck." The words just poured over him, Rock almost incoherent.

Yeah. Hot and male and his beautiful fucking Marine. Rig groaned, pushed his tongue deep, piercing that sweet hole.

Rock groaned, hand grabbing that fat prick and starting to jack it. "Yeah. Fuck."

He moaned, his hands joining Rock's, looking to drive Rock out of his goddamn mind. Rock's knees buckled and then locked, their hands moving faster together.

"Soon," groaned Rock. "Fucking soon."

Hell, yes. Come on, Blue. Gimme. His own hips were fucking the air, cock dripping at the tip. His tongue went deep and Rock's ass squeezed it hard, a cry sounding as Rock shot over their hands. He groaned, shaking hard, forehead on Rock's ass as he jacked himself hard.

"Let me smell you, Rabbit."

"Blue..." He shot hard enough that his thighs burned, his head falling back as he groaned.

"Oh yeah, that's what I'm talking about." Rock's ass flexed beneath his forehead.

"Uh-huh." Thinking good.

Turning and resting his ass against the counter, Rock grabbed his arm and tugged him up, settling him against the hard body, between Rock's legs. Those blue eyes smiling at him.

"Hey." His heart was just pounding away.

"Mmm. Hey." Rock brought their mouths together, lips parting his, tongue pushing in deep.

He was a lucky son of a bitch, balls to bones. Rig just opened to the kiss, rubbing nice and easy. The kiss went deeper, Rock just taking his mouth, diving right in.

"You're trying to grow that damned mustache back," Rock growled.

"It looks good on me." And trying was a strong word. He'd just stopped shaving it, really.

"It doesn't look bad." Which for Rock was almost an honest to God compliment. "Like it better gone."

Well, how could a man argue with that logic? Fuck knew that he wanted Rock to keep looking. "I'll shave, then."

And that damned smile that lit up those blue eyes was more than worth going without the lip hair.

"Yeah? Gonna do it now?"

"Now? You don't want to shower?"

"Yep, shower's definitely going to happen. Doesn't mean you can't shave the fuzz off first." Rock crossed his arms and grinned, body warm and solid against him.

"Pushy Marine." He chuckled and grabbed the shaving cream and his razor.

Rock laughed, watching him. "Nah, if I was pushy you'd have shaved it off at the beginning of the week."

"We were both too busy." He lathered up, started shaving. It was kinda weird with Rock watching.

Sexy, but weird.

"We have at that." Rock grinned suddenly. "You could keep going with that. Shave the lot."

"I haven't been growing my beard in, turkey." Still, he worked the stubble off, leaving himself clean-shaven.

Those blue eyes slid over him, from head to toe and back up. The look long and slow, sexy as fuck. It ended with a wink from Rock. "I wasn't talking about your beard."

His cock jerked, bobbing up against Rock's belly, just like that.

One of Rock's eyebrows went up, Rock just grinning at him. "Oh, you like that."

He sort of snorted, bent down to wash his face off. "I don't know what you're talking about."

Rock's fingers slid over his belly and tugged gently at the curls around his cock. "No, you don't know what I'm talking about at *all*."

"Nope." Pervy Marine. Sexy bastard.

"No? You're hard again because you're shaving off that mustache?" Rock's eyes met his, hot and amused at the same time. "I don't think so. I think you like the idea of baring it all for me."

"I'm hard again because the sexiest fucking Marine on the east coast is right fucking here and naked."

Rock puffed up at that, doing his best 'yes, I'm a studly god' imitation. "We should do it anyway."

"Huh?" Fuck, his prick was hard.

Rock chuckled, fingers reaching out to slide over his hot cheeks. "I said we should do it anyway."

"Do what?" He leaned into the touch, tongue flicking out.

Rock rumbled for him, eyes watching his mouth. "Shave you. Down there." Rock's eyes flicked down to his cock and then back up to his mouth. Oh, Jesus. His tongue dragged over Rock's fingers again, cock hard as stone. Rock nodded. "Yeah, I say we definitely should do it." He got a long, slow grin. "I won't cut you."

"You won't..." Rock wouldn't. It would itch like a son of a bitch growing in, though.

"Nope, I won't." Rock grabbed his razor, grinned. "So how do you want to do this?"

"I don't. Shit, Blue. I don't know."

Rock grabbed a couple of fresh towels and laid them out on the floor. "There. Lie on them."

Rock was serious. Like, about to shave his crotch serious.

"This is..." A little weird.

A little hot.

"Don't make a big deal out of it, Rig -- just lie down." Rock's voice was a little rough, that lovely, fat prick starting to perk up.

Yeah. Don't make a big deal. Just lie down. Lord. He settled, legs sprawled a little, balls drawn up tight. Rock grabbed a cloth and tossed it at him before hunkering down next to him with the shaving cream and razor. One big hand slid over his thigh, hot and solid, touching him.

"Mmm." He relaxed a little, that touch just fine.

The shaving cream was cold, but Rock's fingers as he spread it around soon had him warmed back up. Two short squirts covered his balls, Rock cupping and rolling, teasing.

"Perv." He winked, spread, let Rock know he was playing.

The slightest hint of color hit Rock's cheeks, but those blue eyes were dancing when they met his. "Takes one to know one."

"I won't tell anybody if you don't." Like he'd confess this to a soul.

Rock snorted. "Who am I gonna tell?" Then all of Rock's attention shifted back to his middle, the razor looking small in Rock's fingers.

"Nobody. Damn, this is. Yeah." Rig grinned, trying to seem all assured and not at all wigged out.

"Pervy." Rock winked at him and the razor touched his skin, slid over it, leaving a bare patch behind.

Goddamn. His toes curled, that bare skin so fucking pale. Rock used the cloth to keep the razor clean of hair, returning to his skin again and again. Slowly, but surely, his short and curlies were shaved away, Rock not saying a word. Rig didn't know what to say, so he didn't. He just watched. Stared.

Wanted.

The more Rock shaved, the more intense his looking got, the more Rig could smell how much Rock wanted, that fat prick leaking for him. "Almost done." Rock's voice had gone all husky and deep.

"Yeah." His own cock slapped against his belly, leaving wet kisses.

Rock nodded, fingers hot on his cock as they pushed it aside, Rock paying real close attention as the razor slid next to his prick.

"Fucking sweet," muttered Rock.

"I. Fuck. Rock, it fucking tingles."

"Yeah?" Rock grinned up at him and then tossed the razor up into the sink and used the cloth to clean the excess shaving cream off his skin. "Wow. It's so fucking smooth." Rock's fingers slid on his skin, making the tingles bigger, better.

His toes curled up and Rig jerked, arching toward Rock's touch.

"Oh, fuck." Rock chuckled, the sound good and husky and deep. Then he touched again, fingers just skating over the newly bared skin. As if that wasn't enough, Rock bent and licked a line next to his cock.

"Blue..." His thighs parted, muscles going hard as rock, balls drawing up even tighter.

"Uh-huh." Rock's nose slid over his skin, deep breaths pulling the scent of him in. "Smell good, Rig." Then Rock's tongue took a couple more swipes.

"Like shaving cream?"

Rock's chuckle sent warm air wafting over him. "Yep, but I was talking about *you*. Pure fucking male."

"You... Bed, Rocketman. Now." He fucking needed.

"No shower?" Rock asked, but his Marine was already standing, hand held out for him, eyes hot and eager.

"I can wait." Rock hauled him up, their bodies slapping together, Rock's prick sliding on his shaved skin. "Goddamn."

"Fuck, yeah." Rock's mouth crashed down onto his, tongue pushing in, taking his mouth hard enough their teeth clicked together.

He almost didn't notice Rock backing them out into the hall. Rig got all lost in the kiss, hips bucking, rubbing away at Rock's prick as Rock muscled them down toward the bedroom. Rock growled and rumbled, feeding the vibrations into his mouth, hands all over him.

It came as a surprise when Rock's lips pulled away from his and he was pushed back to land sprawling on the bed. "You're all worked up." Rock ground out the words, sounding pretty fucking worked up himself.

"Yeah. Fuck, Blue. I need." He started jacking himself off, just fucking his hand.

"Just look at you," growled Rock, prick reaching up toward Rock's amazing belly, jerking a little as Rock watched him. "All that smooth skin -- like you're more naked than ever."

He felt his cheeks heat, his entire body rippling at Rock's words. God fucking damn.

Rock climbed up between his legs, eyes flicking between meeting his and checking out his package as he jacked himself. "Gonna fuck you. Gonna have that ass and watch your totally naked cock when you come."

"Uh-huh. Hard. Need it." He rolled up, slammed their lips together again for a brief kiss that made his eyes roll. "Quit fucking teasing."

"Who's fucking teasing?" Rock asked, pushing him back down onto the bed and lying heavily on him as one hand slid beneath the pillows. Rock's sudden grin said he'd found the lube.

He groaned, nodding, just about to beg. At this point he'd take cock, fingers, hand. Anything. Now.

Two slick fingers pushed into him, Rock moving down to flick that hot tongue across one nipple and then the other. The second touch to his tit came just as Rock's fingers curled and hit his gland.

He shot so hard the world grayed out, Rock's name echoing in the bedroom.

Rock hummed, fingers continuing to work him, mouth moving down to lick the come from his chest, his belly. He just whimpered, hips shifting, ass sliding on the sheets. Then nose and lips were on his newly shaved skin, Rock exploring him thoroughly, keeping his prick nice and hard. His fucking universe just hiccupped, his focus on the pleasure rocketing through him.

Two fingers became three, Rock working him hard, lips and tongue making the sensitive skin they'd bared just scream. Every now and then Rock's nose would bump his cock or his balls, that tongue sliding hot and wet over him.

"More. Rocketman. Please. I need more."

"Gonna give you more, Rig. Gonna fuck you into the mattress." Rock's fingers pegged his gland on the last word, and then the thick fingers disappeared altogether.

He couldn't have helped his moan if he'd tried. Christ, he was empty and aching, ready for that hard cock to peg him deep.

"Spread 'em wider." Rock's hands were right there on the backs of his thighs, pushing his legs further apart and then settling them on the muscled thighs. The fat head of Rock's prick slid along his crack, rubbed past his hole a few times.

"Blue! God *damn* it!" He arched and pushed, taking that prick in so deep it made his eyes roll.

"Fuck!" Rock cried out, hips jerking, sending that thick cock a little bit deeper. "Greedy *and* impatient."

"You know it." He nodded, riding Rock like the man was a prize stud at the county fair.

Growling, Rock met each and every move, thrusting into him nice and hard. Blue eyes blazed down at him, keeping them right there, together. Fuck, yes. Just what he needed, right fucking now. His beautiful goddamn Marine. Rock slid one hand over his belly and on down, not going for his cock, but for the freshly bare skin, fingernails just grazing as Rock stroked.

His orgasm came barreling down his spine like Marines storming a beach. Rock was right there with him, hips snapping hard, cock spraying heat deep inside him.

Oh, fuck him raw, that was.

Yeah.

Damn.

"Fucking good, Blue Eyes."

Rock slowly lowered onto him, weight good and solid, Rock propping up somehow so he wasn't crushed under his Marine. "Always fucking good, Rig." Rock's fingers were back at his crotch, feeling him up.

"Uh. Uh-huh." Damn. Damn, that felt like magic.

"Think that shower can wait 'til morning," murmured Rock, just playing and playing with his skin.

"Yeah. Yeah, Blue Eyes. We got time." Days off. Each other.

He was a lucky son of a bitch.

\*\*\*

Rock was trying very hard not to grumble.

He fucking hated shopping. And usually he didn't have to tag along. Rig usually took care of this crap on Saturday mornings while he was still in bed. But they were going to the fucking beach tomorrow, so here they were, Friday evening after a long fucking week and they were running errands.

Rig had a goddamned list and everything.

He shoved the dry cleaning into the truck and shot Rig a look, hoping like hell stopping somewhere for a fucking beer was on that fucking list. "What's next?"

"Flowers. Mother's Day." Every fucking year it was Mother's Day and every fucking year Rig went to the florist's and every fucking year Rig asked him what his mother wanted. Goddamn it.

He did grumble this time. Growled and groaned. He wanted that fucking beer, yes he did. In fact, he was fast approaching deserved it. He slammed the truck door and growled. "Let's go then." He had a fucking plan this year.

"Don't worry, Marine. Being in close vicinity of roses will not reduce your testosterone levels one bit."

"Can I get a guarantee on that?" He followed Rig down to the florist, nose wrinkling at the sweet smell inside.

"Yep. It's a promise. Look at the size of those roses. Good lord."

"Texas sized?" he teased. "What are you spending on Charlene this year?" He had a hundred in his wallet. There was no way Rig was spending more than that. He'd just add his money to match Rig's, get Charlene a bigger bunch of flowers and avoid the whole 'you have to get your momma something, it's Mother's Day' argument.

"Fifty, I guess? If I spend more, she'll call and bitch about me spending too much. If I spend less, Daddy'll call to make sure I still got a job."

He pulled out his wallet and handed over two twenties and a ten. "You sign my name to it, too." He didn't know why he hadn't thought of this sooner.

"Yeah? You... I could put in some for one for yours, too, if you want?"

He should have known it wasn't going to be that easy. He shook his head. "I thought we'd just go with the ones for Charlene this year." His mother wasn't interested in anything from him. Unless it was a picture of his new wife and kids.

"You're good to her. She appreciates it." Rig looked completely fucking confused. The man simply didn't *get* it.

"Charlene's a good woman, Rig. You got a good one." He turned Rig toward the counter. "Look at the books. Pick out some shit you think she'll like."

He hadn't even bothered with a card since the year after he joined up. It had become pretty clear pretty quickly how the land lay with his mother. Hell, Rig talked to Charlene every fucking Sunday; he supposed he couldn't blame his Rabbit for not getting it. Still, that was no reason for Rig to harp on it every fucking year.

"You know her, she likes purple flowers." Rig nodded and smiled at the little girl, charming her right off the bat, ordering irises and lavender and shit for Charlene. The man was attached at the goddamn hip.

Rock leaned a hip against the counter, idly watching Rig in action. He couldn't wait to get out of the flowery little shop. He decided the next thing on that list was beer and burgers. Even if he had to fucking write it in himself.

"You sure you don't want to send her something little, Rocketman?"

He growled. "What did I say?" She didn't want shit from him. Hell, she'd never seemed that thrilled with the stuff they'd made her in school when he was just a kid.

Rig's lips went tight, thin cheeks flushing dark. "Well, then. That'll do it, honey."

He didn't know why Rig was pissed -- he was the one who was having to repeat himself, getting hassled to do something he had no intension of doing.

"Can we go now?" he asked as the little salesclerk handed Rig's receipt and change to him.

"Yep. Thank you, ma'am. I appreciate it." Rig nodded, pulled the brim of his ball cap down and headed out. It fucking looked like rain.

Icing on the fucking cake. "I need a beer." He looked around, catching sight of a Hooters the next block up.

He grunted and pointed to it. "That'll do."

"Woo. T and A. That'll reverse the damage of possibly smelling like roses."

He was not in the fucking mood. "Can't drink roses," he pointed out as evenly as he could. They had decent munchies at Hooters, too.

"Actually, the petals are edible."

Smart ass.

"Pretty fucking expensive meal."

Almost fucking there. Thank the fucking lord.

The hostess was all tits, and Rock was sure if that was what wet his whistle he'd be in heaven, but he just wanted a goddamned beer. Now.

Rig didn't say much of anything, just sort of looked at the menu and ordered a beer and a shot of tequila.

"Hey! Rocketman!"

Rock bit back his growl as one of the guys in his unit stopped by their table. He nodded instead. "Wilson."

"Great fucking place, isn't it?" Wilson laughed, obviously a few beers ahead of him. Maybe more than a few. "This is my brother, Billy. He's old enough to buy beer for himself now."

"Looks like he's old enough to buy you beer now, too, Wilson." Where was *his* fucking beer?

Wilson, obviously oblivious to his fucking mood, nodded at Rig. "Nice to meet'cha. See ya, Rocketman."

"Not if I see you first."

Wilson seemed to think that was fucking hilarious and he was still laughing as he walked out the door, his brother Billy supporting him.

"Jesus," Rock muttered, shaking his head. "Where the fuck's our beer?"

"I'll go check." Rig wandered up to the bar, giving the little chick a warm smile, nodding and bullshitting and managing to down two shots before bringing the beers over.

He growled out a 'thank you', taking a good, long swig out of his bottle, damned near finishing it, too. Shit, that was good. They should have come here first and done the rest of the fucking shit after. He'd bet that flower shop would have been far more tolerable with a cold one in him.

He waved the bottle at the waitress, holding up a finger to show he wanted another. "I want a burger," he told Rig. "We can finish your list after we've eaten."

Rig nodded to him, finishing off the beer and getting Little Miss Nearly Naked to bring another for him, too. Rig always knew how to charm people. It was something to see.

He grunted his thanks, sitting back and letting his foot touch Rig's leg under the table. One beer in him, another on its way, and the promise of a burger before he had to deal with God knew what was next went a long way to improving his mood.

Long as Rig let the subject of Mother's Day drop...

"So, you ever gonna say *anything* about your folks, Rock? We've been together for awhile..." Curious bastard.

He drank some of his second bottle and wiped the back of his mouth with his hand. "What do you want me to say, Rig? What do you want to hear?"

"Well. Are they good folks? Do you got kin?" Rig tilted his head a little, caught his eyes. "I mean, you ain't got to tell them nothing about me. I get not wanting them to know, but I don't get why you don't want me to know."

He shook his head. Jesus fuck. "It's got nothing to do with not wanting them to know about you, Rig." He finished off his beer. He hated this fucking crap. Why couldn't Rig just leave this door closed? "You don't need to know people like them, Rig."

"How bad could they be, Jim? They made *you*."

"And they made me wrong."

"There's nothing wrong with you." The fucked up thing? Rig sort of believed that.

"Not according to them." Just because he hid who he fucked in the bedroom, didn't mean he was ashamed of it, it just meant he wasn't stupid. But that wasn't how his mother and father felt, now was it? "Not everybody brings their gay son a washing machine when he moves house, Rig."

"I'm their son. Period. Not their *gay* son."

"Right." And that was the fucking point.

He waved the waitress over. "I want a burger. No fucking green stuff on it. Fries on the side. And another beer. Thank you. Rig?"

"I'm good with another beer, honey. Thanks."

Rock rolled his eyes. "Make the fries a large." Rig would pick at them the whole time he ate.

"So what's next on the list?" he asked, once Miss October sashayed off with their order.

"I have to get charcoal and shit for the cooler, dog food. I was going to look at tents for the beach."

"Oh, we can find a Motel 6 or something, can't we?" A tent for the fucking beach, that dog no doubt pushing his way in, to boot.

Rig's eyes flashed a little, lips going tight. "I reckon. Hell, you don't have to go, you don't want to. I'm going to go get me another shot." Then Rig was up like a jack-in-the-box, heading back to the bar.

He growled. So he didn't like sleeping in the fucking sand. He'd had enough of that when he'd been a grunt, when they got deployed. There was nothing wrong with wanting to sleep in a bed with a fucking mattress. To fuck without worrying about the damned dog hair or sand in places where they didn't belong.

And if he didn't want to split open a vein and bleed about his fucking asshole family, he wasn't going to and Rig should just... deal. He drummed his fingers on the fucking table, waiting for their food, or for Rig to come back. He wasn't feeling particularly picky on which one came first.

The food ended up there first, Rig flirting and playing with a group at the bar. His Rabbit drank a couple of shots, then someone offered him a cigarette, the cherry lighting up Rig's face under that hat brim.

He growled. Filthy fucking habit. And he was going to have to make this his last goddamned beer -- Rig wasn't driving anywhere.

He started working on his burger, watching the Lakers pound on the Suns on the little TV over the bar. That it happened to be right over where Rig was sitting was pure coincidence. He almost - almost - got pissy when some guy grabbed a double handful of cowboy butt, but Rig backed right off, hands up. That's right. Rig didn't play like that. Rig played with him and the cherries.

Then his Rabbit headed toward the table, headed right for him. He managed to find a smile for Rig, swallowed first and everything, nodded. Then he pushed his plate of fries over a little and took another bite of his meat.

Rig plopped down, smiled back, and took a fry. "Burger good?"

"Yeah. No green crap." He pushed the plate a little closer to Rig. "Was hungry."

"Yeah? Fries are good. You want something sweet?"

He nodded. "Something chocolate."

He finished up his burger, watching Rig eat a good portion of his fries. Leaning back, he stretched out and let his foot rub up along Rig's calf.

Rig looked over at him, eyelids heavy, a little dazed. "Hey, Marine."

He gave Rig his best smile. "Hey, yourself." He rubbed that calf a little harder. "You think we can wrap the rest of these errands up quickly?"

"I think they'll hold 'til the morning, even. It's a vacation. There ain't no hurry." Oh. Oh, hell yes.

He wiped his mouth and nodded at the waitress, signaling for the bill. He met those grey eyes again. "I don't really need dessert. At least nothing they serve here."

"No?" Rig tipped his hat brim back, grinned a little. "I'm betting I can figure something you want."

He chuckled. "Yeah? I imagine you might just be able to at that."

The busty waitress brought him his bill, and batted her eyelashes. Rock just snorted and put some money on the table. Not waiting for his change had more to do with wanting to get home with Rig than wanting to leave her a good tip.

He figured he was in a good place when Rig handed over the keys to the Jeep without him asking. He had to fight the urge to wrap his arm around Rig's shoulders, just bumped them instead, leading the way back to the Jeep. He didn't even try to change the radio station, just turned it down a little.

"Be home in fifteen."

Rig's hand slipped over his thigh, heading north toward his cock. "Fifteen minutes works."

Grinning, he let his legs spread a little, settled more comfortably into the driver's seat as they hit the highway. He glanced at the speedometer, making sure he was sitting just at the speed limit.

Those long fingers moved up and up, brushing nice and easy over his balls. Oh yeah... the evening was definitely looking up. "Careful now. I'm driving."

"Mmmhmm. Pay attention." Rig scooted closer, humming nice and low. "Want you to fuck my mouth."

His hands curled hard on the wheel, his eyes riveted to the road as his whole body went tight. "Love that mouth."

"Mmmhmm. Makes me fucking hot when you take it, let me feel you." That goddamn drawl was thick as honey.

"I've got it right here for you." His own voice was down to a growl, and he didn't look away from the road for a second, knew if he did he'd run them right off it.

"You gonna stay hard for me? Going to fuck me through the wall?"

"You fucking know it." Like he'd leave his Rabbit wanting.

Rig stroked his nuts, the horny son of a bitch's breath hot on his neck. He risked widening his legs a little, his prick aching as it pressed hard against his zipper.

"Want it hard. Deep. Want to feel you all fucking weekend." The heel of Rig's hand rubbed his prick, driving him out of his fucking mind.

He groaned, foot momentarily pressing harder on the accelerator. He eased up on it again, breathing through his nose. "You won't be able to walk straight."

"Promise?" Rig pushed close, bit his earlobe once, quick and sharp.

"You fucking know it."

He put on the blinker, turning off. "Five minutes," he growled. "And that ass is mine."

"All yours." He could feel Rig vibrating against him.

His knuckles went white on the wheel. A minute or two more and he'd be able to hold that ass in his hands. He shifted, hips pushing automatically against Rig's hand.

"So fucking hot." Rig worked him, that goddamn hand knowing just where to touch him.

"That would be you."

He turned again, slowing the Jeep down for the last couple of blocks. Rig took advantage of it, too, working his zipper open and pulling his cock right out.

"Want that mouth," he groaned, turning onto their block and slowing the Jeep further.

"Uh-huh." Rig slipped the seat beat off, slid down into the floorboard, tongue sliding up his prick. Goddamn.

He managed to get them into the drive without crashing the car, his hand sliding from the wheel to Rig's head as soon as he turned the engine off.

Rig didn't play around, head bobbing, lips wrapped tight around the base of his prick. Fuck, yes. Rabbit. He pushed up with his hips, giving Rig exactly what his Rabbit had asked for, fucking that mouth as best he could.

All that teasing meant he was ready to go and he could feel his orgasm gathering in his balls. "Soon," he growled, fingers tightening in Rig's blond curls.

Rig answered by swallowing around the tip of his cock, hands pressing on his balls, rolling them. That was fucking it. His hips slammed up, his cock shooting down Rig's throat as his orgasm rocked him. Deep hums vibrated his cock as Rig cleaned him off, kept him hard.

His hand loosened its hold on Rig's hair, fingers sliding around to stroke Rig's cheek, Rig's lips. "Inside. My cock has a date with your ass."

Rig nodded, lips on his fingers, sucking them in. He pushed his fingers deep, fucking Rig's mouth with them for a moment, holding the grey eyes. Then he grinned and undid his seat belt. "Race ya."

Rig snorted, fumbling his way up out of the floorboard. Rock laughed and grabbed the fucking dry cleaning. He stopped to open Rig's door, but he knew better than to haul Rig out of the Jeep. Once he had his hands on that redneck, there would be no stopping him.

Rig did the in-out thing with Grim, dumping food in the mutt's bowl, ass in the air as Rig bent to the task.

He groaned, and went over to grab that ass, grinding his still hard prick against it. "You about done with that mutt?"

"Uh-huh." Rig nodded, braced against the counter. "Done. Fuck."

"Right here, then."

He slid his hands around Rig's waist, tugging open the button on Rig's jeans, making slow circles against Rig's ass. The tight denim fought him, but there wasn't anything that was going to get in the way of him getting that ass. He was careful with the zipper though, no way was he going to damage the goods.

Finally, Rig's ass was naked, legs hobbled by the jeans. He slid his finger along Rig's crack, his other hand grabbing Rig's hard cock and jacking it slowly.

"Blue..." Hard and leaking, Rig's cock was fucking hot. Desperate.

"Oh, now, you need to wait for me..."

He spread that hot liquid around, thumb sliding across the tip. His other hand worked his own jeans open, tugged them down so he could rub along that sweet crack.

"You. You want me to wait... when... when you're doing *that*?"

"Yep. It'll make you tough." He sucked on his fingers and worked one into Rig's ass, loosening his fingers around Rig's cock and jacking lightly.

"Fucking need you." Rig squeezed him tight.

"I've got what you need right here." Rock pushed a second finger in, spreading Rig wide, getting him a little wet. "Got what we both need." Because fuck. He needed inside that tight heat.

"Uh-huh. Deep and hard, Marine." Hot, tight-assed slut. *His* hot, tight-assed slut.

"You know it." He'd have taken his time, drawn it out, made Rig beg, but that would have meant waiting and Rig's ass was too good to wait for. He bit at Rig's shoulder as he tugged his fingers out. "You ready, Rig? Ready for my prick?"

"Fuck, yes. Ready. Do it." Demanding ass.

He guided his prick to that little hole, rubbing against it a bit, loving the way the hot, wrinkled skin slid against the head of his prick. Then he pushed, sliding right in. Still so fucking tight, even after so fucking long. Rig fucking drew him in, made him grunt with the pressure. He leaned his forehead against Rig's back, panting as he went in as far as he could, their bodies frozen together, fucking joined at the goddamned hip.

As soon as he knew he wasn't going to go off like a fucking Fourth of July rocket the minute he started moving, Rock pulled out and thrust back in, hard. His hand wrapped tight around that sweet cock again, letting each of his thrusts drive it along his palm. It wasn't going to take Rig any time. The man was half-drunk and all the way to needing him, but if Rock was lucky, Rig'd stay up through a hard fuck.

His free hand wrapped around Rig's hip, holding on tight as he banged Rig with all he had. So fucking good. There was absolutely nothing like Rig's ass.

"Rock. Rock. Blue. Fuck." Rig started shaking, entire body shuddering for him.

"Right fucking here, Rabbit. Right fucking here." Harder, faster, he just gave it to Rig. Gave his Rabbit everything.

Just like that, Rig gave it right back, ass milking his cock as his cowboy came for him. He roared as he came, hips jerking, pushing his prick deeper as he shot. Moaning, he kept moving, hips just sort of circling a little, making them both shudder a time or two before he stilled, head on Rig's shoulder.

"Hey." There was a wealth of information in that one word.

He rubbed his cheek against Rig's shoulder, staying buried, staying right fucking there for just a moment longer. "Hey."

Then Grimmy started snuffling around his ankles and he groaned, his prick sliding out of Rig's ass.

"Shower?" Rig nudged him with one shoulder.

"Yeah, that sounds about right."

Time to enjoy the creature comforts while he could. Oh, he liked the beach well enough, but a hot shower big enough for them both would not be in the cards the next couple of days.

He grabbed Rig's face and tilted it, taking that mouth in a hard kiss. Rig hummed, tongue sliding against his, sweet as fuck. He lingered, enjoying the taste of beer and himself in Rig's mouth, enjoying the way Rig smelled less like Stetson and more like *Rig* just now.

Then he smacked Rig on the ass. "Come on. Let's get wet."

# Chapter Three

Rig hauled his ass up out of the Jeep, headed into the house, tired down to the bone. It hadn't been a long trip -- not at all, just a week -- but it had been ugly and long and sleepless and Rig was ready to be home.

Clean.

Fed.

Rested.

Fucked.

He dumped his stuff on the kitchen floor and headed for the bathroom, grunting a little at Rock and whoever the fuck was in there shooting the shit with his Marine.

Shower.

Shower, first.

Then everything else.

He was halfway through it, the water blessedly hot and *wet* and good, when Rock appeared behind him, hot and hard, solid.

"Hey." He kept his face to the water. He didn't care who'd been here, didn't care what was up or whether Rock was having a good day or anything. He just needed that strength.

Rock grunted in reply, hands wrapping around his hips, that heat and strength right there behind him. "'Bout time you're back." The words were spoken against the skin of his neck, Rock sucking the water right off his skin.

Yeah. Yeah, it was. He nodded, head falling forward as he moaned. He just needed some of this. Right now.

Rock's tongue slid over and around his spine, the fingers at his hips moving, sliding across his belly and up. Headed for his nipples in that take no prisoners way his Blue had. Rig just stood there, watched his nipples tighten in anticipation, watched those big goddamn fingers move up his ribs.

A low rumble vibrated against his spine as one of Rock's fingers reached his nipple. "Just look at that. Love the way you beg..."

"Need." He didn't have to say it; Rock knew, but he said it anyway. Meant it.

"Got what you need right here." Rock's prick slid along his ass. Hot and slick, it promised to give him everything he needed.

His head was suddenly tilted back, Rock's mouth covering his, Rock's mouth taking his. Fuck, yes. That tongue pushed into his lips as Rock's fingers found his nipples and rolled and tugged, lights sparking off behind his eyes.

That fat prick rubbed and taunted, not letting him forget for a second that Rock needed as much as he did. One of Rock's hands slid away from his chest and found his ass, fingers pushing at his hole. Rig grunted, pushing sounds that meant more and please and fuck, yes into Rock's lips. One pushed right in, going deep, circling, twisting inside him.

"Fucking want you."

"Uh-huh. Please." Every fucking muscle in his body felt tight, hard, too tense.

A second finger pushed into him, stretching him out, a little bit of soap on this one, barely helping ease the way. It felt good though, right, and he just wanted more, now. So Rig turned and crawled right up Rock's body, not even worrying about whether Rock could hold his weight. His Blue could.

His back slammed up against the wall as Rock pushed hard against him, the fingers inside him disappearing. The heat of Rock's prick pushed against him and then spread him wide -- so fucking thick.

"Blue." Rig's eyes rolled, heart pounding in his chest as he found Rock's rhythm, moved with it.

"Right here, Rig. Right fucking here." Each word was punctuated by a thrust, Rock's whole body pressing against him as the thick cock pushed deep. Yeah. Right there. In him. Filling him up. Christ.

Rock's mouth covered his, tongue sliding into his mouth, echoing the rhythm of their hips, of Rock's hand as it wrapped around his prick. Rock was fucking everywhere. It took a bit before he got into it completely, before his brain shut down and he could just be Rig. Just be him. Rock seemed to know, the hand around his cock tightening, Rock's thrusts getting faster, cock finding his gland and nailing it.

"Fuck..." He was going to crawl out of his fucking skin. He was.

"Yeah. Give it to me, Rabbit. Show me how fucking good it is."

"Just what I need." His body went tight and he shot, bucking and riding Rock's prick.

That fucking roar he hadn't heard in a week sounded, heat pulsing deep inside him as Rock came. A low, soft groan followed the roar, Rock leaning against him, hot and solid, holding him up against the tiles.

"Hey." He held on, eyelids heavy, muscles going lax.

Rock's lips slid across his, tongue sliding out briefly. "Glad you're back."

"Yeah. Me, too." Real glad. Damn.

That fat prick slid from him, Rock sighing and making sure he was steady on his feet before turning off the water.

"Let's go to bed and you can show me just how glad." Those blue eyes were watching him, looking at him, seeing him.

"You know it, Marine." Rig fucking hoped Rock didn't have any plans for tomorrow that extended beyond the fucking bedroom.

Rock draped a towel over his shoulders and knocked their hips together. "You think you remember how to use that mouth?" He got a wink, a shit eating grin.

"I might. You never know with me..." He licked his lips, grinned.

"I sure as fuck hope so." Rock leaned in and licked the path his own tongue had taken, the big hands rubbing the towel over him, drying him off.

Oh. Better.

"Fucking good to be home."

Rock grunted and dried himself quickly. "Rough one?"

"Yeah." He rubbed the back of his neck. Yeah. Too many dead Marines. Too many walking wounded. Too much fuckupedness for one week.

One of Rock's big hands pushed his out of the way, warm and good, rubbing his neck for him. "How about a couple beers, a backrub and I'll fuck you into the mattress." Rock knew how to put him to sleep when he needed it.

"Fuck yes. Please." He nodded, head dropping forward as he let Rock touch him.

Rock grabbed his hand and tugged him toward the bedroom. "Forget the beer, I've got everything you need right here."

"Promise?" He went easy, needing to know that Rock would take care of him.

"You know it."

Rock tugged and pushed and got him into the bedroom, shoved him down onto the bed. The sheets needed changing, the scent of Rock fucking strong on them. Then Rock straddled his ass, fingers starting to dig into the muscles of his neck and shoulders.

Fuck.

Fuck, he was going to die.

Or cry.

Or something.

"Don't stop."

Rock snorted. "Not planning to. Not until you're melted into the bed." Bending over him, Rock whispered into his ear. "That's when your ass is mine."

Rig shuddered, moaning deep and low, words just sorta lost as he nodded.

Rock ran a thumb slowly down along his spine, pressing against the bone, each vertebrae getting the same slow pressure. He could feel the strong muscles of Rock's thighs bracketing his ass, the heavy balls sitting right in the small of his back. Rig's muscles tried to fight it, but they relaxed, Rock making them wake up and pay attention.

"That's it," murmured Rock, sliding back along his ass, that fat prick hot and hard now, just dragging over his skin. Rock settled on his thighs, cock nestled in his crack, fingers working out from his spine to his sides.

He stretched out, moaning low, arms reaching up to hold onto the headboard.

"Sexy fucker." Rock's hands landed on his ass, the thick fingers hot as they dug in and worked his glutes.

"Yours." His thighs spread wide.

A low, sexy rumble came from Rock, the thick thumbs spreading his crack. "Love the way you beg."

"Me? Beg?" He hummed, butt pushing up to feel more.

"Uh-huh. The best kind of begging." Rock slid slowly down his legs, and Rock's breath slid along his crack, full of promise.

"Oh. Oh, Blue..." He pulled his knees up under him, spreading wide to ask Rock for more.

Rock licked from the top of his crack down past his hole and all the way to his balls, and then blew on him again.

"Hot." He rested his face against his arms, heart just pounding furiously.

A grunt was his only answer, Rock's tongue back on his skin, almost teasing before it settled at his hole, licking, the tip pushing in. The roughest sounds pushed out of him, his entire focus on his ass, on the heat flooding him. Rock groaned and pushed that tongue right into him, tongue fucking him with strong, quick jabs.

He started rocking, pushing right back toward Rock's face, just needing this. One of Rock's hands wrapped around his hip, pulling him back, encouraging him to keep moving, keep rocking. A low hum vibrated the tongue inside him.

"Fuck. Fuck. Blue. Blue, please. Need you." Fuck, he was going to fucking explode.

Rock's tongue disappeared, his Blue's heat spreading out over his back. The blunt, hot head of Rock's prick slid along his crack. "You got me."

"Yes." Don't fucking tease. In. God. The fucking room was spinning.

Groaning, Rock's prick sank into him, slowly, but surely, filling him up. He let Rock in and in and in, eyes closing as the pressure made him soar. Rock's hands spread his legs a little wider, shifted his ass, and that fat prick sank in just a bit more. They stayed like that for one heartbeat, and then another, before Rock started to move, each stroke long and slow, pure, amazing torture.

He just breathed with it -- in when Rock pulled out, out when Rock pushed in. Rock's hands slid up along his sides and over his shoulders before following his arms. Fingers twining with his on the headboard, Rock picked up the pace, spreading him wide again and again.

"Oh. Oh, hell yes. Blue. Just like that." Just what he fucking needed.

"All fucking night long, Rabbit." Or at least as long as he needed it, that fat prick spreading him open and pushing deep and fucking owning him, making every single other thing non-existent.

Rig just went with it. Floated. Burned.

Rock was as good as his word, making it last and last, until finally one hand left his, wrapping around his prick and jacking him with sure, hard strokes. He damn near sobbed with it, the sound more overwhelmed pleasure than anything. "Close."

"Then give it to me." Rock's tongue dragged from mid-back up to his neck, following his spine before shifting over to nip lightly at the sweet spot on the side of his neck. "Just give it up to me."

"Yeah..." The world shattered and he came, melting all around Rock.

Rock just kept pushing into him, making it last and last, like one orgasm rolling into the next until finally that fat prick jerked inside him and filled him deep with heat. Rock's weight came down on him, heavy and right, quick panting in his ear, hot breath on his neck.

The world faded away, sleep taking him just like that.

Finally.

He was home.

\*\*\*

The alarm went off and Rock growled, slamming the top of the clock-radio to shut it off.

He fucking hated mornings.

Of course this morning found him with his own redneck octopussed around him, something that hadn't happened in a fucking week.

Oh, now, he hadn't had a *proper* wake-up call in seven days... he should have left the alarm ringing for longer. He grunted and moved his arm, shifted.

Rig groaned, stretched, white eyebrows drawing together. Yeah, that was it. Time to wake up and start the day right. He shifted again, making sure he jolted a bit. He didn't poke or anything, but he didn't see why there couldn't be happy making sucking happening...

"Mmm. Mornin'." Rig grabbed the headboard, back popping with the arch, sheets sliding over that gold skin.

He reached out, stroking a hand along Rig's belly. Fucking sexy. His cock jerked, begging for Rig's attention. "Yeah, fucking alarm's gone off."

"Yeah?" Rig licked his lips, smiled slow and easy. "You woke up before me?"

"Looks like. How the fuck did that happen?" He shifted to rub against Rig's thigh, his prick just aching for that mouth.

"Been working hard." Rig nuzzled his jaw, started slowly sliding down.

"And not sleeping 'til last night," he growled. He knew how his Rabbit worked when away. All work and smoking and patching guys up.

"Uh-huh." Rig kissed his nipple, then licked down each rib.

He groaned, back arching, pushing into Rig's mouth. So fucking good. He slid his fingers through Rig's curls. Man needed a haircut. Still, this gave him something to hold onto.

"Mmm. Smell good." Teeth scraped along his belly, his toes curling with the burn.

His fingers tightened, then loosened -- much as he wanted to just push Rig down to his cock, he wanted this, too, wanted it however Rig was going to give it to him. Rig's tongue slid over the tip of his cock first, lips wrapping just around the head and tugging. God fucking damn, there was nothing on earth like Rig's mouth. He gave a long, low moan, his hips moving automatically, jerking.

Those lips opened up and took him down to the root. No stress, no tension, just Rig and suction and heat. His head went back, eyes closing as he just lived in his cock, in Rig's mouth. His balls ached, Rig's swallowing him and making his whole body shudder. Rig's hands cupped his ass, thumbs rubbing his balls, pushing just hard enough to ache.

"Fuck yeah. Fuck." He grunted the words out, both hands wrapping around Rig's head. His hips starting to push, fucking Rig's face.

Just like always, Rig took him in. Fuck. Those grey eyes stared up at him, sparkling. Wanting him. He wrapped his hand around Rig's cheek, moving faster, so close already. It had been too damned long for it to last. Then Rig moaned, the sound vibrating all along his cock. Jesus.

His eyes rolled in his head, his thrusts turning into a few graceless jerks, and then he was coming, the pleasure from that mouth just too fucking much.

Rig hummed, settling down against his legs, cock hard against his calf, cheek soft on his thigh. He slid his hand through Rig's curls. "I've got some time, what are you needing?" he asked, deciding to skip his PT. Give Rig an orgasm, have some coffee. Enjoy the fucking after blowjob glow.

Rig hummed, rubbing against him, smiling like a kid at Christmas. "Touch me, Blue Eyes?"

Oh, he could do that. He wrapped his hands around Rig's biceps and tugged the lean body up, dragging it along his own. He licked at Rig's lips, tasting himself there as his fingers slid down over Rig's chest, deliberately missing those sweet, little nipples. Rig tried not to respond, but his own personal cowboy's breath hitched, pupils dilating.

Chuckling, he stroked Rig's belly, following the curves of lean muscles. He was touching, wasn't he?

Of course, his Rabbit arched and smiled, pushing up into his touch. "Feels good."

"Yeah? How about this?" He circled Rig's nipple with one finger and then slowly slid it across the tight, needy, little nub.

"Oh..." Rig's eyes rolled, cock throbbing. He'd bet he could make Rig come, just from this.

He pinched a little, rolled the hard bit of flesh, watching as he pushed his thigh between Rig's, giving that sweet prick something to rub against. Rig groaned, belly tight against him, cock giving his belly wet kisses.

He slid his finger over to Rig's other nipple, rubbing it gently, and then with more force. "Such fucking sensitive, little titties."

"Uh-huh. Uh-huh. 'S good." Rig's teeth sank into that sweet bottom lip.

"Just good?" He pinched and then slid his fingers down along Rig's side, just hard enough it wouldn't tickle.

"Good. Fuck." Rig shifted, stretched, fingers rubbing his own nipples.

"Hey now, that's cheating." He took Rig's wrists in his right hand and tugged them up above Rig's head. Oh, now. Look at that pretty, tanned skin go all rosy. Rock fucking approved.

"These," he murmured, plucking at Rig's nipples with his free hand. "Are mine to play with."

"I. Oh. Are they?" Rig's body just reached for his hands.

"Looks to me like they are, Rabbit."

He pressed their lips together, tongue pushing into Rig's mouth, taking it. His thumb slid across Rig's nipple as he devoured that mouth over and over again. Every touch made Rig ripple, cock throbbing against his leg, deep groans pushing into his lips. He tightened his grip on Rig's wrists, tugged them higher to stretch Rig's body out for him.

"Blue." Look at those pretty, tight titties just begging for it.

"You need more? I've got more for you." Bending, he took one into his mouth, worried it with his teeth.

Fuck, he could live on that low, desperate sound for fucking *ever*. He sucked and tugged, tongue flicking across the tip, fingers digging into Rig's hip, pulling him in close.

"Need. Jim. Jim. Fuck." Score. When Rig used his name, he was either fucked or golden.

He let Rig's nipple go, tongue licking across it a couple times before moving on to the other one, giving it the same treatment. Fuck, Rig tasted good. Smelled good, too. All fucking man. All his. Rig was fucking the air, his thigh, anything, head rolling back and forth. Yeah, that's it, Rabbit, show me how fucking much I make you need. He hummed around the tittie in his mouth, letting the vibrations go from him to Rig.

Heat splashed up along Rig's belly, the cry echoing, just ringing through the air. He raised his head, kissing Rig hard as he ran his fingers through the mess on Rig's belly. Then he brought his fingers up, pushing them into Rig's mouth. Rig groaned, sucking hard, eyes closed.

Fucking sexy.

He licked at Rig's fingers and lips, loving the taste. Rig cuddled right in, moaning low and octopussing around him. He chuckled. Damn, he'd missed this as much as the blowjobs.

"Got about twenty minutes before I gotta go."

"But it's Friday, so we can go play pool tonight, huh?"

"Yep. Been too long since I beat your ass at a game or three."

"I bet I can win one out of three."

"You think so, do you?" He grinned and rolled over so he was on top of Rig. "What's the bet?"

Rig stretched under him, just rubbing away. "What do you want, Blue?"

Well now, that was a good question, because he'd bet a month of blowjobs Rig'd do pretty much anything he wanted. In bed.

"Chocolate pie."

Rig laughed, body shaking against him. "Deal. If I win, I want pancakes."

"You're on." He rubbed against Rig. "I should get dressed. Go yell at baby Marines."

"Lucky them." Rig sighed. "I guess I should get shit done, huh?"

Rock grunted, gave Rig one last hard kiss before getting up and stretching.

"Coffee?"

"I'll get it. You can shower, if you want." He could see the weight of the last week on Rig, see it in the slow motions across the room.

"No. Let's go to the donut shop on Watson. I'll buy you breakfast."

"Yeah? I could go for that." He got a quick grin, those grey eyes warm as fuck.

He nodded. "Then let's go." Let the Rocketman give you what you need, Rabbit. Sex, food, a chance to forget about the crap.

"Right behind you."

Fuck, yeah.

"That means you've got a hell of a view." He winked and walked out, feeling those eyes on his ass all the way.

# Chapter Four

Rock pulled his truck up next to Jeremy Roberts', turning off the engine and grinning over at Rig. "Wake up before your Momma gets out here and decides she needs to take care of you."

They'd both managed to get just over a week off for the holidays this year, Rig trading shifts like a crazy man. Rock thought Rig might even be booked to work twenty-four hours straight over New Year's Eve. The drive was a bitch, but they'd shopped on the way, and he liked having his own wheels, not being dependant on getting lifts and shit.

He gave Rig a shake. "I said we're here."

Rig blinked away, staring up at him. "Shit, man. I'm sorry. I just dozed off."

Rock snorted and then laughed. "Rig, you dozed off four hours ago." Rig'd been snoring away to beat the band. It was kind of cute.

"Longview is boring."

Charlene came out of the front door, apron covered in flour, hair dyed bright red and piled on top of her head. "Boys! You're home!"

"Good lord, she's been attacked by Miss Clairol."

Rock bit his lip, but there was no way he was going to be able to keep from laughing at that. No fucking way. Sure enough, he lost it. But he climbed out and went to get their luggage, and by the time he got to the porch, he was just smiling wide for Charlene.

"Hey, Jim, honey." She kissed his cheek. "Merry Christmas. Y'all look good."

He put down the bag in his right hand and gave her a one-armed hug. "You do, too. You've done something different to your hair."

"Oh, God. Julie decided to go to hair-do school." Charlene's eyes rolled, making him laugh harder. "She dropped out last week, before she decided I needed a perm, thank god."

"Well it's Christmassy anyway." He gave her a wink. "All you need's a few lights. I bet Rig could rig something up for you..."

"Don't make me beat you, son." She laughed, went up on tiptoe, and kissed his cheek.

"Yes, ma'am." He kissed her cheek in return and took the bag back up. "Where do you want us?"

"Alex's old room, honey. It's all set up for y'all."

"Woo! Back in the garage!" Rig grabbed his momma, swung her around. "Hey, beautiful. Are there cookies?"

"Only if your daddy is napping."

Rock laughed. "Let me get our shi-- stuff in Rig's room and then I'll come help with that cookie situation." He gave Rig a look that clearly said he expected there to be at least a couple saved for him.

"I'll help. Otherwise Momma will peek at the presents." Rig ducked Charlene's swat, her laugh ringing out.

"You two get a move on, I'll put some coffee on. Jeremy'll want a cup with his cookies."

"Thanks, Momma." He wouldn't dare call her Charlene to her face, not since that time she'd explained how rude it was that the man she considered her son-in-law couldn't bring himself to call her Momma. She'd said it in a joking manner, but Rock was pretty sure that glint in her eyes meant she was heart-attack serious, and when he'd next called her Momma she'd beamed at him.

"We won't be long."

Between him and Rig they made it in one trip, dragging clothes, presents and all up the little stairs. The little room was the same as always -- pictures of Rig riding horses, posters of football players and bulls and some nearly naked blond man that Rig insisted was a famous wrestler from when he was a kid.

It was kind of like stepping back in time, but then he thought that anytime they came here. Rig's family wasn't like his, and despite the arguments that occasionally broke out, it always managed to feel almost like a fairy tale about how families were.

He grinned over at Rig. "Glad we came?"

"You know it." Rig grinned over, grey eyes twinkling. "You gonna go riding with me this year, Blue?"

"Now, Rig. You know I go riding with you all the damned time..." Of course he was pretty sure Rig actually meant on a horse.

Rig's laugh rang out, that tight fucking cowboy butt sashaying by on the way to the window. "We could have a little trail ride..."

He followed that ass, just like a horse led on a halter, and pressed up against Rig's back, cock starting to take notice as it settled against Rig's butt. "I'll ride your trail anytime you want."

"Mmm. Merry fucking Christmas, Marine." Rig always relaxed right up when they came here, just as comfortable as could be.

He nodded, looking out over Rig's Daddy's place. They probably wouldn't see snow, but it would be cold enough to have a fire going, for the kitchen to feel warm and good and inviting, the smell of all that amazing food almost as good as eating it.

"We should go say hey to your Daddy." Get their cookies and coffee, and if he knew Charlene at all there was some chocolate pie in the fridge that she'd made 'just in case they needed an extra dessert'.

He rubbed against Rig's ass, his prick reminding him just how long they'd been driving, the truck smelling like Rig and him not able to touch.

"We should." Rig looked up and back at him, that grin just fine. "He's got himself a new pistol and he's dying to show it off."

He bent and took a kiss, being good and keeping it from going deep and hard. He couldn't keep his cock from firming right up, though, and he rubbed just a bit more against Rig's ass. "Well if a man's got a pistol to show off, we shouldn't keep him waiting..." They could come back to bed early tonight -- it had been a long enough drive to cite being tired early on.

"I'll make it worth waiting for, Rocketman." Rig turned, pressed close, moving against him like the man was dancing.

He groaned, the tease ratcheting everything up a few notches. "You sure? You're setting yourself a pretty tall order." His hands slid along Rig's back, cupping his ass.

"I can handle it." Rig's fingers slid around his arms, just holding on.

"I'm looking forward to you... handling it." He gave Rig a wink and brought their mouths together again.

Pulling back before he could get too lost in Rig's mouth, he took a step back and cleared his throat. "Come on now, I don't want your Daddy thinking we're up here fucking each other's brains out instead of saying hello." It was the one thing he didn't like about coming down to visit -- he liked having free access to that lean body.

"Ew. There's no reason to use the words daddy and fucking in the same sentence." Rig winked and grabbed a sweater, tugging it on over his t-shirt. "Come on. We need cookies."

He laughed, and followed; he had a reason all right, getting his cock, and Rig's, to play nice so they could be good.

"You think your Momma made those pecan ones?" They were his secret vice; anything with lace in the name wasn't a man's cookie, but damn they were good. He shoved his fingers into his jeans' pockets as they crossed over to the house, there was a definite chill in the air.

"You know it. She's been cooking up a storm. Julie'll be over some time tomorrow with the girls, so Momma's preparing." One of the dogs came barreling over, barking his head off and wagging at the same time. Stupid beast had nothing on Grimmy. Too bad they'd had to leave the beast at the kennels this time 'round, silly mutt would have been in heaven here.

A wall of warm air hit them as they opened the front door, the smells enough to make his stomach growl. "Oh, damn, I do love it when your Momma cooks."

"Of course you do, Jim. That woman's got talent." Goddamn, if he ever wanted to know what his Rabbit would look like in thirty-five years, he just had to look at Jeremy Roberts. Craggy and skinny, skin like leather and lively, grey eyes, Rig was the man's spitting image.

"Hey, old man. I like your new truck. You decided to go with the king cab?"

Jeremy grinned, nodded. "Ain't she a beaut?"

Rock nodded and added his two cents. "Yeah, she is. I like the red, too. I suppose that shows up the dirt as much as the dark blue did."

Rock shook hands with Jeremy and gave the man a one-armed hug. He liked Rig's Daddy, he surely did. "Merry Christmas."

"Merry Christmas, boys. Charlene says she'll make Chex mix and cheese balls for the ball games. Alex, you like the Cowboys for the game?"

"You know it."

"Jim?"

"Hell, no, they don't have a chance this year." Didn't much matter who they were playing, either, that was going to be his answer. Arguing over who was going to win and cheering for opposite teams was something he'd learned to enjoy the hell out of last Christmas. He met Jeremy's eyes. "You want to make it interesting?"

Those grey eyes lit up and he got a nod, a hooting laugh. "You know it, I got a pool written all up here in the front. Come on, now. Y'all can pick your squares."

The pad of paper was snatched from Jeremy's end table, the squares carefully drawn out, scores written out for each quarter, each game. Twenty picks later, he was in for a $20 and so was Rig, Charlene taking her picks as well.

"It smells really good in here," Rock told Charlene as he settled in the big chair next to Jeremy's. He gave her his best smile outside of the one he saved just for Rig and that sweet as fuck mouth. "I bet you've outdone yourself again this year."

"Oh, yeah." Charlene plopped down on Jeremy's lap, the old man's arms wrapping around her waist. "We're having an all-soy-fu Thanksgiving."

Rig snorted. "Momma! If you're going to tease, get it *right*."

"Oh, it was worth it son, to see the look on Jim's face."

Rock shook his head. "That was just plain evil, Momma. You better be careful or you'll get coal in your stocking." Soy-fu'd sounded right -- or evil anyway -- to him, until Rig'd pointed out it was wrong.

"I'm hoping for earrings this year." Charlene kissed Jeremy's cheek, winked.

"Lord, woman. You're gonna break me."

Rock bit back his grin. Not only was Charlene getting her earrings, he and Rig had bought her a necklace to match. "You need lots of good karma for earrings, Momma. I think some cookies and coffee for a poor starving Marine would earn you plenty of brownie points."

His stomach growled loudly as he said it, emphasizing his point and making them all laugh.

"Lord, lord. I can't have my son-in-law starving. You want a plate, too, honey?" Lord, those two were still just all into each other.

Rock chuckled and let his foot touch Rig's thigh, his Rabbit sitting next to him on the floor, leaning against his chair. "I don't know how you manage to stay as skinny as you do, Jeremy."

"Us Roberts men have to eat a lot, else we get all scarecrow skinny. You shoulda seen my daddy, Jim. The man was tall as Alex and half as heavy. Was sorta scary."

"No way. Skinnier than this one? There couldn't have been anything to the man." Man, he bet the three of them -- Alex, Jeremy and his father -- would have been a sight next to each other, like seeing triple.

"He was a helluva guy. Rode saddle broncs when he was young, then settled right here."

Rig nodded. "Momma and Daddy ran his feed store before me and Julie showed up."

Jeremy chuckled. "Yeah, well. We could work around Bobby, but you two hooligans? Needed your momma full-time."

"Oh, I knew you were a troublemaker, Rig." He grinned over at Jeremy and winked. "Some things never change."

"Don't make me kick your butt, Marine." Rig stretched out on the floor, one of Charlene's little frou-frou dogs settling on his belly.

"I'd like to see you try." He could see it, too, Rig coming at him, that little dog on his shoulder like a demented parrot, and he stared to chuckle, tickled by the thought.

"Lord, lord. You two be good." Charlene was laughing, too, carrying a big assed tray of cookies and coffee cups.

"Oh, let me help you, Momma." Rock got up and grabbed the tray from her, setting it down on the little table between him and Jeremy. There were half a dozen different kinds of cookies there, including a big pile of his favorites. "These look really good."

"Of course they do. They're Christmas cookies." Rig grabbed a little round one, dusted in powdered sugar.

Rock grabbed a mug and two of the pecan ones, happily stuffing both into his mouth. Oh yeah, they were the fucking best.

The TV came on, Charlene settling on the sofa, Jeremy taking some cookies. The Christmas tree was twinkling, the fire just crackling in the fireplace. Rig's head came to rest against his knee and Rock grunted contentedly. There wasn't any pressure to fill the quiet, nobody was going to comment on him and Rig touching as long as they didn't start making out. Well, he assumed that last part and sure as fuck wasn't going to test it.

He finished his coffee and at least one of every type of cookie, a couple more of his favorites, and then he grunted again. "Rig tells me you've got a new weapon, Jeremy?"

"Oh, Jim. I do. I got a couple things in the workshop for y'all to see." Jeremy's eyes lit up, the man leaned forward and started talking. Guns, tools, horses, workshops -- they all talked and talked until the sun went down, Charlene heading off to the kitchen again to make supper.

It was a great afternoon, relaxing and enjoyable. He liked Rig's family. That feeling only increased when they were called to the table for supper, an amazing spread making him moan.

"You sure do know the way to a man's heart, Momma."

"Honey, I've been feeding Roberts men for more than thirty years." He was handed a carving knife, a roast pushed in front of him. "You do the honors, Jim. Alex, get your daddy a glass of milk."

"My pleasure." He gave her a smile. "Make mine a beer, Alex honey." He started carving, nice thick slabs of meat. Damn, it smelled good.

"Alex honey..." Rig looked at him, one eyebrow raised. "Momma, did you make green beans? Rock loves those." Oh, bastard.

He shot Rig a look back that promised retaliation. "Not as much as Rig loves roast." He cut an extra thick slice and put it on Rig's plate.

"Rig loves my biscuits." Charlene chuckled, patted Rig's arm. "I got sausage for in the morning."

"Yum. I imagine we'll be sleeping in, so don't start them too early." He had plans for Rig's mouth.

"I've got to run into Dallas. I'll leave them in the oven warming for y'all."

"Dallas?" Now that would give them most of the day just the two of them. He could handle that.

"Yeah. I need to shop so Aggie and Missy and me are going in together for the day."

Jeremy snorted and rolled his eyes. "Leave your purse here, honey."

"You should go with her, show her how to really spend it." He winked and settled in front of his full plate.

"No!" Charlene's eyes went wide, head shaking. "I have to. Uh. Pick up. I mean."

"Daddy hates shopping, Rock."

Rock laughed and grinned over at Jeremy. "Just another reason to like you. Maybe Rig should go with her and you and I can continue our conversation."

"No." Charlene glared at him. "I am going with the girls and you boys are staying here."

"Why, Momma, does that mean you won't take me if I ask very nicely?" It was hard to keep a straight face, but he did his best.

"Jim South, you are not too big to turn over my knee."

He tried to swallow his chuckled, "Yes, ma'am."

Rig just cackled, plopping down in a seat next to Jeremy, both of them enjoying the hell out of this.

He waited until the laughter had died down and they'd all had a bite or two. "But being left out of this Dallas trip just might scar me for life."

"Really? Then you'll have to take me for the after-Christmas sales. Jeremy hates the crowds and I get so nervous with all the traffic."

Oh.

Oh, goddamn.

Oh, why did he think he'd just fucked himself?

"Well now, that might depend on how much spiked eggnog I indulge in -- I wouldn't want to drive hung over and get you into an accident." He could salvage this. Maybe.

"Bullshit." It was Jeremy that came to his rescue. "There's football on then, honey. You call Aileen and I'll pay for y'all's gas, but these boys are gonna sit and watch with me. I bought the good beer." Rig's Daddy? Was a damned good man.

"I would prefer the football, Momma. I'm about as fond of shopping as Jeremy."

Charlene chuckled. "It was worth a try."

"Pass the potatoes, Alex, and get your momma to sit down and quick teasing your man."

"Momma, Daddy says sit down and quit..."

Charlene whapped Rig good and hard. "I heard him."

Rock bit his lip and tried hard not to laugh. He had a dinner to eat and his teasing with Momma'd already nearly gotten him into big trouble. "This is really good, Momma."

"It is. Can I have another biscuit, please?" Rig and Jeremy dug in, letting him feel comfortable eating seconds and thirds.

By the end of his meal he was stuffed to the gills and he sat back with a groan, patting his belly. "I don't think I could manage another bite. Unless you're hiding some chocolate pie in the fridge." The only person who made better chocolate pie thank his Rig was Rig's Momma.

"There might be a couple in there..."

A couple.

Hell, yes.

He'd make that trip to the stores the day after Christmas for that. He was lucky enough he didn't have to. "You're the best, Momma."

"Of course I am." Charlene chuckled, patted his hand. "There's cherry for Alex and Jeremy, too."

"Oooh. Really? Homemade?"

"Charlene, you spoil them."

She rolled her eyes, stuck her tongue out at Jeremy. "Yes, like I spoil you."

Rock chuckled. "What's your favorite, Jeremy?" He'd bet dollars to donuts Charlene'd made that as well.

"Pecan."

Rig chuckled, nodded. "Momma makes a fabulous pecan pie."

"Right. Could I have a slice of cherry and pecan as well as the chocolate, Momma?" Never let it be said he gave up an opportunity for extra dessert.

"Whatever you'd like, son. I made them for y'all to eat."

He sat a little straighter and beamed at her. "Thanks, Momma."

It didn't take long to polish off each of the slices of pie Charlene gave him, and he was truly about to pop once he was done. Jeremy suggested they retire to the comfortable chairs in the front room. Rock made a half-hearted offer to help with the dishes, beaming at Charlene when she told him to go on and visit, Rig could help her.

He gave her a kiss on the cheek and soon he and Jeremy were comfortably ensconced, digesting their dinners. Jeremy didn't bother him with small talk, just found something with cops and robbers on the tube and watched about ten minutes of it before the man was sound asleep, snoring softly.

He dozed himself, waiting on Rig to be finished with Charlene. They had some unfinished business back in the room over the garage.

The smell of coffee woke him, Rig and Charlene sitting and chatting, a cup of black sitting at his elbow, just waiting for him.

He drank some, waiting for those grey eyes to find his and then smiling over.

"Coffee's good." He debated whether or not he could get away with asking for a cookie or two when he noticed a pair of the pecan lacy things sitting next to where the coffee cup had been.

Grunting, he grabbed one and munched happily. Rig nodded, smiled over and fuck, but that was a good feeling. Belonging right here. Felt good enough he didn't hurry Rig along, just half watched the cops and robbers, half listened to Rig and Charlene catching up on everything and everyone.

Of course by the time the news came on, he figured he'd been good long enough and deserved his reward. Standing, stretching, he yawned. "'Bout that time, Rig."

"Yeah. Been a long day. You have fun tomorrow, Momma. We're gonna take a day to just relax, be lazy." Those eyes promised more than just relaxation.

"Night, Momma." He kissed her cheek, got a hug and a pat from her.

He linked his arm through Rig's and they headed out, Jeremy snoring up a storm behind them.

Rig shivered as they wandered, that wind just biting right through. "Oh, goddamn. It's chilly. You have a good evening, Blue Eyes?"

Rock slid his arm around Rig's shoulders, tugging the lean body in close to keep him warm. "I did."

"Good." Rig hummed, pressed close. "Want you, man."

"Fuck, yes. Been wanting you all day."

They climbed the stairs, his cock getting a little harder with each step. Rig's hands squeezed his ass, hurrying him up.

He only waited long enough for them to clear the door before he wrapped his hands around Rig's skull and took a kiss. Rig tasted good -- coffee and pecans and tart cherry. Fuck, yes. Rig stole his fucking breath away, tongue sliding into his lips, making his head spin. It was sweeter, hotter because they'd had to wait all day, because he'd wanted to pound Rig into the mattress when they'd brought up their bags and hadn't.

He pushed Rig back up against the door, hips grinding into Rig's.

"Blue. Jesus. You're hot." Rig crawled up his body, one leg wrapping around his hip.

"On fucking fire for you." He grunted, grabbing Rig's T-shirt in both hands and spinning Rig, manhandling his Rabbit right over to the bed.

"Cookies make you horny?" Rig was laughing into his lips, hands tugging at his shirt.

He snorted. "They do when delivered by this nurse I know." He raised his arms, let Rig pull the shirt up and off.

"Want you, Blue. Been watching you all evening."

"Yeah? You obviously liked what you saw." He flexed for Rig, showing off before undoing the top button of his jeans.

"What's not to like, Marine?" Rig's fingers danced right up his belly, teasing and tickling.

"Not a fucking thing." Rock's voice sort of growled, six-pack jumping beneath Rig's fingertips. "You're wearing too many clothes."

"I am?" Hot fucking tease.

"Yep." Rock got his zipper down, his prick pushing out eagerly against his skivvies. He pushed them down just enough to give Rig a good view of his cock. "Take 'em off, Rig. I want skin."

Rig nodded, starting wiggling, peeling the denim off. Putting his hands on his hips, Rock watched, all that wiggling making his cock just throb. Now he could watch that all night. He got a nice, long look at lean legs, a full, hard cock, those pretty nipples tight and stiff.

He licked his lips and pushed his own jeans down past his hips, letting gravity take them. "Looking good, Rig."

"Yeah? You like it? It's all yours."

"You know I like it. You know I do." He watched a moment longer, hand dropping to his cock, fingers wrapping around it, sliding.

"I know." Rig's eyes lit up, fastened on his cock. Watching. Lips parted.

Fuck, he loved that mouth. Fucking loved it. "You want it, don't you? Come and get a taste."

"I do. You know how I need." Rig headed toward him, mouth open, tongue wetting those lips.

He licked his own lips, groaning, fingers sliding on his cock. He squeezed the head, watching as a drop of liquid pooled from the tip.

"Mine." Rig's tongue just traced his slit, stealing the drop.

"Fuck, yes." His fingers wrapped around Rig's head, tugging gently, encouraging a stronger touch. That tongue pushed against his slit again, fucking him so carefully, making him shake. His hands dropped to Rig's shoulders, holding on as his knees hit the bed.

"Mine." Rig went down on him, long and sweet, the touches making him crazy as fuck.

"Uh-huh." No argument from him.

"Been waiting all fucking day for this."

Rig didn't say another thing, just sucked him like he was Rig's entire goddamn world. Head falling back, he moaned, let Rig hear how fucking good it was. No matter how many times Rig did this, it was still so fucking good.

He loved the sight of Rig's head bobbing over his cock, loved the way those lips dragged and pulled, loved that swirl of the tongue. He slid his fingers across Rig's cheek, thumb tugging on the swollen lower lip. Rig's answer was a sweet groan, that sound as happy as anything he'd ever heard.

His hips started to move -- no way anyone could keep still with that mouth working them, no fucking way. In and out, his prick hitting the back of Rig's throat, his balls drawing up. Fuck. Fingers tugged his balls, rolled them, Rig demanding he give it up, give it over.

He wasn't about to deny Rig, or himself, for a second, he just gave it up to that mouth, groaning as he shot hard. His hips kept moving, sliding his throbbing prick along Rig's tongue.

His Rabbit let him slide free, lean body stretching out on the bed. "Good."

"You said it." He moved between Rig's legs, crawling up to lie over his Rabbit. "So's this." He rubbed a little, his prick going from half-mast to full again, just like that. Oh yeah, Rig was something special.

"Mmmhmm." Rig shifted, rubbing right back, the motion lazy and sensual, hot as fuck.

He licked Rig's lips and took a long kiss that had his toes curling and his hips moving. "What do you want?" he asked.

"You." Rig took his hand and put it on that hard prick.

"Mmm..." He wrapped his fingers around that heat, stroking a couple of times, feeling the veins, the harness beneath the hot velvet. "Done -- you've got me."

"Oh..." Rig arched up, fucking his fingers nice and slow.

Moaning softly, he buried his face in Rig's neck, licking at Rig's warm skin, at that spot that made Rig shiver. Soft, random words filled the air, nothing he had to listen to, because it all meant yeah and more and don't stop. He rubbed his own prick against that dip next to Rig's hip and licked his way down, finding one of Rig's sweet, little titties and worrying it with his teeth.

"Fuck, yeah. Blue. Jim. Fuck." That ratcheted the heat up, Rig starting to slide from seductive to hungry.

His thumb pressed into the tip of Rig's cock, slid back and forth and then dragged down along the hot length. He grabbed hold of Rig's balls and tugged, twisted them just enough to keep Rig from coming. "Not yet. Wanna fuck you."

"Uh-huh. Uh-huh. Please. Close." He teased a little bit longer, forcing Rig back from the edge so they could have a good ride.

He rubbed that sweet hole with his thumb, spreading Rig's pre-come over the wrinkled skin, and then pushed his fingers into Rig's mouth. "Nice and wet for me, Rig."

Rig nodded, sucking his fingers with as much enthusiasm as his prick had received. He slid them on Rig's tongue, his cock jerking in empathy.

"Gonna take you good and hard, Rig. Gonna make you come so hard you see stars."

"Promise?"

"Fuck, yeah." He sealed that promise with a kiss, too, pushing his tongue into Rig's mouth, both of them wetting his fingers.

Then he tugged them away and they slid out with a pop; he deepened the kiss. One of Rig's legs wrapped around his hip, Rig humping up against him. It spread Rig for him, opened those ass cheeks right up and he pushed his wet fingers in, groaning at the way Rig's body grabbed at him. He stretched and fucked Rig's ass, working faster now, wanting.

"Deeper. Deep. Oh. Oh, fuck. Right *there*." Rig's eyes rolled back in his head, lips parting.

He pegged the spot a few more times, watching Rig's face, loving the way Rig's hips rose and that cock jerked against him every time his fingers slid past the sweet, little gland. He didn't spend a whole lot of time there, though. No, he wanted in. He let his fingers slide away.

"Blue..." Rig grabbed those bony knees, pulled up and out, spreading himself wide.

Just look at that. "Slut," he murmured, grinning, settling between those spread legs and just nudging Rig's hole.

"Yours." Rig nodded, held his eyes.

"Hell, yes."

He sank into Rig's body, into that perfect fucking heat, not stopping until his hips were pressed up as hard and tight against Rig's ass as they could be. Rig held him tight, those muscles fluttering and shifting around him, enough to make him gasp, to make his hips want to jerk forward, push even deeper. He bent down, pressing Rig's legs back further so he could bring their mouths together. The kiss was quick and hard, a promise of what was coming.

Then he started to move. Rig rocked up, ass taking him, sliding along his shaft and riding him. His groan was low and needy, his body moving slowly, finding Rig's rhythm. The slap of their skin together was fucking sweet music. Rig groaned, stretched out beneath him, calling his name over and over.

So fucking sexy.

He moved faster, harder, demanding that that sound, his name in that ecstatic voice, come again and again. The old bed creaked and groaned, making them both chuckle, even as they arched, bucked, groaned. Their lips brushed, and he breathed in Rig's air, shared his own.

So fucking good.

So fucking... "Shit. Soon."

"Uh-huh. Please. Damn." Rig's head tossed, fingers digging into his shoulders.

He got his weight settled on one arm, wrapped his other hand around Rig's cock. "Come on my cock, Rig."

Rig's eyes went wide, entire body flushing. His cock was squeezed hard and he cried out, shouted Rig's name as he jerked, spunk shooting deep. Rig's come coated his fingers, Rig's cock throbbing in his touch. He pushed a few more times with his hips, a shudder going through him.

"Rig..." Groaning, he collapsed onto the lean body.

"Yeah. Yeah, Blue." Rig's arms slid up his spine, Rig just holding on.

He managed to grab the edge of the covers and half tug them over onto them. "Gonna stay right here for a moment."

"'Kay. We can sleep in tomorrow, huh? Take it easy." Rig octopussed and cuddled in, humming low.

"Uh-huh." He kissed the nearest patch of skin, nibbling. "Jeremy's gonna have plans."

"Uh-huh. Daddy always does." Rig didn't sound upset at all.

"So long as I get my morning wake-up." He winked, eyelashes tickling across Rig's skin.

"There's a reason the garage door locks." Rig chuckled, nuzzling right into him.

"Damn, I didn't lock it on the way in." He shifted reluctantly.

"Mmm. I'll get up early and do it. Stay."

He hummed, kissed Rig's cheek. "You're good to me."

"Mmmhmm. You're my Marine."

"All yours. And Uncle Sam's." He grinned, nipping at Rig's neck, fingers sliding along Rig's ribs.

"Yeah, yeah, yeah. Uncle Sam has you on leave for a few days." Rig chuckled, swallowed under his lips.

He chuckled, nodded. "You've got first dibs."

"Good. I'm going to keep you."

"Works for me."

It sure as fuck did.

# Chapter Five

"Catch the fucking ball!" Rig hooted as Daddy hollered, him and Rock battling hard over the final score.

Momma'd gone to hide or to Aunt Katie's or shopping or something after setting them up with beer and Chex mix and sausage balls. He'd gone in at halftime and made popcorn and queso. They were all a little buzzed, all full and all loving the concept of all-day games. Despite the shouts and noise over the score and the plays, Rock looked relaxed and happy. His Marine just plain got along with his Daddy like a house on fire.

A time out was called and Rock turned to him, grinning and looking hopeful, shaking an empty long neck. "Beer?"

"You know where the kitchen is, Marine." He rolled up and headed to grab three more. It was his turn.

Momma'd left chili in the crock-pot, the bowls of cheese and onions already cut up and waiting.

Looked like Rock *did* know where the kitchen was, that big body suddenly pressed up behind him, mouth sliding on his neck.

"Oh." His head fell forward, ass pushed backward, the action easy as breathing.

He could feel the rumble in Rock's chest against his back, his Marine's breath a little beery. Rock's solid hands slid over his belly, one moving up to tease his nipples through his shirt, the other headed south, cupping him, squeezing.

"Got another commercial or two," murmured Rock, licking the lobe of his ear.

"Jesus. You. Damn, Blue." His cock just went boing, filling and pushing toward Rock's fingers.

Rock laughed. "Could smell you sitting next to me. Missed my half-time blow. Hell, I missed two of them."

"Uh-huh. Takes something out of football."

"'S'okay, I'll put them on your tab." Rock's hand squeezed him through his jeans, worked him a little, making him hard as hell.

"I have a tab?" Goddamn it, he needed.

"Yep. You owe me two blowjobs and a fuck, and that's just today." Rock sounded a little breathless, and that hand let him go to push into his waistband, fingers just brushing the tip of his cock. "Look what I found."

"Oh, shit. Rock. You're gonna make me ache and I'll have to go back in a second." Daddy wasn't stupid.

"I know." Rock rubbed against his ass, letting him feel how much Rock wanted, too.

Daddy called from the front room. "We're back, boys!"

"Gotta go," growled Rock, letting go of his cock and grabbing one of the bottles.

"Bitch." He grabbed the other two, setting one hard against his cock.

Rock winked and adjusted himself in his jeans. Then that son of a bitch reached out and tweaked his nipple through his t-shirt, winked again, and headed back to the game.

He growled and grumbled, then took Daddy a beer, settling way out of the way of Rock's hands. Rock shot him a look and mouthed "coward" at him, but those blue eyes were just dancing for him.

He rolled his eyes, grabbed a handful of Chex mix. Asshole. Beautiful fucking asshole.

"Your momma leave us supper, boy?"

"Yes, sir. Chili. It's all ready whenever."

Daddy nodded. "She say when she was coming home?"

Rig shook his head. "No, sir. She's shopping."

Rock shook his head. "Football on and she's shopping. I never will get women."

"Oh, now. You see, she'll go spend my money, get herself gussied up and happy, and then she'll make my life easy for a bit. That's a nice thing -- a couple of pairs of shoes fixes all her woes." Lord, Rig was glad Momma wasn't here to hear that.

Rock just laughed. "I know all about woe fixing, but shopping's got nothing to do with it." Those eyes met his again, full of heat.

"Shit, son. That may be the only reason to go for bulls instead of cows. Less jewelry buying."

Rig almost snorted.

"Nope. Not the only reason. Not even close." Rock winked at him and by the time Daddy'd swung around to look at Rock, butter wouldn't melt in his Marine's mouth.

Oh, good lord. Rig fought his laugh with everything he had, just holding it in as hard as he could. Daddy just stared at Rock for a long second, one eyebrow raising.

Rock took a long drink of beer, licked his lips, and looked over at Daddy. "You're missing the game, Jeremy." There was a muscle in Rock's jaw that was just twitching.

Thank God the Cowboys intercepted the ball right about then, sending them all screaming and hollering as this tackle started trying to run down the field. They settled back in after the play, watching the tail end of the game.

Rock shook his head when it was over. "I backed the wrong horses this time around. What do you say, Jeremy? Double or nothing on this last game?"

"You got it, Marine. What do y'all say we get some chili during the pre-game? I've had a beer too many."

"Yeah, that sounds good. We got cornbread, Rig?" Rock stood and stretched for him. "Why don't you stay comfy, Jeremy, I'll help Rig dish up." Rock's eyes met his.

"I can make some up real quick. It'll take a half hour, or so."

"Yeah? I'll head out and get the feeding done then, son. We'll meet back here in thirty." Daddy stood, stretched a little.

"You sure, Daddy? I can do both."

"Nah. I'm good. You make cornbread as good as your momma's?"

"No sir, but it's not bad."

"Only cornbread I've tasted that's better is Charlene's. You need some help with that feeding, Jeremy?" Rock even sounded like he wanted to help, bless him.

"Nah, you help Alex out. I got a routine." That and Rock wasn't the most bull-friendly human being on earth.

"If you're sure. We'll see you in thirty -- be ready, my team's gonna wipe the floor with your boys this time." Rock nodded and grabbed their empties, carrying them out to the kitchen, giving him a fine view of that ass.

Daddy chuckled, headed for his jacket and work boots, and Rig followed that ass. Rock was good, let him get all the ingredients for the cornbread dug out and ready before the teasing started again. It started out slow, Rock brushing by him as he went over to get to the bowls out, then brushing by again as he set them next to the slow cooker.

He'd just measured the ingredients into the bowl when Rock pushed up against him again, arm reaching past him to grab a glass out of the cupboard, cock solid as an iron bar against his ass.

"You are an evil man, Jim South." Rig adored him.

"Hey, I offered to help your Daddy with his chores. I deserve a reward -- he could have taken me up on it!" Rock rubbed against him as he spoke.

"He could have. Then that big old bull could have hunted your butt." He rubbed right back, cock hard as a rock.

Rock groaned. "Yep. And then how could I have hunted yours?" Rock's hands slid around his hips, fingertips just brushing the sides of his prick. "Hurry up and get that made, Rig. We're on the clock."

He threw cornbread together in record time, melting butter and beating eggs like a madman. And all with Rock "helping" him, that fine body staying close, rubbing against him anytime he shifted, hands sliding across his belly or his hips for a touch before disappearing again.

"You're driving me fucking crazy, Blue." His balls were aching as he put the cornbread in the oven.

"I'm being *good* -- I'm letting you get that shit in the oven before I fuck you over the fucking table." Rock grabbed his hips and ground against his ass.

"Oh, Jesus. Rock. This is." His eyes went wide, just shocked.

"Charlene's gone shopping and Jeremy very nicely took his ass out to do the fucking chores, Rig. We've got," Rock glanced at the clock on the oven, "twenty minutes to get this done and I don't know about you, but I am not sitting through another game with a raging hard on."

Rock spun him, took his mouth. Rig's eyes rolled back in his head. He felt like a fucking teenager, making out here while his folks were close. Fuck. Solid hands landed on his ass, tugging him in closer, their cocks meeting through two layers of clothes as Rock's tongue pushed in deep.

"Bathroom. Rock. Just in case." He didn't want Daddy seeing them and dropping his teeth.

"Long as it gets done." Rock started backing up, hands tight on his hips and drawing him along.

"Uh-huh. Hard and fast, want to feel you all through the game." He wanted that hard cock buried in him, needed to feel Rock.

"Jesus fuck, Rig, that kind of talk's going to get you fucked, but way before we hit the bathroom." Rock growled, pushing him up against the wall, their mouths crashing together.

His legs wrapped around Rock's hips, body jerking, humping against his Blue like a horny puppy. Rock's hands landed on his ass, his Marine moving them, getting them into the fucking bathroom.

"Need. Damn it, Blue. I need you."

Rock slammed the door closed and put him down. "Get fucking naked."

"Bossy." He locked the door and stripped off, working fast, cock slapping his belly.

"No. Horny." Rock's own jeans hit the floor, his Marine grabbing for the hand lotion.

Rig nodded, bending over the sink, thighs spread. "Yeah. Goddamn."

Two fingers pushed into him, slick and wide, Rock working him hard and fast. "You ready?" Rock asked, already tugging his fingers out.

"Fuck, yes. Now, Marine. *Now.*" He felt like he was fixin' to die.

Rock didn't finesse, didn't take his time, just bumped the head of that thick cock against his hole and pushed, shoving right on in and stretching him wide. Groaning, Rock stopped long enough to grab his hips, and then they were off. Hard, hot, the burn and stretch the best thing he'd felt in days. Days. The sink rattled and he could see them both in the mirror, Rock's eyes drilling into him.

Faster and harder, Rock kept plowing into his ass, one hand sliding around to grab his cock, tug it just as hard.

"Jesus. Blue." He jerked, going up on his toes, ass clenching tight.

Rock grunted and kept pounding into him, shifting just enough to hit his gland. Rig shot hard enough that the edges of the world grayed, his entire body shaking. Jesus. Just. Jesus. Rock kept pounding into him, thrusts turning into graceless jerks.

He kept squeezing, trying to give Rock all he could. "Come on. Come on, Marine."

Rock's mouth pressed against his shoulder, muffling Rock's cry as heat filled him in several long pulses. Panting, Rock rested against him, hands still holding him tight.

"Jesus. You. We. God *damn*, Blue." His grin was going to split his face.

Rock laughed, breath hot against his neck. "Fucking sweet, Rig. Sexy motherfucker."

"Yours, huh?" He stood up, squeezed Rock's prick one more time.

Groaning, Rock nodded. "You better fucking believe it."

That fat prick pulled away, Rock sighing.

"Let's get cleaned up. This next game's going to be way more relaxed." Hell, he might eat and take a nap.

"Fuck, yeah." Rock turned him and took a long, slow kiss.

"I might actually be able to care about this game."

"Yeah." He hummed into the kiss, the smell of cornbread in the air.

Rock grabbed a washcloth and cleaned them both up and then tucked him back into his jeans, tugging up the zipper. Those thick fingers brushed against his belly as Rock did up that top button.

"You go on out first. I'll be right behind you." Lord. He'd just.

In his folk's guest bathroom.

"Checking out the view?" Rock took another kiss, long and lazy. "Use the spray -- place smells like us."

"Yeah. Yeah, I will." He just kept grinning. Goddamn.

Rock rubbed a thumb along his lower lip and then headed out back toward the kitchen, whistling cheerily.

Yeah. This next game was going to be way more relaxed than the others.

Way more.

# Chapter Six

Rock was beat, but he had a fucking three-day coming up and that made up for a lot. He pulled into the parking lot at Bud's, eyes finding Rig's red Jeep. He hoped Rig had a beer waiting for him. A nice, thick burger would be good, too.

He hauled ass into the bar, eyes sweeping the place for his skinny cowboy. Rig was in a corner, hat pulled down low, two bottles in front of him. Good man. He made his way over, tugging out the stool next to Rig's. He grunted a "hey there."

"Hey." Rig nodded, gave him half a grin. "You look beat."

He nodded and grabbed the beer farthest away from Rig. "Long day." And somehow the fucking baby Marines were getting younger every day.

"You hungry?"

"Yep. Want a burger. Or a steak. You?" They usually played pool Friday nights, but he had to admit he wouldn't mind giving it a miss tonight.

"Steak sounds good. You want to go somewhere with good ones?"

He took a long swig of his beer, feeling it settle in his belly. Oh, yeah, he'd needed that. "Fuck, yes. You got somewhere in mind?"

"Charlie's? Texas Roadhouse?" Rig shrugged. "Hell, we could get it to go and take it home."

"Yeah? That way there's great food and great fucking." He had another swig of his beer, feeling more relaxed already. "How was your day?"

"Not half bad. I'm glad it's over. There's a message for you up at the house. From somebody that says she's your sister."

He snorted. "Yeah, right." Like Shelly'd be calling him.

"I left the message on the machine." Rig shrugged, drained his beer.

"Probably one of the guys playing a joke." He finished his own beer. "The bill settled?"

"Yup." Rig grinned, winked. "You can buy supper."

"You got dessert for me back home?"

Those grey eyes lit up, sparkled for him. "Are we calling it dessert now?"

"Hell yes, and it better include chocolate." He stood, rolling his neck, trying to get the renewed tightness to back off. He was gonna kill the jackass who thought it was funny to leave prank messages.

"Chocolate and massage oil and a hot shower, I'm thinkin'."

He shot Rig a look. He must look really rough if Rig was pulling out all the stops. "Add a blow and I'll buy you the biggest damned steak we can find."

"Works for me." Rig sashayed out of the bar, that tight, little ass like a beacon. He followed happily, fuck, he'd been impressed with that ass from moment one.

It didn't take long at all before they had their steaks and were pulling up at home, his truck hot on the Jeep's ass.

And didn't he just follow that ass straight in. If it wasn't steaks in the take-out bag, he'd have been all over Rig the minute the door closed behind him. But a man couldn't pass up a prime piece of meat when he was hungry. There was a potato and mushrooms and oh, damn, it smelled so fucking good.

He growled at Grimmy when the beast took undue interest in the bag. "You've got kibble."

"Oh, now. If you could have steak or kibble, which would you pick?" Fucking cowboy was laughing at him.

His eyes narrowed and he started stalking Rig. "Do I look like a dog?"

Rig stepped back. "Is this where I go 'ruff, ruff'?"

He snorted. "This is where you tell me to sit down while you feed the mutt and get the beer. And steak knives. Or I could just do you up against the wall."

"I like walls." And poking Marines, apparently.

"And here I thought you were hungry." He certainly was, but whether he was more hungry for food than for Rig... well, that was up for grabs now.

His eyes slid down over Rig's body, finding the telltale bulge in the tight jeans. Oh, yeah. Food was a poor second to what he could have up against the wall. He kept stalking, letting Rig lead him toward the kitchen.

"Starving. Haven't eaten anything good since this morning."

"Oh, I've got your favorite meal right here." He grabbed his crotch with one hand, and managed to get the bag containing their supper on the counter with the other. "You want what I've got?"

"You think you can fill me up?" Oh, Rig was willing to play.

"Fuck, yes." He backed Rig up against the wall next to the fridge. "You decide where you want to be filled."

"I have a few ideas." Rig pushed against him, the kiss hard and deep, making his head swim.

His groan was the only reply he made, one hand going behind Rig's neck, tilting his head just a bit so the kiss could go deeper, the other finding Rig's ass and tugging their cocks together through their clothes. Rig's hands worked his shoulders, digging in even as that kiss stole his breath.

It felt so fucking good, Rig relaxing him even as his cock pushed hard at his zipper.

"Mmmhmm." Rig watched him, eyes hot, needy, staring right into him.

He shoved their hips together hard, Rig's ass hitting the wall with a thump. Fuck, but Rig made him need.

"Come on. Want you." Rig didn't make him wonder, gave it up for him, over and over.

"Right here, Rig. All yours." He pushed Rig's T-shirt up, thumb tips pressing against those sweet tittles as they went by.

"Good." Rig bit his bottom lip hard enough to sting, to burn some. "My beautiful fucking Marine."

"Yep. You know it." Rig always knew how to make him feel like the stud he was.

He got the T-shirt up and worked open Rig's jeans, grabbing the sweet prick that practically leapt into his palm. He got a groan for his troubles, Rig's hips jerking, humping his hand just like that.

"Gonna suck me once I'm through here?" he asked, looking into those grey eyes as he squeezed and tugged. "Gonna have dessert first?"

"Fuck, yes. Want you to fuck my mouth, Blue. Need it."

"I will, Rig. Gonna take your mouth and you're gonna be tasting me for days." His hand moved faster, thumb sliding across the tip of Rig's prick.

Rig's eyes rolled, head knocking back against the wall. "Don't stop."

He chuckled and leaned in, breathing across the sweet spot on Rig's neck. "Not gonna stop, Rig." He licked a line along Rig's neck to ear as his thumb pressed into Rig's slit. "Gonna make you come and then you're gonna make me come."

"Fuck, yes. Want you." Rig nodded, groaning, cock pressing up toward his hand.

"All you gotta do is come, Rabbit, and it's all yours." He squeezed tight, jacking Rig's prick hard.

His own personal redneck gave it right up, heat spraying over his fingers, male and musky and hot. Groaning, he pressed a kiss to Rig's lips, the scent flavoring the familiar taste. His hand glided over Rig's prick, slick and easy now.

Rig hummed, rubbing against him, kiss gone hot and lazy and deep. He tugged Rig's lower lip out as he ended the kiss, rubbing the come into Rig's belly. "My turn."

"You know it." Rig was working his jeans open before he could think, sliding down the wall.

"Yeah. Yeah." He nodded, hands bracing on the wall, eyes on Rig, watching that mouth as it got closer to his prick.

Rig smiled, licking his lips. Hungry bastard. "Want it."

"Me, too." He grinned, smiling back. They were fucking well suited, that mouth just made for his prick. He curled his fingers against the wall, hips pushing forward. "Come on, now. Take it."

Those lips parted, slid over his cock like a goddamned rubber, close and tight and covering him all the way down.

"Fuck. Fuck." His head fell back, a low moan coming from him as he pushed forward with his hips, the pleasure spreading out from his cock. He stopped thinking, stopped breathing, just fucked Rig's mouth. He could feel those lips squeezing around him, could feel the back of Rig's throat every time the tip of his cock hit it. Fucking good. Groaning, he watched his prick slide in and out of Rig's mouth, watched those sweet lips sliding on him. "Fuck. Rig."

Rig's fingers circled his nuts, starting stroking and petting his sac, making him feel that much more. Leaning his forehead against the wall, he sawed his hips fast and hard, Rig taking it, taking him and not backing down for a second.

With a low, needy sound, he came, hips jerking as his prick pulsed. Rig didn't lose a drop. Hell, that hungry mouth sucked him dry and then cleaned his prick. He dropped his hand down to Rig's face, stroking, thumb sliding across the swollen lips.

Rig rose up, leaned against him, and the kiss he got was soft and hot as hell. "Mmm. Needed that."

"Yeah. Was hungry." He gave Rig a wink and a pat on the back before tucking himself away, closing up the fly. With any luck the steak would still be warm. He grabbed the bag and a couple knives and forks. "You bring the beer and plates."

Yeah, he was feeling good now, just hungry for the steak and potatoes. Bringing this stuff home had been the right thing to do.

"You got it. You want this leftover brownie, too?"

"Chocolate? You know it." He grinned and headed for the living room, dumping everything on the coffee table. The answering machine was flashing, so he hit it while he turned on the TV.

There was a message for Rig from the hospital, which he didn't pay attention to, and a hang-up, and then the machine started in on the messages it had saved, some woman asking for him. Frowning, he went over and pressed the button to restart the message.

"James? Um. I'm looking for James South. It's Shelly. Your sister. Grandma South died and you've been named in the will. You'll need to come." Well fuck a duck, that *was* his sister. Rock's shoulders tightened right back up and he growled. He had nothing bad to say about Grandma South, but he really wasn't interested in going back there and seeing people who didn't want to see him.

"Oh, shit. I'm sorry to hear that." Well, he knew why Rig'd been so careful with him.

"Thanks. I hadn't seen her in awhile." She was actually the only one who'd kept in touch with him, sending him Christmas cards for a few years after he'd joined up. It had stopped after a couple years and he'd always assumed she'd finally been told that he was a fag and she'd disowned him like everyone else.

He ran his hand over his face, and tried not to growl again. "I don't know why I'm in the fucking will." She must not have gotten around to changing it.

"You're her kin." Rig shrugged, sat down. "You the older brother?"

He nodded, still staring at the answering machine like it was going to start up again and he was going to hear Shelly's voice. Or worse, one of his folks. "There's just me and her, though Uncle Dave and Aunt Cerise have kids. Fair bit younger than me and Shelly."

He went and sat, his appetite suddenly half of what it had been.

"I'm sorry. Were you and your granny close?" Rig opened dishes, spread out the food.

He shrugged. "Not really. Maybe. I hadn't seen her since I joined up. But we used to see her every Sunday for dinner and in the summer I'd make extra money doing odd jobs around her place. So I spent a fair bit of time with her." And he'd liked her. She'd never smelled old like a lot of his friends' grandparents had.

But he hadn't seen her in a long time and had to figure she was as disgusted with him over his lifestyle as his immediate family was. He wasn't sure how upset he was supposed to be.

"What was her name?" Rig dug in, eyes watching him, sort of curious, sort of concerned.

"Grandma." He gave Rig a wink, but it felt forced and he shook his head. "Esther South. She was... hell, I asked once and was firmly told that it was impolite to ask a woman her age, especially if she was old enough to be a grandma. But she had to be in her nineties, I'll bet."

He cut himself a large piece of steak and the minute it was in his mouth, his body remembered it was hungry, his stomach making a loud noise.

"I like to hear that a person that lived a good, long life."

He nodded and rubbed his neck and took a mouthful of potatoes. "She used to do stuff, too. Her husband died when I was little. He was her second husband, too. But she was always going on coach tours and stuff. Saw most of the US that way."

"Was she your momma or daddy's people?" Rig put his fork down, moved around, and started rubbing his shoulders.

"Daddy's." He groaned and let his head fall forward, those fingers just making him feel good.

The truth was he was more tense about having to deal with Shelly and his family again than over Grandma dying. Not that he was going to tell Rig that. He knew he was supposed to be broken up about it. Kind of hard to be, though, when his family'd basically been dead to him since they'd found out.

"You look like your daddy's side? I always think that's neat, how families look like each other." Yeah, well, Jeremy Alexander Roberts, Jr. couldn't look any more like Jeremy Alexander Roberts, Sr. if he tried.

"Yeah, you'd know my father if you met him." Which he was pretty sure was part of the problem -- not only was the man's son gay, but they looked alike. Rock was *supposed* to be a South clone. And he wasn't. Not that him being gay meant his father was, but try telling the man that... Thinking about it just got him more tense, so he shoved some more food in his mouth and tried to concentrate on Rig's massage, let those fingers work their magic.

"You got yourself a lucky momma, then." Rig scooted closer, legs wrapping around his hips.

Well now, didn't that just make him feel like a god? Grinning, he rubbed back a little. "You think so, huh?"

"Yup. You got it going on, Marine." Rig kept touching and licking and just keeping him close.

He had a few more bites, relaxing back into Rig. "You want a bite?" he asked, offering over a forkful of mashed potatoes with a piece of steak on the end.

"Yeah." Rig pushed up, stole the bite off the fork, just rubbing against him.

Oh, he was feeling better already, the food and Rig's attentions easing him just like that.

"I guess I'll have to call her back." Thanks to Rig his shoulders didn't immediately tense up over that, and he was able to have another bite of what really was a great steak.

"Yeah. Tomorrow. It's late tonight." Rig nuzzled the edge of his hairline.

He nodded. "You're right." And with that he could relax the rest of the way, let Rig make him feel so fucking good.

"This is damned good steak," he noted, offering another bite over his shoulder to Rig.

"Yep. I never can get it like that on the fucking grill. They've got to have some secret."

"Drugs," he suggested with a grin, popping another piece into his too-thin cowboy's mouth. Hell, there was still more than half a steak on Rig's plate, the food abandoned in favor of the massage he was currently enjoying the fuck out of.

"Maybe. Whatever it is, I like."

"Yeah." He gave Rig another bite and finished his own steak off. "You could bribe the chef to find out." Not that he didn't grill a mean steak himself, and not that he didn't like it when Rig made it.

"Wonder if he gives trade secrets for blowjobs."

Rock snorted. "The steak's not *that* good."

"No? You sure like it." Rig stole another bite.

"Oh, it's good. But it's got nothing on that mouth."

He rubbed his ass back into Rig's crotch and speared the rest of the steak on Rig's plate, moving it to his own. They could share what was left. He could feel Rig's smile against his shoulder, feel Rig's pleasure in the way those hands stroked over his skin.

He made short work of cutting the steak up and piled potatoes, gravy, and steak on the fork, offering it over to Rig. The TV droned on in the background, but couldn't do anything to drown out the little yum sound Rig made as he ate.

"What have you got planned this weekend?" Rig always had a list a mile long.

"Grilling. The guys invited me to the beach, but I wasn't sure if you were going to be around."

"I'm sleeping in tomorrow." Just in case there was any question about that. Not that he'd been up that early on a Saturday he was off in ages. Rig usually did half that long list before he got up. "Otherwise, I'm free and clear. Although I was hoping for a date with a certain cowboy butt."

"I bet I could handle that. Ocean isn't going anywhere."

"You usually do handle what I've got." He rubbed his ass back again, and ate the last bite of the steak, washing it down with his beer. "You wanting some of this brownie?" For Rig he'd share.

"One bite, maybe." Weirdo.

He broke off a corner and handed it back to Rig, then rested back against Rig's lean body as he munched on the rest of it. Steak and chocolate and Rig. It was a pretty fucking good evening, all told.

Barring that blinking light on the answering machine.

Goddamn it.

# Chapter Seven

So, there was that message.

And he knew it wasn't his to worry on, but damn.

It was Rock's *granny*.

Rock's people.

So, when they'd settled after supper on Sunday night, Rig cleared his throat and just asked what he wanted to know. "So, you goin' back to see your people?"

Rock grunted. "Yeah. They need me to go up for the will thing. Funeral was Wednesday last week, so it's just a matter of when I can get the time." The funeral was Wednesday, but Shelly's call'd been Friday...

"They not know where to find you?"

"They got a hold of me, didn't they?" Rock gave him a wry grin. "Don't stress it, Rig -- they didn't want me at the funeral. The only reason I'm going now is I'm in the will."

"Yeah, but..." Damn it. Rock was their *kin*. It wasn't right. It just *wasn't*.

"Just leave it, Rig." Those blue eyes met his. "You got a few days coming to you?"

"I do." Now, he didn't expect that at all. Surely, Rock wasn't asking him along to meet folks... Not after all the growling and pissing.

"Old Orchard Beach's not that far. Beach would give you something to do when I go to the lawyer's."

"Yeah? Sounds good. You want me to make some phone calls?" Okay. Damn. Odd, even, but okay. He'd go to Yankee land.

"Yeah, after I clear the days with my CO. I should be able to swing Wednesday through Sunday. I'll make the appointment with the lawyer for Thursday and we'll have the long weekend to play."

Rock cracked his knuckles and stretched his arm out on the couch, fingers sliding over Rig's shoulder.

"I'm a fan of playing, Marine." He was sort of shell-shocked, really.

"Then it's a date." Rock voice was gruff, face set, telling him the discussion was closed. The hand on his shoulder tugged a little though, bringing him closer to all those muscles.

He leaned in, lips brushing Rock's jaw. "Man, you need to shave."

"You volunteering for the job?" Rock asked, scratching at his chin.

"Mmm. I could. Make you all smooth for me." He grinned as Rock's eyes dropped right to his crotch. The man loved to have him shaved, to see him naked. Perv.

"I'd do you after," Rock suggested, voice low, husky. "Quid Pro Quo."

"Why do I think you're not talking about my jaw, Rocketman?"

Oh, that was a shit eating grin and those blue eyes just shone at him. "Because you shaved this morning?"

"Shithead." He felt his cheeks heat, cock just starting to throb.

"Uh-huh. You know you love it."

"I don't know what you're talking about." Butter wouldn't melt in his mouth.

"No? I guess you need a reminder."

Rock reached for the remote and turned the television off, nudged him. "You can do my face first."

"Come to the bathroom." He was hard, aching a little, willing to stretch this out.

"Yeah, I'm not going to miss this."

Rock's arm went around his shoulders as they made their way to the bathroom, hip bumping his, those blue eyes warm as they looked over at him.

"You assume I'm going to let you do it." He grinned, winked, taking the kiss Rock offered.

"You will," Rock told him as their lips parted. "You'll bitch and call me a perv and get harder and harder every fucking second."

"Will not." He swallowed his groan. "Perv."

Rock just laughed. The fucking beautiful bastard.

"Where do you want me?" Rock asked, pulling off his shirt, standing there bare-chested and all stud in the middle of the bathroom.

"Mmm. Sit on the pot, I guess. That way I can reach." He couldn't help reaching out to touch.

"Mmm. I do like it when you reach." Rock let him touch for a bit and then moved to sit on the can, shit-eating grin on his face.

Rig rolled his eyes, started whistling away as he got a new razor out, filled the sink up with hot water. He liked the smell of the shaving cream -- always had -- and he spread it on real careful. Those blue eyes watched him, like a touch, keeping him close. There wasn't a spot of doubt in them, though -- Rock trusted him to do this implicitly.

He took his own sweet time, dragging the razor over the strong jaw, stubborn chin. He didn't nick Rock once, just cleaned that face right up. He could feel the heat pouring from Rock's skin, those little nipples going tighter and harder for him with every drag.

He finally settled on Rock's thighs, pushing close, doing the detail work. Those big hands slid around his waist, one moving right back to slide into his jeans pocket, tug him a little closer.

"You are one fine son of a bitch." He went real careful on Rock's upper lip.

Rock rumbled for him, looking pleased as punch, and that hand in his pocket squeezed his ass.

"Almost done, Marine. You'll pass inspection."

Those blue eyes met his. "Yeah? You gonna inspect me real close, Rig?" Rock's voice was low and husky, just dragging across his nerves and making promises.

Rig wiped Rock's face off, the wet towels good and hot. "You know it."

"Felt like you did a thorough job. 'Course I wouldn't expect anything less." The hand not in his back pocket rubbed his crotch. "I'll be just as thorough."

He shook his head, tongue dragging along Rock's jaw and testing. "Perv."

"Yours," Rock pointed out, fingers squeezing his cock hard, hot even through his jeans.

"You know it." Worth leaving Texas for.

Rock's face turned this way and that for him, letting him taste and test thoroughly before those hands squeezed again. "Okay. My turn."

He groaned, cock throbbing. "It. I."

Fuck.

"Hush now, you know you want it."

Rock started undoing his jeans, fingers making short work of the button, the zipper. "Get rid of all these pretty, blond curls and leave you smooth and sensitive. Fucking love how it makes you shiver when I touch."

He groaned, thighs going tight and hard in his jeans. "Blue..."

"What?" Oh, those blue eyes just danced, Rock knowing exactly what he was doing.

Those knowing, warm hands tugged his cock out, pumping lightly. "I'll stop the second you stop loving it."

He wanted to argue, but damn, that hand. Just. Damn. His head rolled, hips jerking in random motions.

"Yeah, that's what I thought." Rock's lips landed on his neck, breath warm against his skin, tongue licking a line of fire around to his Adam's apple.

Rock sucked on it for a moment and then put their foreheads together. "No more stalling, get up and get those jeans the rest of the way off."

"Stalling? Who's stalling?" He stretched, just to get more of that touch.

Chuckling, Rock let go of his cock, moving to peel off his T-shirt instead. Oh, that was a satisfied, happy noise that Rock made as his fingertips slid across Rig's nipples.

He arched, almost tipping himself right off the back of Rock's knees. "Damn. Careful. No falling."

"Not going to let you fall," growled Rock, one hand sliding around, fingers spread wide on his back. Leaning in, Rock licked across his right nipple.

His fingers dug into Rock's shoulders, holding on tight. "Good. So fucking good."

"Gonna make you fly, Rig," Rock promised, hand sliding up along his breastbone.

He didn't doubt it. His Blue made him fucking nuts. That tongue played over his nipple again, and then bit it none too gently, leaving a sharp sting behind. Then it was gone and Rock stood, placing him gently on the floor, holding his hips.

"Shaving first, Rabbit."

He was fucking vibrating, breath huffing from him.

Rock pushed his jeans down his legs, fingers dragging along his skin all the way. One big hand wrapped around his right ankle, encouraged him to step out of the jeans, and then the left. Rock looked up at him and smiled, a fucking wicked, little smile.

"You think you can stand while I do it?" Rock's voice said he didn't believe Rig could.

"You cut me and I'll have to hurt you." He could fucking stand. It might kill him, but he could.

Rock chuckled and reached over for the shaving cream, spraying the foam on his pubes and on his cock, so fucking cold against his burning skin. He stepped back, ass hitting the wall, cock bobbing.

"Look at that pretty prick." Rock grinned up at him and then reached for the razor. "Hold still, now."

"Perv." His skin was already tingling.

Rock laughed, then bent to press a kiss to the tip of his cock. Straightening, Rock slid the razor slowly across his skin. Rig didn't moan, but it was a close thing, the slight sting making his toes curl. Rock did the outer areas first and then went for a new razor, holding his prick back now as Rock moved in closer to it. "Just look at that."

The first time Rock'd done this, he'd damn near died. It was so...

Yeah.

Each stroke was careful but sure -- he might have joked about killing Rock if he got cut, but he knew Rock wouldn't let that happen. This way and that, Rock pushed his cock, the razor scraping, removing all his pubic hair. Then his ballsac was stretched, Rock so careful, scraping the sparse, near-white hairs away.

When he was done, Rock squeezed gently, rolled his balls in those big fingers, and grinned up at him. The heat in those blue eyes was near to burning him up. Rig couldn't even speak; his hips rolled, so needy he couldn't hardly bear it.

"Yeah, that's what I'm talking about." Rock's voice sounded like he'd gargled with stones, it was so rough.

Then Rock ran a cloth under the water and started to clean him off, the cotton warm, but fucking rough against his newly bared skin. Rock's tongue wasn't, though, when Rock leaned in to follow the cloth's path.

"Blue..." He went up on his toes, nerves sparking madly, lights behind his eyes.

"Your legs aren't going to give out are they? Because you said you could stand." The tease would have worked better if Rock hadn't sounded so desperately turned on.

Rock's warm, sure fingers joined lips and tongue, moving over his so sensitive skin.

"I. I can. Fuck, I need you." His cock was throbbing, pre-come sliding down and making his shaft wet and slick.

"I'm not going to leave you wanting, Rig." Rock's mouth moved to take one of his balls in, tongue sliding on his skin, making him fly.

No. No, his Marine wouldn't. Oh, sweet fuck, yes. He was damn thankful for Rock's hands holding him up, because his knees buckled. He felt the low chuckle around his ball, the vibrations making him ache. Rock let it go and took in the other one, tongue just working him, knowing how fucking big the sensations were. This time it was a low hum that vibrated his sac.

He grunted, hands curled around Rock's shoulders. "More."

Mouth sliding away, Rock grinned up at him. "Oh, you want more now, do you?" Just before Rock's mouth closed over the skin between his hip and his prick he heard the word "perv".

"Am not." Maybe he was. It didn't matter.

Rock didn't answer with words, just sucked on his skin, hard enough to leave a mark right there next to his cock. Oh. Oh, fuck. He came without any more than that, lips open and cock jerking. Rock moaned softly, pulling off his skin to look at the mark, to lick through the come on his belly. Each touch of that tongue was adoration, seduction.

"Fucking sexy, Rabbit," muttered Rock.

"Yours." He was still hard, still needing it.

Oh, that slow smile was something else, and all his. "I know."

Rock stood up slowly, eyes dragging up over his skin, fingers following.

"Bed." He went up on his tiptoes, drawn by that touch.

"Can you wait that long?"

Rock started moving, though, walking slowly backward, fingers moving to undo his pants, opening the button first and then dragging the zipper down. The head of Rock's prick was pushing up out of his underwear, red and wet-tipped.

Rig groaned, licking his lips and watching that pretty cock. "Want you to fuck me."

"The only thing that's going to stop that from happening is if a bolt of lightning hits the house and sets us on fire." Rock made it to the hall and crooked a finger, still walking backward.

"We have an extinguisher." Beautiful, sexy motherfucker.

"Well then come on. Nothing's gonna keep me from that ass."

They hit the bedroom and Rock started working those pants right off, letting him see the amazing muscles in those legs, letting him see the whole fucking beautiful package. Rig groaned, reaching for that cock, fingers brushing over the tip.

Rock moaned for him, hands reaching to wrap around his arms and tug him closer. Their mouths met in a hard kiss, teeth clicking together. He let his fingers push down over that heavy cock, rubbing and stroking, even as their kiss made him crazed. One of Rock's hands wrapped in his hair, tilting his head to make the kiss deeper and harder. That other hand was busy sliding over his shaved skin, barely touching one minute, pressing hard the next.

It was like a stand-off to see who could make the other break for the bed and the actual fucking first. And they were both going to win. Afterward, he wasn't sure who broke first. Hell, he wasn't sure he cared. All he knew was that he was kneeling on the bed, Rock's fingers pushing into his ass. Thick and hot, they spread him wide, curling to find his gland. Once found, Rock kept working it, making his body rock to his Blue's beat.

Then just as suddenly Rock's fingers were gone. "Now, Rig."

"Now. Now, Jim." In him. Deep. Now.

"Right here." And Rock was, that thick cock spreading him open, filling him so deep.

Fuck him. He grabbed the headboard, driving himself down on that fat prick, jonesing on the burn and stretch. Rock's hands wrapped around his hips, adding that strength, tugging him back into each solid, bone-jarring thrust.

They didn't say a word between them, both growling and grunting, fire pouring between them. Rock pumped in harder, faster, like Rock was trying to crawl into him.

Yes. Yes. Yours. Please. Fuck.

One big hand slid around to grab his prick, working it just as hard as Rock was working his ass. "Come on, Rabbit. Give it to me." The words were short, breathless, demanding.

Rig just nodded, cock throbbing and jerking as he shot. Rock pushed deeper inside him, cock emptying. That roar echoed as he was filled with heat. He leaned back into Rock's strength, damn near shaking it felt so fucking good. Rock's arms wrapped around him, pulled him up so they were kneeling together on the bed, that thick prick still buried deep.

One hand slid down to glide over his shaved skin. "I like it," growled Rock, nose sliding along his neck.

He squeezed Rock's prick, skin goosepimpling up.

Fuck, that felt.

Yeah.

Rock groaned. "Gonna make me hard again. That what you want? Want me to fuck you until it's time to get up?"

"It's Saturday. We have thirty-six more hours."

"Oh, I'm not sure your ass would survive that."

"I'm not either, but it would be one hell of a way to go." They both started laughing, Rock's body shaking with it.

Rock's cock slid away and they collapsed together, Rock hot and hard behind him, around him. He brought Rock's hand up, kissed the palm. Damn, he was one lucky son of a bitch. Rock made a soft noise, fingers curling to stroke his face.

A kiss landed on the back of his neck. "Mmm." Yeah. Good. Very good.

Nap.

Then they could play again. And pack.

He was going back east with Rock. Imagine that.

# Chapter Eight

The plane ride had been a fucking nightmare, with delays for the first flight, delays for their connecting flight. Turbulence and a fucking baby screaming its head off almost the entire damned flight. The car rental place had screwed up their reservation and he'd barely fit into the little compact they'd been given.

At least there hadn't been any hitches with the beach house they were renting. Rock tossed their bags into the bedroom and contemplated just stretching out on the bed and going to sleep. He didn't fucking want to be here in the first place.

He went over and looked out the window. They really were right on the beach. Rig would be happy.

"You hungry, Rocketman? I could order a pizza?" Rig's hands slid down his spine.

"I want a couple beers, too." He leaned back a little, pushing into Rig's hands. If it hadn't been for Rig, he'd have turned around and been on the first flight home when the rental agency gave them the wrong damned car.

"I bet we can manage that." Those fingers dug in harder, easing him right up.

He groaned, head rolling forward. Fuck that felt good. "You think this whole trip is jinxed?"

"Nah. Just busy, and we're not here for fun, so it feels like it."

"Hey, you can have fun. It's a beach -- you like those." He wasn't going to drag Rig into any shit.

"I do, but I'm here 'cause you're here."

"Well, I've got to go to the damned lawyer's tomorrow, but I'm all yours soon as I'm done there." He couldn't wait for this to be over with.

He kept wondering what he'd do if his father was there, what he'd say. He didn't like this fucking introspective crap at all.

"You want me to come with you?" Those hands moved down, stroking his lower back.

He shook his head. "You don't need to worry about this shit." Rig's family was different. They were good people.

"Whatever you want, man. I've got your back." And his ass. The back of his neck.

"You do. What're you going to do with it?" he asked, Rig's hands working enough magic that he was... well, not mellow, but he wasn't going to strangle the next person he came across now, either.

Rig chuckled, lips on his shoulder. "Prob'ly love on it 'til you can't bear it, but I'm open for suggestions."

He hummed a little at the touch. "Oh, I thought yours was pretty damned good. Though I can't imagine me ever not being able to bear it." Quite the opposite -- he never got enough of that mouth, that ass.

"It'll be fun to try." Those fingers slid around his belly, petting him.

He tried not to smile. He tried hard not to smile. It had been a shitty day and he was in a bad mood. Damn it. He grinned. "It would be."

Rig chuckled, nodded. "We got great ideas, Marine. Great fucking ideas."

"Nah. What we've got is great asses and cocks." He rubbed his ass back against Rig's cock to prove his point.

"Mmmhmm. Fine fucking ass." Rig nodded, rubbed right back.

"Pizza'll wait, right?" He threw the words out casually, hand sliding to press Rig's tighter against his belly. Some things a man needed more than food.

"We got time." Rig worked his jeans open, fingers stroking right under his bellybutton, finding the hot spot and playing it.

Rock groaned, leaning back a little harder. He reached back with both hands, sliding his fingers up along Rig's sides and down again to grab onto Rig's hips.

"Mmm. Right there." Rig whispered into his ear. "It tastes good there, yeah? And I can smell your cock, smell you when I lick you there."

Oh, fuck. He jerked, hands squeezing Rig's hips. He could still hear the ocean, but he couldn't see it anymore, his eyes watching their watery reflections in the window.

"Rig..." Damn that mouth was magic.

"Uh-huh. Fucking get off on it, your cock in my mouth, the way you taste."

Oh, yeah. He got off on his cock in Rig's mouth, too. "Uh-huh," he managed to grunt, his prick pushing hard enough to poke out the top of his underwear now -- just begging for Rig's attention.

Those fingers heard him, stroking across the tip of his cock, pushing the briefs down. "Love when you fuck my mouth, when I got nothing to worry on but fucking and you."

His hips jerked again, his cock making its own comment. "Yeah, Rig. Our own fucking private heaven."

Heaven was that mouth, that ass, and he wanted nothing more than to sink into either, both -- he wasn't picky.

"Mmmhmm." Rig started jacking him off, hand moving nice and easy, thumb working the tip over and over. Oh, fuck, this wasn't exactly hell on earth, either, now was it?

Rock shuddered, body soon moving with Rig's hand, his own opening and closing over Rig's hips.

"You want me to keep going? You want to fuck me?"

"Fuck, yes." He nodded. Yeah, this was good, but that ass. "Want you, Rig. Want to fuck you."

Rig took a step back, hand disappearing. "Then come on. I need."

He didn't need to be told twice.

He turned and stepped up to Rig, pushing off the man's t-shirt and slowly walking Rig back toward the bed. Rig went easy, lips parting, tongue sliding out to tempt him. Never one to pass temptation by, especially when it came in the form of Rig, he leaned in, lips wrapping around the pink tongue and sucking. Damn, but Rig tasted good. Even after a long fucking day.

The moan that pushed into his lips was even better, Rig right against him, rubbing nice and easy. He got Rig's jeans open so their pricks could slide as they stood by the bed, bodies moving together. That lean body felt just right.

Rig didn't bullshit with him, just worked at getting him naked, getting them ready. Getting them hot.

"Slick?" he asked, hands reaching for Rig's butt, fingers sliding along that hot crack as his palms rubbed over that fucking sweet ass.

"In the ditty bag." Rig hummed, and arched for him.

He groaned and pushed Rig back down onto the bed. Following, he spread Rig's legs, tilting those hips up so he could get to that sweet hole. "We'll just do it this way."

"Oh, sweet fuck. Yes." Rig nodded, spreading for him. His rabbit was still bare for him, that skin sensitive and smooth.

He tongued Rig's balls first, licking the smooth orbs, sucking on them before he slid his tongue down along the smooth, hot flesh that ended at Rig's hole. Sweet fuck, Rig smelled amazing.

"Blue..." He grinned, knowing if Rig was begging like this now, in a few minutes, he'd have pure bliss.

He teased the wrinkled skin that surrounded Rig's hole with the tip of his tongue, backing off to lick along the sweet patch of flesh between balls and hole before going back to the teasing touches. His fingers kneaded the skin of Rig's thighs, his ass. The taste was male and heady, but a little sweet somehow, and it made him linger, trying to figure it out.

He repeated the caress again and again, making Rig writhe, seeing Rig's hands slide and twist in the sheets. Finally, he jabbed the tip of his tongue into Rig's body, piercing the tight muscles to feel the silk inside Rig's body clench around his tongue.

"Jim!" Rig's hands twisted in the comforter, knees sliding up underneath the man.

He rumbled his pleasure, pushing his tongue deeper, face pressed up against Rig's ass. Rig didn't pull away, just rode it, pulling his hand up to touch that soft, bare skin. He just moaned, tongue fucking Rig's ass, fingers sliding over that amazingly soft skin. All he could smell was Rig, all around him, making the bed theirs.

"Blue. Blue, I can't. You're gonna make me."

He didn't stop, instead he pushed harder with his tongue and ran his fingers over Rig's hard, burning hot prick. If Rig came, he'd get his cowboy up again. Heat sprayed over his fingers, Rig jerking and moaning, body tightening around his tongue. Oh fuck! His own hips jerked and he grabbed for his balls, squeezing tight.

He tongued Rig's ass a bit longer, and then dragged his come-covered hand over his prick, kneeling up behind Rig. "You ready, Rabbit?"

Rig nodded, still panting, thighs spread.

"Yeah, you're ready for this." Rock pushed in, groaning at the tight heat that surrounded his prick.

He started thrusting as soon as he was in, too turned on by making Rig come to go slow. Rig's body wrapped tight around him, squeezing him, muscles rippling.

"Fuck, yes." He pounded into Rig, and everything else just fell away, didn't exist while he was right here, buried inside Rig.

Rig pushed up, climbing the headboard and fucking riding his cock. Those thighs slapped against his, their skin sliding. He fucking loved that, loved how Rig never just took it, always let him know how much Rig wanted it, needed it, loved it.

Rig's head fell back, landed on his shoulder. "Good. Fuck, Rock. So good."

"I know." He wrapped his hand around Rig's prick, tugging it insistently back to life. He was good to go long enough to get Rig off again.

He fucking loved that grin, all wild and wanting and pure fucking happy. The sound of their bodies slapping together was the best fucking music, Rig's moans, his own grunts, perfect harmony. He thrust and thrust, hand tugging and pulling, jacking Rig as he fucked the sweetest damned ass ever.

Rig shook right before he came, hips jerking, ass milking Rock's prick. It made him roar, just like it always did, Rig's ass just demanding his orgasm. He came hard, hips pumping into Rig.

They sort of stilled, both resting together, panting. He pulled out with a groan, the sound turning to laughter as Rig's stomach growled loudly.

Throwing himself down on the bed, he chuckled, letting his fingers linger over the bare skin around Rig's cock. "Sounds like you're wanting that pizza now."

"And the beer. You're exercise, Marine."

He snorted. "Is that what we're calling it now?" It worked -- they'd both worked up a sweat. Speaking of... he leaned up and licked a drop from Rig's belly, the taste of salt and male mingling on his tongue.

"Yep. Good old fashioned exercise."

He murmured something agreeable, lost in the flavor of Rig's skin, the salty, sharp sweat of man under his tongue. Nothing fucking like it.

"Order us something for dessert, too."

"Cinnamon something?" Rig arched for him a little, skin flushing a sweet pink.

"And chocolate?" he suggested hopefully, tongue sliding in the hollow by Rig's hip. That tasted of sweat and come and that something that was just Rig that nobody else had.

"Mmm. If they have chocolate..." Oh, that was a pretty damned stretch and all for him.

He licked the line from Rig's hip all along the long belly, along skin stretched tight over Rig's ribs and right up to that pretty, little nipple. He didn't touch it with his tongue, just let his breath slide over it, watching as it tightened up for him, the skin around it going all puckered.

He chuckled, glancing up at Rig as he slid his tongue out of his mouth, but didn't quite touch that little bit of flesh that wanted it so bad.

"Tease." Rig shifted, working it, just trying to reach.

"Me? I'm just being good. Waiting for you to order supper without distracting you." He gave Rig his best grin.

Rig's laugh just rang out. Fucking nobody thought he was funny like his Rabbit. "You expect me to think with your mouth on me."

"It's not *on* you right now," he pointed out, breathing across Rig's nipple again. He licked his own lips, knowing he was being an evil tease, knowing Rig would eventually pay him back in the best way possible.

"Don't make me kick your ass, man." Rig rolled, reaching for the phone book, taking that nipple right out of reach.

Damn it.

Of course, that presented him with Rig's side, all stretched out for him, a hint of that sweet ass right there. Bending, he nibbled the curve of Rig's hip.

He heard the flipping of the pages stutter. "I'm trying to find a pizza joint."

"Good. Want a meatlovers." He slid further down the bed and licked the edge of the crease between Rig's ass and the back of his thigh. "Don't let me stop you."

Rig chuckled, scooting away and grabbing the phone. "That tickles."

He spread out on the bed, hand reaching for that skin, just touching idly, letting Rig's voice flow over him as he stared up at the ceiling. It was funny, kinda, how used to this he was. To Rig taking care and having the man around to talk to, fuck around with.

He tugged Rig over as soon as the phone was hung up. "How long's it going to be?"

"Forty-five minutes to an hour."

"That long?" Damn, he was hungry, too. Of course the extra time meant extra time for a little more tasting of his favorite appetizer. He moved his hand over Rig's hip, just feeling the shape of it.

"You wanted dessert." Rig stretched out, one long leg draped over his.

He slid his hand along that leg, just feeling the lean muscles up. "You get us something good?" Like Rig would let him down.

"Pizza. Brownies. Beer. That work?"

"It does indeed." He squeezed Rig's thigh, his other hand sliding up Rig's spine.

"You bring that map with the directions?"

"Yeah. I brought that whole folder deal." Rig's lips parted as he massaged, face going slack.

"You like that?" He massaged Rig's shoulders, fingers digging in.

"Uh-huh." Oh, fuck. That was pure bliss.

Grinning, he kept touching, kept making Rig look and sound like he'd died and gone to heaven. Oh yeah, he did it for Rig.

He was the stud.

He touched his lips to Rig's, sharing air.

"Hey, Rocketman." That grin felt fucking good.

"Hey yourself."

He looked into grey eyes, licked at Rig's lips. Fuck, those kisses made his goddamn head swim. Rig just pushed into them, made the whole goddamn world stop. He tugged the lean body over fully on top of him, hands sliding down to grab Rig's ass, humming into the kisses.

Rig's fingers worked his temples, rubbing and relaxing and fucking melting him, bone-deep. He didn't worry about their pizza or the fucking meeting tomorrow or his family or anything. He just let Rig's touches work him over.

"Mmmhmm. That's it. Just let it go."

"Gonna have me asleep," he pointed out, eyes closing slowly. It just seemed right to drift off.

"S'okay. I got you." A kiss brushed his forehead.

He rumbled a little. He didn't need anyone to look out for him - - he looked out for others... for Rig...

'Course Rig's words seemed just about right, and he relaxed, letting the growly day slip away entirely as he fell asleep with Rig keeping him warm.

# Chapter Nine

"So did you grow up here, Blue?" He was stretched out on the sofa there in the room, wearing nothing but a pair of shorts and a beer bottle. The pizza had been damned good, the brownies nowhere as good as his.

Rock looked over from the pseudo easy chair he was watching tv in, one eyebrow going up. "This very spot? Nope."

"You know what I mean, asshole. Is this where sweet baby James grew up?" Lord, the man was closed mouthed.

And that eyebrow managed to climb even fucking higher. "Sweet? I don't think anyone's ever accused me of being that, Rig..." He didn't think Rock was going to answer the damned question, either, but then his Blue nodded. "Folks still live in the same house I was born in a few towns over. We used to come to the beach for picnics on the Fourth."

"Yeah? That's cool. Momma and Daddy's house looks different, because they built on and all, but it's in the same place." He drained his beer. "You must not've liked it much."

Rock shrugged, frowned a little. "What do you mean?"

"Well, you don't talk on it. Don't ever mention coming back. Hell, you've been home with me. I point out every fucking thing that's changed."

Rock grunted and took a long swig from his own beer before setting the bottle down on the little coffee table with the brochures in front of him. "It was fine." Rock shrugged. "I never thought on it much growing up - whether or not I liked it -- it was just home. And then it wasn't anymore and the place itself didn't matter any."

"Yeah?" It just didn't make sense to him, not a bit. Texas was home -- from the bluebonnets in the spring to the smell of the hay to the corny dogs at the State Fair and he just couldn't get it.

"Yeah." Rock grunted again, looked back at the TV. He almost missed what came next, would have if he hadn't been listening for something... more. "Was made clear it wasn't my home anymore and that was that."

Oh, now. That just got his back up and he growled a little. "That fucking sucks."

"It happens." There was that shrug again that he knew was supposed tell him that Rock didn't care, trouble was he wasn't buying it.

"Yeah, I reckon." He chewed on his bottom lip, trying to figure out what to say. "Is it the queer thing?"

"That would be a more polite way of putting it than my father ever managed." Rock looked over at him, spoke quietly. "You've got real good folks, Rig. You know I'm proud to call your mother Momma."

"I know." He did know, balls to bones. "She thinks of you as her own." Momma loved Rock with a passion and Daddy was right fond of the Marine.

Now that smile was a real one. "Long as I don't have to spend my *entire* Sunday afternoon jawing on the phone..." Rock winked, the tease fond. It didn't happen often, but he'd seen Rock sitting in his chair, phone at his ear, nodding and going "yes, Momma", "no, Momma", for longer than he'd have ever thought possible.

Rig laughed, nodded over. "That woman can *talk* and I think she wishes we were closer."

"I'd get fat if we were," Rock noted, flexing for him.

"I'd just have to work you harder." Fat. Right. The uberMarine.

"Oh, now, I like the way you work me." Rock's interest was clear in his voice, in the look that had come into his eyes.

"You can't be wanting again, Marine. No way." But it would sure be fun to try.

"I had a nap. Dinner. Chocolate." Oh yeah, the brownies hadn't been nearly as good as his own, but Rock had managed to put away all but one of the half dozen that had been delivered. Those eyes pinned him to the couch. "And I'll rise up to that challenge."

"You think you can?" God, he loved teasing the bear.

He loved that growl he got when he'd managed to tease just right. "You think I can't?"

Rig spread, just a little, just enough. "You better prove it."

There was that growl again, right on cue, and Rock stood, stretched, letting him see the big muscles encased in jeans and nothing else. He happened to know that Rock was going commando, too -- just the one layer between him and that fat prick.

Rock's belly rippled, and the hard pecs jumped for him. "I think I will," Rock said. "Prove it, that is."

Oh, fuck yes.

His thighs went hard and his cock jumped, one hand dropping to disguise it. "Bring it on, Marine."

Rock's hand also dropped, cupping his package, showing it off. "I've got what you're looking to see right here, Roberts." Rock stalked toward the couch, covering the space between them slowly, letting him looking his fill, drawing it out.

Every fucking nerve in his body was firing, heat flooding him in a rush. That's it, Marine. Come play with me. Need it.

"You'd better put that beer bottle down," Rock suggested, eyes sliding from his face to his toes and back up again. "And I hope you're not fond of those shorts."

He licked the mouth of the bottle once, then put it aside. "They're real comfortable."

"They're in the way."

"In the way of what?" Look at that man.

"Me. Fucking you. Into the fucking floor." Rock's fingers dropped to tug open his jeans, the zipper coming down just as nice as you please and letting that fat prick out of its cage.

If he'd tried, he couldn't hide the groan, the way he licked his lips.

Rock chuckled, the sound rich and deep, dragging over his skin like a touch. "You want a taste of this, Rig? Want me in your mouth?"

"Didn't you get a blowjob this morning, Marine?" Like he ever didn't want it.

"Did I? It was so long ago..." Rock stroked himself, hand slowly working that magnificent cock.

"Mmmhmm. Fucked my mouth good and hard before you had your first cup of Joe."

That beautiful cock jerked hard at his words, Rock groaning for him. "I guess you don't need another taste then."

"I..." He licked his lips, almost able to taste it. Oh, fuck, that smile was knowing, smug. Rock kept stroking lazily with one hand, fucking teasing him.

Rig leaned back, stretched, lips open. He could do his own share of teasing. Bingo. Rock groaned, moved closer. His hand landed in his hip, stroking so slow. Come on, Rocketman.

With a growl, Rock put a hand to either side of his shorts, tearing them off with a single quick, sharp motion. Jesus. He arched up, cock slapping his belly. Hello.

97

"That's better," muttered Rock, hand sliding along his thigh and then wrapping around his cock.

"Uh-huh." Fuck him raw. He pulled Rock down, brought their lips together with a groan.

The kiss was hard, full on, Rock taking his mouth as that big, strong body covered him. Rig just pushed into the kiss, fucking Rock's lips, hands wrapped around those strong shoulders. Rock's prick slid along his belly, and against his own cock, hot and silky, gliding as Rock's hips moved.

He wrapped his legs around Rock's hips, humping up, driving them together. Come on. Give me more, Blue. Please. A growl slid into his lips, one of Rock's hands dropping down to slide along his crease. Then it disappeared, but before he could protest, two fingers pushed into their kiss, sliding against his tongue.

He sucked good and hard, head bobbing as he licked and groaned and wet those fingers. Rock groaned and moaned, body moving with his. When Rock's fingers popped out of his mouth, they both bucked, arched and moaned.

Then those wet fingers pushed right into him, the teasing over.

"Yeah. Fucking need you." He was done playing.

"Got me." Those blue eyes met his, held them, dead fucking serious and full of heated need. Rock stretched him, making it good, pegging his gland just like that.

His head fell back against the back of the sofa, throat working. "Hurry. Fuck."

"Gonna fuck you, but I'm going to take it nice and slow, make it last." His gland was pegged again, Rock playing him like an instrument. Fuck him raw. It was all he could do to whimper, nod at Rock's words. Rock nodded back, fingers sliding from him. "I know what you want now."

"What I need." He held Rock's eyes. "Come on."

"I won't make you wait." And Rock didn't make him wait for a second longer, that fat prick pushing into him just like that, stretching him, spreading him wide.

The angle was perfect, Rock over him, pushing deep, buried in his ass. A low, needy groan tore from Rock's throat and those blue eyes held his as Rock started to fuck him. Slow, steady strokes filled him with Rock's prick over and over again. Hell, yes. Rig nodded, just sort of caught in it all, happy as all get out.

Rock's lips slid to his neck, finding the sweet spot there and nuzzling, making his skin just sing with it. His Blue's hips kept moving, like a machine that was never going to stop.

"Mmm... worth leaving Texas, Blue-eyes." Hell, yes. Just. Yeah.

Rock grunted, a breathed 'yes' warming the skin of his throat. Shifting, Rock's weight settled on him a little more, fat prick sliding deeper as his own was engulfed in one of Rock's hands. The push and tug worked together, Rock making everything else just disappear.

"Mmm. Just like that. Just like that, man." His own hands slid down Rock's sides, rubbing good and hard.

It went on and on, or maybe it only went on for a second or two, he couldn't tell and it didn't matter. Rock's head lifted, their lips coming together again as Rock's eyes met his. So blue, so hot, and all for him. He shot, entire body shuddering as his balls emptied, Rock fucking everywhere around him.

That fat cock kept pushing into him, swelling and getting harder as Rock jerked a few times before filling him deep with heat and collapsing onto him. A low groan vibrated against his skin, Rock's breath coming hot and fast.

He just held on, octopussing and relaxing.

"Told you," murmured Rock sometime later, just about when he thought Rock was maybe asleep.

"Uh-huh." He wasn't sure what Rock'd said, but yeah. Okay. Cool.

Rock grunted suddenly and hauled himself up. "Bedtime, Rig."

The big hands wrapped around his arms and pulled him up, too, Rock supporting him, practically carrying him into the little cottage's bedroom.

"Uh-huh." He was all about bed now. He'd left his bones behind somewhere.

Rock pushed him down and under the covers, joined him with a groan. "Not as comfy as ours, but it'll do."

And given the way Rock relaxed and his breathing quickly slowed, it seemed it would do just fine.

# Chapter Ten

Ten-thirty and Rock was about ready to crawl out of his own skin.

The appointment wasn't until eleven-thirty, and it shouldn't take more than forty-five minutes or so to get there, but he wanted to leave enough time for finding parking. He wasn't going to be late to this. He was going to go, find out what the story was, and get out.

There was a lobster place just up the road from the cottage they were staying in and he was planning on treating Rig to a fine surf and turf dinner, and they were going to start having some fun. But first...

Growling a little, he stood, stretched, and rolled his neck back and forth, trying to ease the stiffness. Goddamn, he wished Grandma'd just taken him out of the will like everyone else had. "I guess it's time to get going." Sooner he did this, the sooner he was back here with Rig, implementing his dinner plans.

Rig's hands landed on his shoulders, working him good and hard. "You sure you don't want company, Marine? I'm happy to tag along."

He shook his head, ready to tell Rig no again, even as those hands eased the hardness in his muscles. He didn't want to drag Rig into this. Wouldn't. "Yeah, okay." He snorted at himself.

"Cool. Let me put on a good shirt." Lord, his cowboy was going to stick out like a big, sore, Southern thumb.

He rolled his eyes, but nodded. "I'll wait out by the car." Because he couldn't just stand around waiting anymore. He was too keyed up.

The sun shone outside, bright and cheery. It made him growl. Rig should be out on the beach enjoying this. Hell, they both should have been. He stood by the car, glowering at the road.

Rig didn't take but a minute, coming out in a snow-white shirt, good straw hat on his head. Fuck, those were even the dress boots.

He just shook his head and climbed into the car. They weren't going to know what to make of Rig. It made him smile as he started up the car. "You can navigate," he told Rig, nodding at the map on the dashboard.

He knew where he was going, but figured it would give Rig something to do.

"Surely." Rig grinned and did just that, easy as you please. He kept waiting for Rig to push and Rig just didn't.

He grunted, pleasantly surprised, easing a little.

The car ate up the miles, each one bringing them closer to this meeting with the lawyer. With his father and who knew who all. He hadn't seen his mother and father in... well not since he'd joined up. His hands went tight on the steering wheel, his foot pressing down on the accelerator.

Rig watched him, one eyebrow lifted. "You want to stop and get a Coke? We're making good time."

He eased up on the gas, looked around, surprised to see they were already at the edge of town. "Yeah, okay."

The street the lawyer was on had a bunch of stores and stuff on it, and he figured there'd be somewhere to eat there. A few minutes later he turned onto Slater Street, and sure enough, there was a little cafe with an outdoor patio a few buildings over from the lawyer's office. They were in luck when it came to parking, too, a spot right by the cafe.

He pulled in and nodded. "Bet they'll have something sweet to munch on, too."

And Rig could wait for him there while he went in and dealt with business.

"I'm all about munching. You wore my ass out yesterday." Oh, that grin was wicked.

"You better make sure you fill up today then, because yesterday's got nothing on what I've got planned for that ass today."

He winked and locked the car up, checking his watch. Hell, yeah, they had time for him to get a coffee and something sweet.

"You think I can get coffee here that's black?" Rig grimaced, and he laughed. Yesterday'd been an adventure, Rig ordering coffee and getting it with cream and sugar.

"If you ask for it that way." He made sure to keep out of range of Rig's hand when he said it.

"What type of folks don't give coffee black?"

Rock grinned at him and threw Rig a bone. "Yankees," he mouthed.

"Oh, God help me." Rig hooted, rolled those grey eyes.

He shook his head, chuckling at his cowboy. He was glad Rig'd come along, he'd have been driving himself up the wall right now if not. He watched Rig work, charming the hostess, the waitress, the businessmen in the next table. The man jabbered and chattered like a magpie, making sure people paid attention.

Rig just made things easy and before he knew it, they were sitting out on the patio, a huge gooey brownie in front of him, along with a pair of steaming hot coffees. It almost made him want to bring Rig up to this meeting with him.

"That looks damn good, man." Rig had a piece of cherry pie and was eating it, one cherry at a time.

He put a chunk of his brownie on his spoon and held it out to Rig. "Try some."

Rig took the spoon, ate, moaning just a little. "Oh, man. That's fine. You reckon they'd give up the recipe?"

Oh now, that would be something. "If anyone could charm it out of them, it would be you." He took another bite himself and almost moaned. Yeah, he could handle Rig having the recipe to this.

"I'll do my dead-level best." Rig's voice dropped, so he could just hear it. "I like watching you eat it."

He nearly dropped his fucking spoon. Instead, he scooped up some more brownie, slowly eating it off the spoon.

"Man, you're dangerous." Those grey eyes flashed, went hungry.

"Yep. Me and my deadly spoon of chocolate brownie. A real badass." Fuck, but he wanted to spread Rig out and give him what those hungry eyes were begging for. They could go now. Just drive back to the beach house and forget this whole will thing.

"Jimmy? Jimmy is that you?"

Jesus Christ. His sister had gotten old.

His back went stiff and he put his spoon down. He got up and stood stiffly at attention. "Shelly."

"I didn't think you'd come. I really didn't." She hugged him, eyes on Rig.

He hugged her back awkwardly. "You said I had to. That it would tie up the will if I didn't."

Her hair was... crunchy. And looked sort of like Aunt Irene's. Scary. "Well, yes. But I still didn't... Is this your new... friend?"

Jesus fucking Christ. His friend. Rock snorted. "He's not new. And he's not my friend." He nodded toward Rig. "Alex Roberts. Rig, this is Shelly South."

"Pleased to meet you, ma'am." Rig stood, held one hand out.

She stared at his hand a moment and Rock growled softly, his teeth grinding as she finally, carefully, shook Rig's hand. "It's Shelly Webber now, actually."

Rig nodded, smile not fading a bit. "Would you like to have a seat, honey?"

Oh fuck, Shelly's back stiffened, her nostrils flaring. Rock knew she wouldn't make a scene, though. Not in public. He bit his lip and checked his watch.

"That's a great idea. You can keep each other company while I go to this thing at the lawyer's. Unless you need to be there to, Shelly?"

She shook her head. "No. No, it was just you and Mom and Dad. I drove them over."

"Great." He pulled out a chair for her. He almost felt guilty for subjecting Rig to her for however long this thing lasted. Almost.

"You want to finish your coffee, Rock?"

"Rock?" Shelley's nose wrinkled, and the temptation to shake her was sharp and sudden.

"I do. And the brownie." He sat, hands clenched as he continued with a growl. "Sit down, Shelly. Or get the hell out of here."

"You want me to get you a coffee, honey? Something sweet?" Rig stood and helped Shelly into a chair.

Rock gave her a look, eyebrow raised, just waiting for her to dare to be nasty to Rig.

She stayed stiff, but nodded. "Yes, please. Two creams, two sugars, but nothing to eat."

"Surely." Rig wandered back in to the counter, smiling at the waitress.

"Honestly, Jimmy. A cowboy? Isn't that terribly... cliché?"

Rock bit back his "fuck you", but it was a close thing. "You're an expert now, are you?"

"Of course not, but I've seen 20/20. I keep track of things."

"Keep track of things..." He rolled his eyes. Jesus fuck. "You don't know anything about it, Shel." He pointed at Rig. "That's my partner. You don't like? Leave." He glanced at his watch and stood.

"And don't let the Southern charm fool you -- he can take care of himself."

"Obviously." Her nose wrinkled again, but then Rig showed up, sitting down with a cup of coffee.

"Here you go."

He gave her a hard look, and then turned his back on her. "Hey. I've got to go to this thing." He tossed Rig the keys. "In case you want to go exploring if this goes long."

"Sure, man. Good luck." Rig nodded at him, those eyes telling him that, even here, Rig had his back.

He smiled, tempted as fuck to kiss Rig good and hard. Being careful in public was ingrained, though, and he wasn't going to fuck up their lives just to shock his sister.

"Later." He didn't bother including his sister in the good-bye, just headed over to the lawyer's office, gait stiff, shoulders back, meeting whatever was coming head on.

# Chapter Eleven

They sort of sat there and stared at each other.

Weird, because when Jim met Julie, they'd spent about five minutes sizing each other up, then Julie'd landed in Jim's lap, stealing a beer and laughing.

Somehow Rig didn't think this gal was the laughing type.

"So, you live with James?" Man, that *voice.* It was a good thing Rock'd been south for a while – South. Rig damn near laughed at himself, but he just cleared his throat and nodded.

"Yes, ma'am. We share a house."

Lord, look at that woman's nose wrinkle like she was smelling stinky-feet cheese. "And where did he meet you?"

The temptation to tell her they'd met at a Jello-wrestling competition during a Gay Nude Bar Tour of central Texas was huge, but Rig grabbed onto his polite upbringing with both hands. "San Antonio, ma'am."

"Why doesn't that surprise me?" Those eyes looked at him like Rock's never had, even when they were having a war. "You realize that he's not going to get a dime of Gram's money, don't you? He doesn't deserve a penny."

Oh, now. That was just nasty. "Honey, I'm here because Rock lost his granny. Neither one of us is here to get money." Except Rock sort of was. Damn it. Hell, it wasn't like Rock wanted the cash, Rock just wanted this all over.

"Lie to someone else. I've read about filthy beasts, about the things you do. He's an embarrassment to the whole family."

"Why? Because he's a Marine? He serves his country, now. I won't hear you badmouthing him."

"No. I'm talking about his…" That nose wrinkled again. "Lifestyle."

"Well, honey. He's not looking to sleep with you; I don't see where it's your business."

"It's filthy. My brother in with a bunch of pedophiles."

Now, that was enough. "Rock hasn't ever so much as looked sideways at a kid, now. You need to watch your mouth, lady. Just because you don't like it, that's no reason to lie on him."

An envelope got dragged out of a purse that probably cost more than their mortgage payment and thrown on the table. "I don't want him anywhere near my boys. I told them he was dead."

"You are a sick fuck, lady." He couldn't have stopped his growl on a bet. "He don't need y'all. He's got family in Texas -- nieces and nephews and all. We're not ashamed of him a bit." Hell, Julie and Hank loved Rock, and Momma just took the man right in. Lord, these folks were damn scary.

"Well, excuse me for not being impressed that a bunch of in-bred hillbillies accept him into the fold."

His eyes snapped and he stood, hands landing on the table. "You know, I will put up with you bad-mouthing the Marine because he could kick your ass, and I will put up with you bad-mouthing me because I was raised right and don't have a reason to give a shit what a slimy, bigoted piece of shit asshole thinks. But I will not put up with you bad-mouthing my momma, you homely, ill-mannered, foul-mouthed, closed-minded bitch. You'd best thank God and all the angels that my sister isn't here, because she'd pluck that over-processed hair out of your head."

Mrs. High-and-Mighty hemmed and hawed and flustered. "You. You. I should..."

"No. You shouldn't. Just because I've been nice, don't mean I'll keep on that way." Go on, you evil bitch, before shit starts hitting the fan.

Thank God she managed to stand up, feet pounding on the floor, cheeks just as red as fire as she headed for the street.

"Nice to meet you, honey. Come visit anytime." His voice couldn't get any nastier.

She stopped, looked over, and huffed on out. Lord.

That silly envelope was still sitting on the table and Rig took it, opened it. Pictures.

Lord. About twenty pictures of his Blue – from newborn to teenager. Look at that.

It got him to smiling, fingers tracing that stubborn jaw, those laser-beam eyes. Oh, now. These were worth fighting with that little bitch over. Look at that man.

He lifted his coffee cup up, asking for a refill, turning the photos over, one after another. Just staring.

# Chapter Twelve

Rock made his way next door and up to the second floor, the little secretary at the big desk all efficiency, offering him a coffee that he refused. He wasn't here on a goddamned social call.

He was led into a room with a large table, a man -- the lawyer, Robertson, he assumed -- at the head of it, his mother and father on the man's right. Christ, if he'd thought Shelly'd gotten old, his father was… really old, his mother looking almost just like he remembered, except maybe wound a little tighter. Her hair was certainly pulled back in about as severe a bun as she could have possibly managed.

For a minute, just a couple seconds really, he took a step, intending to go around, to give her a hug, maybe even give them both a hug, some instinct leftover from before he'd left to join up. Then he noticed the way his mother wouldn't look at him and the way his father's lips had curled. Rock's spine went straight and hard, and he put his hands behind his back, just standing at attention and ready to take whatever was dished out. He kind of wished he was wearing his BDUs instead of a fucking suit.

Introductions were made all around, Rock shaking hands with the prim, little man in the dark suit. He sat at the big, wooden table, the veneer on it shining and smooth.

"Shall I just get started?" Robertson asked, and Rock had to work to keep from snorting. There sure as shit weren't going to be any pleasantries. Christ, his jaw ached already.

A secretary was called in to take minutes and the lawyer started.

"There are a few items bequeathed to friends, distant relatives. Ester had them all boxed up and left with me several years ago. I'll be taking care of those separately. Otherwise, all parties with an interest are currently present. She wrote a letter she wanted delivered after her death, James, along with your inheritance."

Rock took the letter passed over to him, eyebrows raised in surprise. Almost more surprised than he'd been about needing to be here in the first place. He tore the seal open, but before he could read it, his father's fist landed on the table.

"You're not seriously telling me that my mother left a penny to him?"

Rock's fist closed over the letter at that, and he looked across the room over his father's shoulder. The paneling had probably cost a fortune.

He ignored the screaming, just let it wash over him. Kind of reminded him of being in basic, or getting an ass reaming for something or other by his CO. His father would have made a piss-poor drill sergeant.

When Robertson continued reading the will, the shouting got louder, the words coming out of his father nasty and hurtful, and Rock just clenched his teeth and his fists on his thighs. Robertson tried to calm his father down, and his mother was sitting there, crying softly, still not looking at him.

Rock hoped it would be over soon so he could get the fuck out of there. He couldn't think of any amount of money that would make any of this worth it.

# Chapter Thirteen

Shit and Shinola, this had been the crappiest day in the history of days.

He pulled off the highway, Rock sitting beside him like the biggest, maddest Marine he'd ever seen. "You hungry?" He figured he'd start with the small shit, then sort of move up.

"No, I am not fucking hungry." The words were low, tight -- Rock so mad he wasn't even shouting.

"Okay." He kept heading for the cabin. Shit. He'd seen Rock pissed. Hell, he'd pissed Rock off, but this was.

Different.

Deeper.

Wrong.

"She say anything to you?"

"Nothing I couldn't deal with." Like he gave a shit about the stupid bitch. He had those baby pictures of Jim in his wallet now; he'd make copies, give some to Momma. Rock'd just be theirs.

Damn it.

"I knew this was a fucking mistake."

"Hey, I'm good. You're done now, right? We'll just do the vacation thing."

Rock looked at him, those blue eyes boring into him for a moment. Damn, he was glad that wasn't actually aimed at him. Then Rock blinked and nodded, stared out the front again. "Yeah. I'm done."

"Okay." Shit. Shit, this was.

How could they.

Jim was their *boy*.

Rock didn't seem to be getting any calmer, either. He was almost vibrating, fingers clenched into fists, the knuckles just white. Rig could practically hear Rock's teeth grinding, too.

He pulled up next to the cottage and killed the engine, just sitting there. "You got a couple choices, Marine. We can go for a run. We can go get drunk and start a bar fight. We can go fuck."

Rock was silent a moment and then grunted. "Run, then fuck. Way my day's going someone'll call the cops before I even get a single good punch in if we choose door number two."

"Works for me. Let's get shorts on and we'll go." He could run Rock into the motherfucking ground.

Rock didn't answer, just got out, slamming the door shut with enough force to shake the whole damned car before stalking up the walk to their cottage.

Fun, fun, fun. Lord, no wonder Blue didn't ever say nothing about his folks, especially if the sister was the good one.

The door to their cottage rattled as well, Rock stalking into the bedroom and changing into a pair of black shorts and a tight, white t-shirt. Every movement was short, economical. He tugged his boots off and grabbed his running shoes and a gimme cap, whistling a little under his breath.

Rock's hand slapped his ass. "Come on, let's hit the beach." That beautiful fucking body jogged out ahead of him.

He followed, running along without a goddamn word. It felt fucking good, feet slapping on the sand, muscles working and working and fighting. Hell, yes. Rock didn't say a thing either, just ran and ran and ran, sweat starting to plaster the T-shirt to all those muscles, shoulders shining in the afternoon sun.

By the time they turned back, he was starting to feel it, muscles protesting the unsteady gait that the sand gave him.

"Keep that ass moving, Rigger. I've got plans for it." Rock didn't even sound out of breath, his chest was working though.

"Shut up and run, Marine." He winked over, staying just out of reach.

Oh, that was nearly a smile. "Don't you worry about me. I can go forever."

Fucker. "Yeah, yeah, yeah. I'm smaller, but I got stamina."

"You can prove that when we get back." Those blue eyes were making him promises.

"You know it, Blue Eyes." Rock was the best motherfucking thing to come from Yankee land.

The cottage came into sight and Rock moved faster, just like a horse catching sight of the barn. The temptation to swat that fine ass was fucking huge. Show off.

And then Rock turned, running backward. "Well, come on!"

"I will kill you, Marine." He chuckled, feeling good for the first time all day.

"You can try. Gotta catch me first." Rock turned back around, pace picking up again.

Oh. Asshole. He put on speed, catching Rock and swatting that tight ass good and hard.

"Oh, that's how it is, is it?" They hit the stairs together, footsteps loud on the wood.

"You know it, Marine."

"I know this," Rock told him, grabbing hold of his arm the second they were through the door and throwing him up against the wall. That solid body pushed up against him, Rock's mouth meeting his, kissing him hard enough his head hit the wall.

Oh, fuck him. Yes. This he knew he could give his Blue. He moaned and opened right up, let Rock take what he needed. One hand wrapped around his head, tilting it so Rock's tongue could go deep as that big, hard body humped against him. Rock was hot and sweaty and felt so damned good. That's it. Give it up, man. He could take it all. Shit, he wanted it.

Rock moaned, free hand pushing his T-shirt up, fingers going for his nipples. He arched and groaned as Rock pinched and tugged, twisted one and then the other.

"More. Won't break, Blue." He never had. Wouldn't, damn it.

With a growl, Rock tore his t-shirt in two, leaving it hanging from his shoulders. Mouth, sliding over his neck, licking at the sweat on his skin, Rock made a beeline for his right nipple, lips soon closing over it. He couldn't hold his needy cry in any more than he could stop arching up into that mouth.

Rock's fingers slid down along his sides, the touch firm, strong, shoving his shorts right down off his hips as Rock nibbled and bit at his nipple, working it ruthlessly.

"Fuck, yes. Shit. Rock. Fucking need you." He was on fucking *fire*.

"Gonna do you right here," muttered Rock, mouth sliding across his chest to his other nipple. "Up against the wall."

"Hell, yes. I'll ride you 'til you can't fucking see." Until that nasty group of stupid bastards that didn't know how to appreciate a good man disappeared.

"Fuck. Yes. Rig." Rock just grunted, and bit at his skin, fingers tugging his shorts down further, one sliding behind to push at his hole. He worked his shorts the rest of the way off, wiggling and rubbing and trying to get more of that mouth the entire time. "Me next," growled Rock. "Naked." The word was breathed out against his neck just as Rock's finger pushed into him.

"Uh-huh." It didn't take anything to get Rock's shorts down, that cock in his hand. Rock made a noise, half broken, half growl, and then his Blue's mouth was on his again, his lips bruising up from the force of it. Rock's need just poured into him, fat prick sliding along his palm, hot and solid, silken fire.

"Mine." The word slipped out of him, but he meant it. Rock was his Marine. His man. His fucking family.

It earned him a low rumble, Rock's mouth wrapping around his lower lip and tugging on it. Those blue eyes bored into his own as a second finger worked its way into his ass, Rock stretching him hard and good. He nodded, bearing down and letting Rock in, fucking demanding more.

"Fucking want you, Rig." Rock's fingers scissored and fucked in and out of him, brushing against his gland every couple of thrusts, while the hard cock in his hand throbbed with Rock's heartbeat.

"Ready. Ready for you." He spread Rock's pre-come over the heavy prick, slicking Rock up.

Rock nodded, hands sliding around his thighs and lifting him up, balancing him against the wall. He wrapped his thighs around Rock's hips, bracing himself on Rock's shoulders.

"Yeah, just like that." Rock's prick nudged his hole, and they both shifted, and just like that he was being stretched, filled. Rock's forehead rested against his, their breath panting together.

They sorta stared, just watching each other for a long second, then Rock grinned and his own smile answered. Hell, yes. Rock's mouth landed on his again, and that cock slid almost out of him before pushing back in with a nice, hard thrust, his cock trapped between them.

"Just like that," Rock said again, starting a good, solid rhythm.

"Yeah." He held on, bucking and riding, head tossing. "Hell, yeah. Blue."

"Uh-huh." The sounds tore from Rock, his hips moving, humping up and into him and up and into him, his back hitting the wall with every thrust. He just held on and rode, body bucking and jerking, letting Rock drive them to the moon.

The sweat they'd worked up running was nothing compared to the sweat they built up now, Rock's body sheening and dripping, their skin slapping and sliding together.

"Rabbit," muttered Rock, hand wrapping around his cock.

"Uh-huh. Gonna. Fuck." His world was coming to an end. Goddamn.

"Do it. Come on my cock." That growl lodged in the base of his spine, pushing the pleasure through him.

"Yeah. Yeah. I. Blue..." He just shorted out, eyes rolling up.

Rock came with him, cock jerking inside him as he milked it, heat splashing between them even as Rock's heat filled him deep.

He just held on, chickens scattered like he couldn't believe. "Damn."

That soft chuckle sounded great.

"Hold on," muttered Rock, hands sliding, one going around his back, the other holding onto his ass as Rock straightened and headed for the bedroom. So fucking strong. He grinned, lips at Rock's throat.

He didn't worry for a second about being dropped, and he wasn't, Rock lowering him to the bed once they were there. Those blue eyes started down at him, looking hard. He looked right up, not hiding a bit. He wasn't going anywhere. Damn it.

A soft smile tugged at the corners of Rock's mouth. "You look well-fucked."

"I am. You're good to me." Rock was looking more like his Marine.

"I know which side my bread's buttered on." Rock grinned suddenly. "You want food or round two more?"

"I can eat anytime, Marine."

Any fucking time at all.

# Chapter Fourteen

They were officially on holiday and he was up at six fucking am, doing goddamned pushups. He hadn't even waited for his standard wake-up call, letting Rig sleep while he did his PT. He was fighting his instinct to get Rig to call and get their fucking tickets changed to go home today. But he'd promised Rig a few days at the goddamned beach and he wasn't going to disappoint his cowboy.

The work-out felt good -- pushing himself, making his muscles work and work, letting all the frustration and anger he'd woken up with out. He rolled over and started doing sit-ups, not even bothering to count, just going and going.

"You're going to wear yourself out." Rig rolled over on the bed, head hanging down, eyes half open.

He grunted. "Didn't want to wake you."

"Mmm. I was dreaming about pancakes." Rig grinned wide, looking lazy as all hell.

He leaned forward and slid his lips against Rig's before going back to his sit-ups. "I'll finish up and take you out to breakfast." They'd find someplace on the highway, he wasn't going back to Old Orchard.

Rig actually pouted. "You're forgetting something."

Chuckling, he pushed their mouths together again as he came up, lips wrapping around that pout and tugging on it. "I am?" he asked, as he went back down again.

"Uh-huh. Something important."

"Hrmm..." He did a few more sit-ups, pretending to think about it.

Rig was playing right along, grinning for a second before pouting dramatically again. He leaned in again, nibbling on that pushed out lower lip. Shifting slightly, he let the teasing touches turn into an upside down kiss, fingers coming up to cup Rig's cheek. Rig hummed into his lips, eyes closing, that kiss sweet as fuck.

Groaning, he ended the kiss with another tug of Rig's lower lip. "I think it's coming back to me now," he murmured against Rig's mouth.

"Yeah? Starting to come back to you?"

"Uh-huh." He rubbed Rig's lip with his thumb. "You coming down to me, or am I coming up to you?"

"Bed's softer." Rig started sucking on his thumb, making it fucking hot, somehow.

"As long as the bed's the only thing that's soft." There were no worries on his end, that thumb sucking thing had him hard.

Rig nodded, moaned, teeth sliding over the tip of his thumb. Groaning, he fucked Rig's mouth with his thumb, his cock jerking in his shorts. He stood, thumb sliding out of Rig's mouth with a pop.

Rig moaned, rolling over, lips parted. "Get naked, Marine."

"You're pretty pushy today." His hands were already tugging up his t-shirt, though, tossing it over his shoulder before he went for his shorts, tugging them down over his hard-on.

"Enthusiastic. The word is enthusiastic." Rig's hand was moving, working that hard cock, the action hidden by the sheets.

He chuckled, eyes caught by the movement. His hand dropped to his own prick, sliding over it, matching Rig's rhythm.

"Uh-uh. Mine." Rig groaned, tongue wetting those lips.

Hand still moving on himself, he climbed onto the bed and straddled Rig's shoulders. "Yours? This?"

"Yes. Mine. That. Gimme." Pushy redneck.

He leaned forward just enough to paint Rig's mouth with the tip of his cock, leaving a couple of drops on Rig's lower lip. Rig's groan made him feel ten fucking feet tall. "Open up, it's all for you." He slowly slid his prick into Rig's mouth, just groaning at the heat.

Rig just... Fuck him. It was like the first time because Rig opened up and let him in and goddamn. A low moan tore out of his throat, his cock sinking in and in until it hit the back of Rig's throat. Bracing his hands on the bed over Rig's heat, he started fucking that mouth, watching as his prick slid in and out.

Rig's hands slid over his thighs, encouraging him to push in, to take what he needed. Hungry cowboy. Those grey eyes stared up at him, just starting the shine. He groaned and grunted, a shudder moving through him. It was so fucking good. There was nothing like Rig's mouth.

He tried not to move faster, harder, tried to hold back and make it last. It was too fucking good, though, and he was soon just going at it -- all out fucking Rig's mouth. His Rabbit pulled him deep, throat squeezing the tip of his cock, nose buried in his pubes.

He lost it, hips jerking as his cock throbbed, pulsed inside Rig's mouth, his spunk shooting down Rig's throat. Gasping, he kept moving, hips slowing, gentling. Rig's tongue cleaned him up and loved on him.

It wasn't fucking easy to pull out, but he did, moving down to lie on Rig properly, to take that mouth that tasted like him and Rig all twisted together in the best fucking way. Rig's cock pushed against his belly, wet-tipped and hot enough to steam.

"Mmm... wanting, Rig? Need the Rocketman to take care of you before we head out?" He ground their hips together, Rig's cock like a brand against him.

Rig fed him a great, little, needy noise, entire body arching under him, want drawn on the thin face. "Blue."

"Right here, Rig. Got what you need." And he did, too, his cock going nice and hard at that look, at the way Rig's body moved against him.

He held Rig's eyes, reaching up for the lube they'd left under one of the pillows last night. "Gonna do you right."

"Hell yes. I'm needing." Rig nodded, spreading like soft butter for him.

"Needing this." Rock let his cock bump Rig's hole while he slicked up his fingers and sent them skating across Rig's sensitive, little titties.

"Uh-huh." There was the barest mark on one from last night. His mark on that gold skin.

His cock throbbed and his hips jerked a little, pushing just the head of his prick into Rig's hot, tight hole. It seemed to cling to his skin as he pulled back out, making him groan. His slick fingers slid from the pretty nipples on down over Rig's belly, dipping into Rig's navel, making them both chuckle. Then two of his fingers were swallowed by the tight heat of Rig's body, as he pushed and stretched, got Rig ready for his cock.

"Mmm. More, Blue. I need more." Rig rode him like he was a prize pony, lips parted, hands braced on his shoulders.

"I know." He did. He pushed in another finger, sliding them deep enough to bump Rig's gland, making that long body jerk and jump for him. He wasn't going to tease; he was just making sure

Rig's ass was nice and slick for him. Hot lips slid up his jaw, Rig's grunt sexy as fuck. "Fucking good."

He nodded his agreement, fingers sliding away. He waited a minute, just poised on pushing in, loving the anticipation. Then he pushed right in, loving the tight, hot squeeze even better. Rig just groaned, arching toward him, ass squeezing his cock.

"Yeah, just like that." He nodded and then started moving, fucking the tight ass like nothing going. He pressed their mouths together, lips moving with Rig's, breath passing between them along with spit and need and groans.

Rig rode and jerked, ass working his prick, tongue pushing into his lips. He braced himself on one hand, the other sliding to find those sensitive nipples, loving the way each touch made Rig jerk, made him ride harder.

"Blue!" Rig flushed dark, arched as he pushed deep, that ass squeezing.

"Right fucking here, Rig." He bent to nose along Rig's neck, tongue coming out to tease the little patch of skin that never failed to make Rig shiver.

Rig gasped and shot, heat spraying between them, happy sound filling the air. He let that sound push him over, let the smell of Rig's come drag another orgasm out of him. Hips jerking, he filled Rig again, draining his balls dry.

"Fuck. Rig." He groaned, lowering his weight onto Rig.

"Uh-huh. Gonna be walking bowlegged."

"Uh-huh. Gonna look like you've been riding the Rocketman." He grinned, it was his favorite look on his Rabbit.

"My favorite pastime. Yee-Haw."

He chuckled, sliding out and slapping Rig's side. "Bitch."

"You know it." Rig's body jerked around him with laughter. "You gonna take me out and show me the beach, Marine?"

He hummed, stretched, kissed the side of Rig's mouth. "I said I would, didn't I?"

Groaning, he rolled and sat, stretched his arms up over his head. "You want those pancakes first?"

"You know it. I want bacon, too. Oh, man. And coffee."

"Lots of bacon. Lots of syrup. Whipped cream." He moaned a little. "Man, that's almost as good as sex."

"Almost." Rig grinned, leaned up for another quick kiss. "Shower?"

He laughed and grabbed Rig's ass. "Slut."

"No shit." He got a laugh, a wink. "Good thing I'm yours."

"Uh-huh." He grunted, nodded and tugged Rig into a hard, quick hug before standing up and stretching. "Come on then, day's not getting any longer."

"Nope. We got a few days to just play, man. I'm a fan."

"Yeah." He smiled, feeling eased in a way doing push-ups couldn't manage. "Me, too."

# Chapter Fifteen

Well, the beach wasn't half bad.

It was fucking cold.

And rocky.

And filled with Yankees.

But not bad.

He grabbed another couple of beers from one of the little bars off the pier and headed back down where the bear was splitting his time between growling and snarling at the other tourists.

Ah, Rock was in *such* a good fucking mood.

"Hey, Marine. Have a cold one."

Rock grunted, hand snagging the bottle he held out. It was half downed in a few quick gulps before he got a grudging, "Thanks."

Rock was sitting in one of the folding beach chairs the cottage they were staying in had on hand, putting his ass about a foot above the sand, his legs spread out in front of him. The aviator glasses looked fucking cool, especially above all the muscles nicely shown off by the white T-shirt Rock wore. T-shirt and PT shorts, pretty much Rock's uniform since they'd been here. Aside from the good clothes he'd worn to the lawyer's.

"So, tell me what the lawyer said, man." He settled himself down, drank deep, not looking at Rock.

Rock snorted. "The lawyer? He said the will says you get twenty-five thousand dollars from Esther South's estate."

"Good lord. Go Granny." Rig nodded. At least somebody in Rock's family was worth something.

"Apparently she was out of her goddamned mind or she would have remembered to change the fucking will to make sure a faggot like me didn't get a goddamned penny." Rock's voice dripped with bitterness.

"Or maybe she was a decent person. Well, you had to get it from somewhere." Goddamn people.

The chuckle sounded startled, surprised. "I suppose you're right. The lawyer said she had changed the will -- after I left home in fact -- and that there was nothing wrong with Esther's mind, which my father damned well knew." Rock shrugged. "He wants to fight it anyway. Doesn't want me seeing a penny of what he says should be his money.

"Robertson, the lawyer, told him it would tie the entire estate up if he did. Told him it was most certainly my grandma's wishes that I got that money, and asked my father to reconsider. You should have seen the old man's face when Robertson told him that.

"If he's going to fight it I'll get a notice, if he changes his mind I'll get a check -- Robertson had me sign all the fucking paperwork I needed to." Rock drained the rest of his beer, eyes out on the ocean. "Not sure if it's worth the trouble if he decides to take it to court."

"Sure it is. It ain't about the money. It's about you being something special."

Rock shook his head and snarled. "Not to him, I'm not. I'm the fucking faggot son they wish they'd drowned at goddamned birth. I just want to get the fuck out of here and never have to see that asshole again." Rock's hands curled, one around the beer bottle, the other around the arm of his chair, knuckles white.

"Okay. Let's go home. Hell, let's rent a car and drive it. We got three days." If he had his druthers, he'd go find Rock's daddy and beat the sorry motherfucker to death.

"Promised you the beach." Rock's jaw jutted out, his body taking on that stiffness it always did when Rock was being stubborn.

"So, we'll follow the coast." He couldn't see the point of sitting here and listening to the big guy growl for days.

"I'm not letting that asshole ruin your vacation."

"And I'm not letting that asshole ruin yours." He sat up, looked over his glasses. "Shit, Blue. Let's go exploring. Rent a convertible and get our happy asses into some trouble."

"You really want to?" Rock looked at his watch. "Day's already more'n half over, we've got to get packed, check out, exchange the rental if you were serious about the convertible..." Rock might have been protesting, but Rig hadn't heard a "No" yet, now had he?

"You go deal with the car. I'll deal with the hotel. We'll grab supper somewhere further south." Hell, they'd need to stop for a map, some beef jerky, and a Styrofoam cooler.

"Well I suppose if it's really what you want to do -- it's your vacation."

"Cool." He finished his beer and stood up, grinning down at the big guy. "I bet we can find a few Elvis CDs at the Wal-Mart for the trip."

"Whatever you want, Rig." Rock stood and stretched up, muscles clenching and releasing beneath the tight t-shirt. And unless he was badly mistaken, the lines in Rock's forehead and by his eyes had already started to ease. "Long as it's not some twangy shit."

"I'll do my best, man." He grinned, winked.

Yeah.

Yeah. Road trip.

That was better.

Rock chuckled and closed both their chairs up, carrying them up toward their rental cottage. "I want car munchies, too. Chips and shit."

"Hell, yes. Chocolate. Cherry sours. We ought to grab a couple of those beach towels, in case we need 'em."

"James. I thought I'd find you here, flaunting yourself like a common whore." Jesus Christ. That son of a bitch looked just like Rock.

But old.

And crusty.

And that nasty, little bitch was with him.

"I take it this nasty bastard used to be yours, huh?" Rig's eyebrow went up, eyes running over Daddy South. He wasn't fucking impressed.

Rock had frozen in place at the sound of his name, but Rig's words had Rock moving again, putting that big, beautiful body between him and Daddy South. "What the fuck do you want?" Rock's muscles were so fucking tense, Rig worried he was going to pop a vein.

"I just came to see what you were taking up with and to tell you you'll never get a dime of that money." Lord, did Rock really used to *sound* like that? Thank God the man had been in the South a while, because damn.

"I'd introduce you to him, but you don't deserve to fucking clean the ground he walks on." Rock spat on the ground at his father's feet. "And you want to tie the estate up for God only knows how long? You just go ahead. I'm not hurting any for it. And I got a lot more years than you left to keep waiting on it."

"Well, there you go. Come on, man. Leave the trash on the beach. Somebody'll come along for it." Yeah, they needed to go, both of them. This place wasn't for him at all.

"You nasty, little piece of backwater, hillbilly trash! Don't you think you can just seduce my brother and not pay for it!" Lord, that woman could scream.

Rig stepped around Rock, got right up in little Miss High-and-Mighty's face. "Look, you hare-lipped little bitch, I'll tell you this once. I'm nobody's trash and I'll fucking seduce whoever I fucking want to. Why don't you take your dried up, nasty self and get the hell away from the best thing your folks ever managed." Jesus. How bad was it if the girl you hit was really a goddamn harpy in disguise? He sure wished Julie was here. She'd kick that gal's ass for him.

"You punk-assed, little asshole." Daddy South spat the words at him, fist coming straight at him.

It never hit him though, Rock's hand was right there, wrapping around it scant inches from his face. The low sound that came from Rock nearly put a shiver down his spine and it was Daddy South who wound up on the receiving end of a punch, Rock knocking the man right down onto his ass.

"Come on," growled Rock. "Get up. I goddamn dare you."

Well, shit marthy. He grabbed Rock's arm, whispering low. "Come on, Marine. They call the cops on you and your ass is grass. We're leaving. Now."

"He started it," growled Rock. "Didn't you, old man? Pretty fucking tough until you've got someone your size standing up to you."

Rock's father was half-sitting, spitting blood from a split lip, the sister screaming like a banshee about how Rock'd hit him.

"Yeah and you finished it. Now, get moving, man. Now." He didn't know how these folks were, but he knew how the Marines were and Rock'd be in serious hurt.

He stepped close to Shelly, hauling the old man to his feet. "Y'all hush, now. Now. I'll take him and we'll go, but I swear to God, honey, you don't stop your screaming and I'll make you cry."

Well, that worked. Thank God. Probably more out of shock than anything else, her mouth opening and closing like a fucking goldfish. But she'd shut up for now.

Rock just growled and stepped around them, headed for the door, back stiffer than he'd ever seen it.

"That's better. Y'all go on, now, and we will, too." He met Rock's daddy's eyes. "You don't have to care for him; he's got family that wants him. Y'all just go on."

"He's not getting a dime of that money. Not a penny. I'll see him in hell first." There was so much damned hate in those eyes that were as blue as his Rock's.

"Oh, man. You just do what you need to. I reckon you'll meet lots of your own in hell, given time."

"Rigger." Rock growled at him from the door, their bags in his hands, clothes all but falling out of them. "We're going."

"I'm right behind you, man." He turned his back on the assholes and followed Rock without another thought.

Rock threw their stuff in the back seat and got into the driver's seat, starting the car up before he'd even climbed in. He could hear Shelly screaming after them, calling them names -- words a Marine would blush at using in mixed company.

"Man, Sissy ought to be here. She'd shut that little bitch right up." He shut the door as Rock pulled out.

"I'd pay good money to see that." Rock followed the road out to the highway, flooring it as soon as they were on their way.

The key to the cottage was tossed at him. "I locked it. Guess we'll have to put that in the mail because I'm not fucking going back there."

"Okay. We'll overnight it. We're good." He looked over. "You gonna be okay?"

Rock shrugged. And then nodded. "Yeah. I am. Better with every fucking mile we get away from there." Rock growled again, not looking that okay at all. "He can say what he wants to me, but I won't have him talking to you like that."

"Works for me." He reached over, hand on Rock's thigh. Christ, it was like touching a log.

"You okay?" Rock asked suddenly, hand dropping to squeeze his for just a moment.

"Yeah. Yeah. I'm good." He nodded. He thought he'd be just fine, thanks, now that he'd got his man away from those people.

Rock nodded at the glove compartment. "Find the map and figure out where the fuck we're going. And I still want my goddamned munchies."

"Hell, yes. Stop somewhere, huh? We'll call the rental car place, the hotel, shop. All that happy, happy."

Then they could just leave this shit behind.

# Chapter Sixteen

They switched the car, picked up munchies and driving music, called the hotel and mailed off the key, all before seven p.m. Fuck, there was nothing like Rig on a mission. They didn't bother with supper, just started driving, putting as many miles as possible between them and those fuckers that were his family.

The music played, Elvis and Aerosmith, Rig drawing the line at AC/DC for some reason. Rig fed him chips and chocolate, candy keeping his mouth busy, keeping him from grinding his teeth together.

It'd been dark for a while when his stomach growled good and long, and he glanced over at Rig. "You hungry?"

"You know it. Let's find something good and then we can hunt a room, if you want."

He nodded. "Yeah. Steak. Fries. A fucking huge piece of cake and lots of beer." Hell, if they found a hotel near a restaurant, he could get rip-roaring drunk.

"Oh, fuck yes. Except I want a baked potato with all the crap. Butter. Cheese. Sour cream. Bacon."

"I'm not sure they do that this far north," he teased, taking the next turn-off. "Keep your eyes peeled for a steakhouse."

"I'm looking. Damn Yankees." Rig grinned at him, eyes teasing.

"You know it." He was going off the breed himself. He figured he'd eaten enough of Rig's chili and cornbread to count as an honorary Southerner. He pointed to a sign. "There's a Howard Johnson's up ahead."

"Woo. Ho Jo's. There'll be pie." Jesus, look at that grin.

"You wanna eat or check in first?" He slowed down, pulled into the parking lot.

"If we check in, we'll end up having sex because we're both frustrated and growly."

"And that's a problem?" Of course his stomach picked just then to growl again. Loudly. "Okay, okay. We'll go get our meat before I slip you mine."

"Slip? Shit, man. I want it hard enough to rattle my teeth. Then I want it again. And again." Rig was vibrating a little, eyes heated.

"Right. We'll check in first." He wasn't ruled by his stomach.

"Hell, there's a Burger King. We can get take out and have a big breakfast."

"Uh-huh. Or room service. Or even those fucking ten dollar bags of peanuts out of the mini-bar." He wasn't fucking picky. Not at the moment.

He got out of the car before he jumped Rig right there, and went around to grab their bags out of the trunk. Stupid things were still bulging open. Rig was gonna have to work that stupid packing magic on 'em. Later. Much, much later.

"I'll get the room." Rig moved fast, tight ass swaying back and forth. He watched until it disappeared through the doors. Damn, that was something.

He might have gotten pissed on in the family department, but if Rig was his reward for that he'd come out ahead. He'd come out so fucking ahead it wasn't even on the same page.

He shouldered their bags and sauntered in, eyes scanning the lobby. Rig was leaning over the fucking counter, signing for the room, legs splayed, pretty ass in the tightest pair of jeans known to man.

Jesus Christ. And people expected him to give that up just because they disapproved. Snorting, he headed over, just as Rig was collecting the keys. "All signed in?"

"You know it. Room service is open 'til midnight." Rig was bouncing, eyes burning into him. "We're upstairs."

"Not yet we're not. But we will be." He hit the button for the elevator and then noticed the stairwell right around the corner. He nodded toward it. "Race you."

"First one up gets a blowjob?" Rig looked around, then kissed him good and hard. Right there. Bastard.

"You're on." Then that jackrabbit was running.

Oh, that cheating, sexy, motherfucking bastard.

Rock headed on up after Rig, taking the stairs two at a time. Rig was hustling, ass moving, those cowboy boots thumping on the stairs. Oh yeah, that's what he liked to see. Still, he didn't want to lose this one -- he wanted that mouth wrapped around his prick. He put on a burst of speed, realizing as he followed Rig through the door into the corridor that he didn't have a clue what their room number was.

Rig stopped in front of a door, hands fumbling with the key. "Damn it."

He caught up, grinning as he pushed up against Rig's ass. "You cheated," he told Rig, rubbing.

Rig nodded, rubbing back. "I want you. The fucking *door* won't open."

He laughed, taking the key out of Rig's hand. "Yeah, I wouldn't be none too steady with a Rocketman special coming my way either." He got the door open, hustling Rig in.

"Jackass." Rig's laugh got cut off by their lips smashing together.

He tossed the bags on the floor, pushing the door closed with his foot, the kiss going deep fast. Rig just crawled up his body, legs wrapping around his waist. He grabbed hold of that ass, squeezing as Rig got hold of his tongue, sucking on it. Rig's hands were holding his head, tilting him so that kiss could go deeper.

He walked blindly until his legs hit the bed, and then he fell back onto it, grunting as they went down hard, Rig on top of him.

"Hey." Rig moaned, kissed him so hard his head was going to pop off.

"Hey," he growled, hands sliding on Rig's ass, up along Rig's back.

"Fuck me, Marine. I need you."

His hips bucked up, rubbing his prick against Rig's. "I owe you a blowjob."

"Yeah. Tomorrow you can blow me and I'll fuck you through the mattress. Tonight I need your cock."

He laughed, flipping them so Rig was beneath him. "Too fucking many clothes, Rabbit." His fingers tugged Rig's t-shirt out of his waistband, pushing it up and off.

"Uh-huh. You, too." Rig pushed his shorts down, fingers wrapping around the shaft of his cock.

Groaning, he pushed down into Rig's hand, hips working as he tried to get into Rig's pants. "You would be wearing the tightest fucking jeans you own."

"They were the closest pair in reach. I did change in the car, Marine."

"Uh-huh." Like he didn't know Rig wore those painted on blue jeans just to get him all worked up. Of course, because they were old and skin tight and worn here and there, that would make them that much easier to tear off. "I hope you have another pair."

"You know how I like my jeans, man." Uh-huh, and he knew how it turned Rig on, him needing that cowboy ass like he did.

"I'm gonna start a fund. Feed it every payday." He winked, getting a hold of the sides of the jeans, testing how strong they were. Oh, there was a weak spot somewhere in the ass because he could hear it tear already. Grinning, he finished the job, his cock just throbbing in Rig's hand.

"You bastard..." Rig laughed, tongue pushing right into his lips, fucking him just like he wanted to fuck that ass.

Rig could call him what he wanted, he was about to be buried in that tight ass that had been teasing him since they'd gotten out of the car.

And if there was a voice in his head that snorted and pointed out that had been all of about five minutes, if that, he squashed it by slicking a finger up on the pre-come dripping from Rig's slit and pushing that finger into Rig's ass.

"Blue..." Rig groaned, arched right into his touch, and started rocking, fucking his finger.

"Yep. Got it first try." His teasing ended on a moan, his prick just jerking at the thought of that ass working his cock like it was working his finger.

He needed the fucking lube or something, but their fucking bags were by the door.

He shifted to kneel between Rig's legs and pushed two fingers from his free hand into Rig's mouth, sliding them in and out just like he was doing to Rig's ass. Oh, shit. That mouth. That amazing fucking mouth. Rig licked and sucked, nuzzled and groaned over his fingers, teeth just threatening.

He liked to think Rig could get him off with that mouth working any number of body parts, but it would be a waste of an orgasm to let it get him off now. He wanted in Rig's ass, and he wanted bad. Groaning, he tugged his fingers out of Rig's mouth and pushed them into Rig's ass alongside the first.

The heat of Rig's mouth had nothing on the heat of Rig's ass.

"Oh, fuck." Rig arched, knees bending and sprawled wide open, ass pumping as it took him in and in.

"Not yet, but soon." The words came out as little more than a growl, his cock throbbing, wanting. He wanted to watch this for a moment longer, though, wanted to watch Rig just lose it on his fingers, body twisting and needy. "Sex on a fucking stick, Rig."

"Make me so goddamn hot." Rig's fingers started working those pink titties, stroking and pinching, Rig just going wild on his fingers.

Oh, fuck.

Groaning, he yanked his fingers out and spat into his hand, slicking himself up as good as he was going to. Then he brought his cock to Rig's hole and let Rig's movements pull him right in. He called out Rig's name, eyes closing at the tight heat.

"Yeah. Yeah, Blue. Yours. Take me."

He nodded, pushing in all the way, eyes opening to meet Rig's. Those grey eyes just shone at him as he started to fuck Rig's ass, taking it like he was storming a fucking beach. Shit, yeah. That's what they needed. Just that. Right. Fucking. There. Rig seemed to be right with him, bucking and riding him, hands gripping him and squeezing hard.

The bed made all sorts of noises, headboard banging against the wall every few thrusts, and it just made it sweeter, as did the needy, little noises Rig made, noises that went straight to his prick.

He could do this all fucking night and never stop.

Rig pulled himself up, mouth on his jaw, moving up toward his ear. Those teeth nipped him just enough to feel, Rig whispering, "Fucking good."

And just like that, he was close to coming, Rig's ass squeezing him good and hard. He wrapped his hand around Rig's cock, jacking his Rabbit off as he took that ass over and over again. "Show me," he growled.

Rig didn't answer, didn't have to. Those eyes went wide, that tight ass squeezed, and then Rig was shooting, spunk splashing on his fingers. The smell of it... Rock groaned. It was pure male and all Rig and there wasn't anything like it. His hips pushed his cock inside Rig's body a few more times, but it was all over except for the shouting.

"Rig!" He jerked once more and let Rig have it, coming with a few full-body shudders.

Long, skinny arms wrapped around him, kept him close. He sank onto Rig, letting the lean body act as a mattress. It let him stay buried deep and he closed his eyes.

"Yeah." Rig nodded, lips on his temple. "Better."

He grunted and nodded.

Why he wasn't fucking enough for his goddamned family? That he didn't get.

But this... he groaned as Rig's tightened briefly around him again. This he understood just fine.

# Chapter Seventeen

He hadn't laughed so hard in years. They'd been meandering south, stopping at every weird, little museum, every stupid tourist trap, every goofy thing they could find. The car was full of crap -- gimme caps and T-shirts, earrings for Julie and Momma, pecan logs and chocolate everything.

Christ, they were having fun.

"Rock! Look! A fudge factory!"

Rock glanced over at him, sun shining off the aviator glasses his stud wore. "Let me guess -- you want to stop."

Rock had moaned and groaned every time they found a new place to stop, grumbling and bitching. And then who had bought the most crap and insisted they buy a disposable camera to take pictures outside every damned place? None other than his stud.

Rock didn't even wait for him to answer, the wind easing as the convertible slowed, pulled into the parking lot of the factory.

"Yep. We need samples and we can mail fudge home to Momma." He grinned over, laughing at the look Rock gave him.

"You're going to make yourself broke, mailing crap back to her." Rock got out of the car and stretched, the tight T-shirt and jeans hugging every muscle.

"Nah. Momma loves it." He hummed, licking his lips. Watching.

"You think they've got different kinds of chocolate?" asked Rock.

"I hope so. I love peanut butter fudge." They headed in, signed up for the silly little tour, the little tour guide staring at Rock with huge, sparkly eyes.

"We get free samples, right?" Rock asked her, turning those blue eyes on her.

"Oh. Yes. Yes, absolutely." She sort of simpered, eyelashes fluttering, and Rig fought his laugh. Oh lord.

Rock just beamed at her. "Chocolate?" he asked, leaning in just a little, tone hopeful, just pouring it on.

Oh, man. He was going to goose that tight ass. Hard.

"Oh, sure. Do you like dark or milk?"

"He likes it all. He's equal-opportunity."

Rock nodded. "That's right. I have yet to meet a chocolate I didn't care for. Especially of the fudge variety. My friend here prefers peanut butter fudge -- can you believe that? Someone thinking peanut butter is better than chocolate?"

She giggled. "We have both. I can make sure you get to sample both, too. Who knows, maybe it's like that Reese's ad on TV -- you just need to run into each other and get your chocolate and peanut butter on each other."

Oh. Oh, man. He was going to bust out laughing.

Rock coughed, *not* looking at him. "Maybe..." Rock coughed again. "Maybe we'll have to try that."

Rig tilted his head, lips twitching. "So, honey. How about showing us where we can... rub our candy together?"

That tickle in Rock's throat got worse, Rock damn near having a coughing fit.

"Oh man, are you okay?" The sweet thing thumped Rock on the back. "Do you want some water? You're not allergic to nuts are you? Because this is not a nut free zone. Not at all."

Rock cleared his throat. Three times. "I'm fine," he finally replied in a strangled voice.

"Maybe you ought to get him some water, darlin'. He looks a little peaked."

See him.

See him not laugh his ass off.

"Okay. I'll be right back!"

She hurried off and Rock finally looked at him. "Allergic to *nuts*? I'd be fucking doomed."

Oh, Jesus Christ. He burst out laughing, holding his belly he cackled so hard. Rock's laughter joined his, his Marine almost choking for real from chortling so hard.

"Sh. Sh. She's gonna come back any second now." Rock had stopped looking at him again, shoulders shaking as Rock tried to stop laughing.

"So... are you peanut butter or chocolate?"

That had Rock going again, and his Blue thumped him one on the arm.

Their guide came back and Rock took the water with a strangled "thanks", drinking it down in a few gulps.

"So, do you two want the whole tour or did you just want the short tour?"

"Honey, we just want the fudge. We've got to get on the road." He carefully didn't look at Rock. "So he can dip his chocolate."

Oh, Rock was going to hurt something if he kept choking like that.

She was starting to give Rock worried looks, but she packaged up a good-sized chunk of several flavors for them, handing them over to Rock and patting his hand. "You take care of that cough. It sounds bad."

Rock nodded and thanked her and made a bee-line for the door, bag of fudge clutched in one hand.

"I'll make sure to take care of him, honey. Don't you worry." Oh, God. That was *funny*.

"You do that. Enjoy the fudge! And if you're ever by this way again just come back and see me and I'll give you the full tour."

Rock called him from the door. "Rig. We need to get going."

"Will do, honey. Thanks!" He managed to make it all the way to the car before his laughter caught him again.

Rock hit him in the arm again. Hard. And then just lost it, almost howling. They leaned together, gasping and hooting and just fighting to catch their breath. Goddamn.

"Oh, shit. The look on your face. Oh. Oh, Blue. That was funny as fuck!"

Rock shook his head. "That was something else. 'Dip my chocolate'." Rock started up the car. "What do you say we look for a place to hang your hat for the night? Find us some steaks, a bed, maybe not in that order."

"Works for me, man." He dug out a bite of fudge, held it up for Rock to eat.

Rock leaned over, mouth closing over his fingers, eyes on his. "Mmm... I do believe my chocolate met your peanut butter."

That set them both off again and by the time they pulled into the Best Western, they were howling.

"They're going to think we're a pair of fucking crazies." Rock didn't look particularly concerned though. Just... amused as fuck.

"Good thing we're not from here, huh?" He pinched Rock's thigh, grinning like a fool.

Rock jerked, and snorted, popping him in the arm again. "Be nice or I won't let you rub your peanut butter into my chocolate."

"You're gonna leave a bruise and I'm going to have to hurt you."

"Oh, look who's a tough guy today." Rock nodded at the hotel. "Come on, Rig. I'm wanting things I can't find a way to say in fudge. Let's go in."

"You grab the bags and I'll get us a room." Rig winked and he hopped out, sashaying and giving Rock a show as he sauntered in. A couple of jokes, a couple of dollars, and he had himself a king sized bed and a key.

Hooboy.

Rock chuckled at him as they went up in the elevator. "You could charm a dead man."

"Can I charm a sexy Marine?"

"I imagine that mouth can do anything it wants to *this* sexy Marine."

"I want to suck my sexy Marine dry, then I want you to make me come so hard I'll feel it tomorrow."

Rock made a noise that was part moan, part rumble, all heat and need. Any reply he was going to make, though, was forestalled by the ding of the elevator, and Rock just grinned hungrily and followed him down the hall. Rig followed that fine fucking ass, his cock filling just at the sight of it.

"Come on now, Rig, open the door so we can get this party started." He loved it when Rock's voice got all husky like that.

"I'm thinking I'm going like this party, Marine." He got the key card in the lock, reaching around Rock to do it.

Oh, his Blue liked that, pushing that sizeable package against his hand. He turned his hand over, distracted, cupping that heavy cock.

Groaning, Rock rubbed against his hand a few times. "Shit, Rig. In. Now."

"Uh-huh." He worked the door open, Rock shoved him and the suitcase in, the door slamming shut behind them.

Rock grabbed his arm and spun him, bringing him up against Rock's hard body. His Blue's mouth landed hard on his.

Oh.

Hello.

Rig opened right up, tongue sliding against Rock's, diving into the kiss. Two big hands landed on his ass, Rock pulling him in nice and tight. He focused on fucking Rock's lips, hips rocking, rubbing them together.

Those blue eyes stared right into him, Rock leaning back against the door, fingers of one hand sliding up under his t-shirt to tweak at a nipple. The laughter and joy of the day just made it all bigger, better, and they were suddenly grinning into the kisses, both of them chuckling.

Rock stripped his t-shirt off, fingers sliding on his skin, tickling and gliding. "Mmm..."

"Want." Rig climbed up Rock's body, hooked his leg around Rock's hip.

"I've got what you want right here." Yeah, he could feel what Rock had for him, straining at Rock's jeans.

"You do. The bed, Marine, you can fuck my mouth."

Rumbling, Rock started walking them over to the bed. "Now that is tied for my favorite flavor."

"Tied?" He licked his way along Rock's jaw.

"Uh-huh. Tied with fucking this." Rock's hands squeezed his ass, pulled him in closer to rub their pricks together.

"Oh. Okay. Yeah. Fuck, yeah." He was a fan. Rig worked his way over to Rock's ear, teeth teasing the lobe.

Rock groaned and those knees buckled, Rock dropping them both down onto the bed, the big body pressing him into the mattress. They bumped together hard, both of them grunting, hips starting to roll.

"Fuck," muttered Rock. Their teeth clicked together as their mouths met again, Rock rolling them, putting him on top of that hard body.

Rig started working Rock's shirt open, hunting for skin, for that amazing fucking heat. Rock was little help, busy squeezing and kneading his ass, one hand pushing beneath his jeans to grab a handful. He got enough skin to get his lips around one nipple, lick and suck it to hardness. Rock bucked up against him, the low rumble vibrating Rock's chest beneath him. The hand on his ass opened and closed, fingers teasing his crease.

"Rig. Yeah."

"Uh-huh." He nibbled and sucked, teeth dragging along Rock's skin. He knew how good that felt.

"Fucking mouth," muttered Rock, body lifting his as Rock's hips bucked up.

Yeah, and he was hungry for it, for that thick cock to push into his lips. The hard muscles beneath his lips bunched and flexed, Rock moving for him, encouraging each lick and suck. Every now and then Rock would groan, fingers tightening on his ass. One played with his hole, rubbing and teasing.

"Want you." He nibbled his way down Rock's ribs.

"Got me." Rock's hands slid up along his back as he moved down, fingers rubbing and touching whatever they could reach.

"Good." That prick was waiting for him, the tip leaving wet kisses on his chin, Rock's belly.

"Uh-huh." There was a hint of impatience in that word, Rock bucking just a little, hands opening and closing on his shoulders now, not *quite* pushing him the last little bit down.

Rig licked and nuzzled Rock's belly button, nipped the taut skin of that belly before his tongue slipped over the tip of Rock's prick.

Rock's legs spread for him, a low moan sounding as the fingers on his shoulders dug in. "More. Fuck."

"Mmmhmm." He licked again, tongue pressing in to taste his Blue. Salty. Bitter. Good.

Happy, give-me-more noises rained down on him, Rock's hands sliding to cup his head, fingers pushing through his curls. Rock's legs spread a little further apart, heels digging into the hotel comforter as Rock pushed his cock in deeper. He reached down, rolled Rock's balls in one hand, fingers tapping the sensitive skin behind.

"Fuck, yeah." His Blue's hips started moving rhythmically, rocking that prick in and out of his mouth as groans and rumbles filled the air.

His fingers slid farther back, slowly stroking the tight muscles around Rock's hole. Rock's body tensed and relaxed with his stroking, the fingers in his hair tightening, Rock's cock pushing deeper. He rubbed and pushed, Rock's body just letting his fingertips in, just opening for him.

Another jerk and Rock called out his name, spunk shooting down his throat. Swallowing Rock right down, Rig hummed and moaned around Rock's cock, cleaning it with his tongue.

Rock relaxed back onto the bed, legs splayed, hands gentling in his hair, stroking. "Keep me hard, Rig, and I'll take care of you."

Keeping Rock hard was something he could so do. Rig just kept sucking and licking, head bobbing as he loved on Rock's prick.

"Yeah, Rig. Fucking love your mouth." Rock's words slowly went from low and sated to needy again, letting him know it was getting to be time.

He let his tongue drag along Rock's shaft, working that still-hard flesh like a big-assed Popsicle. Rock was leaning up on his elbows now, watching, eyes hot as they looked down at him, a rumble just vibrating Rock's chest. Rig closed his eyes and just worked it, up and down, giving Rock all he had.

Soon enough those hips were moving again, Rock pushing up into each lick and suck and touch. "You don't fucking stop that soon and you won't get your ride," growled Rock.

He let go with a pop. "No way. I need it."

Rock's laugh sounded rough. "Then get your ass up here and take it in."

He crawled up Rock's body, cock tapping Rock's belly, leaving wet kisses.

Moaning, Rock circled his cock with those thick fingers, slowly jacking him. "Bring me that sweet, little hole, Rig. Gotta get you ready."

"Yeah... Please. Fuck." Rig nodded, gasped, needing it so bad.

Rock tugged him up, keeping him moving until he was practically sitting on his Blue's face. Then Rock's tongue began to slide along his hole, licking and teasing, pushing into him.

"Oh, fuck." Rig's head fell back, eyes rolling as his cock throbbed. "Rock. Blue. Your tongue."

Rock just rumbled, the sound vibrating from Rock's tongue into his ass, making it huge.

Oh. Oh, God. Oh, he was going to come. "Jim. Please. Damn."

Again and again, Rock's tongue stabbed into him, wetting him, opening him. One of Rock's hands wrapped around his balls, tugging just hard enough to keep him from coming. "Okay, now, Rig. Now."

"Uh-huh. Now. Please. *Please.*" He shook with it, just needing it so fucking bad.

With a show of that strength his Blue had, Rock flipped him, putting him on his back as Rock rose up over him. His ankles were hooked over Rock's shoulders, that fat cock pushing into him just like that.

"Fuck!" He shot, entire body shuddering with it.

Rock's smile was satisfied as fuck as their lips pressed together. "Yeah, Rig. Fuck."

Moving, Rock started to thrust -- long, hard pushes that filled him over and over again, making the pleasure of his orgasm just roll through him in slow waves.

"Uh-huh. Don't stop."

Rock snorted. "Not stopping. Not fucking stopping, Rig." Growling a little, Rock pushed their mouths back together again, taking his mouth with one hard kiss after another. His cock didn't even think of going soft for a second.

Yes. Fuck, yes. His Blue. His eyes rolled, heart pounding, world just spinning around and around. Harder, faster, then slowing, dragging it out, making it last, those blue eyes holding his own. Rig shuddered, their bellies rubbing together.

Finally Rock's hand wrapped around his cock, jacking him as that fat prick fucked him. "Come on -- gimme."

"Pushy Marine." He groaned, gasping as his balls drew up tight.

"Yep. Do it. Come on my cock." Rock shifted slightly, hitting his gland hard.

The world went white, his heart pounding in his chest as his brains shot right out his cock. The only thing he knew was his own pleasure, and the heat of Rock's spunk as it filled him deep inside.

Rig just melted into the bed, let those strong arms hold him tight as Rock rolled to the side and brought him with. And hold him Rock did, body solid and warm, keeping him close.

"Better'n fudge any day, Rig."

"You know it, Marine. Better than *anything*."

"Yep." Rock's fingers moved on him, drawing random shapes, circling his skin. "You think a beer and a steak would make a good follow-up to a nap?"

"That works for me, man. We got nothing but time."

"Oh, I've got a little bit more than time." Rock's arms squeezed him tight.

Oh, now. He could get used to this. In fact, he thought maybe he was already.

# Chapter Eighteen

The were a couple hours away from home, just zipping down the highway, music blaring out of the open top. The last few days had been good, Rig rescuing a beginning that had gone from bad to fucking shitty, and turning it into a fun mini-vacation. Rig was good for that.

"When's your shift tomorrow?" he shouted.

"Six a.m., but I'm only on for a couple hours, then I can come home and nap. I'm on swing all month." Rig rolled his eyes, stuck his tongue out. The man hated working swing.

Rock wasn't too fond of it, either. They usually wound up just missing each other and it made him cranky.

"You wanna find someplace to stop for supper?" If they got home late enough, Rig would be willing to go to bed and fool around instead of cleaning and organizing and shit.

"Oh, hell yeah. That way we don't have to hit the grocery store. I'll even get Grimmy tomorrow."

Oh, fucking A. Being lazy and not having to do shit was way easier if he had Rig on the same page.

He slowed and took the next exit off the highway. "See if you notice something nice. Not McDonalds or anything like that."

He wanted somewhere with good food where they could sit and talk and just fucking be for a bit longer.

"'Kay. I'm thinking Italian, huh? Something nice and spicy." Rig's hand was on his thigh, just petting a little.

He wasn't overly fond of Italian: too many vegetables and not enough meat, but Rig had been indulging him something fierce this trip, so he figured it was time for a little payback. "Sounds good."

Rig smiled, nodded. "Chicken parmesan, man. I love that shit. Oh. Look. Vinny's. Let's stop there."

Covered in fucking tomatoes -- Rig would like something like that. He just grinned and nodded, slowed down the car. He could eat a few vegetables for Rig.

He parked the car and put the top up. "You think they've got some decent brew here?"

"I bet they do." Rig leaned back over the seat, grabbed his hat. "If not, we'll drink whiskey."

Oh, yeah, whiskey and Rig's tongue made a lovely combination.

"What's that dessert I like?" he asked, as Rig settled the hat and they made their way in.

"Tiramisu." Rig grinned over, winked. "You like to watch me eat the cannoli."

"Oh, that's right." His prick jerked just a little at the thought of Rig's mouth wrapped around the end of one of those, licking the cream out... He groaned. Okay, so Italian wasn't so bad.

The place was a bit old fashioned, but the low lighting and intimate seating made up for that. The hostess sat them in a quiet corner and Rock ordered them both a whiskey with a beer chaser before they even looked at their menus.

Rig looked hot and happy, face tanned, little brush of a mustache just to tease him, those grey eyes warm as anything. "Oh, you want an appetizer? They have fried cheese."

He nodded. "Yeah, that sounds good. They have anything meaty on the menu?"

"They've got a steak dinner. Chicken in alfredo?"

"Is that with that white sauce?" He liked the white sauce. Garlicky. He grinned over at Rig. "You'd better get something with garlic, too, 'cause I'm kissing you regardless."

"Promises, promises." Rig's boot tapped his ankle. "I'll get alfredo instead of red sauce with mine."

He laughed, leaning in a little. "You see, I knew you didn't *really* like the vegetables."

"Yeah, I'm still getting salad."

"Freak." He winked, turning his smile on the waitress as she brought over their drinks and a plate of fresh bread with some olive oil shit to dip it into. He went ahead and ordered for them, making sure they were getting that fried cheese and some garlic bread for starters, along with Rig's salad. She flirted like mad with him, obviously bucking for a big tip. He just played it up and she left the table smiling wide.

"You dog." Rig chuckled, sipping his whiskey, cheeks already flushed a little.

"Don't worry -- I'm going home with you."

"You'd better be. She can't give you what I do."

Rock shuddered, only exaggerating a touch. "Fuck no, she can't." He shot back his whiskey, feeling the burn as it went down. "There isn't a mouth in the world can match yours."

"Nope. Everybody's got a talent."

"I do appreciate a man with talent." Just look at those grey eyes shine for him.

"Yep. You've got that appreciating thing down." Rig leaned back when the appetizers showed, stomach growling.

Laughing, Rock waited until the waitress had moved on before picking up a fried cheese bite and popping it between Rig's lips, right into that amazing mouth.

"Mmm." Rig moaned around the bite and the sound was enough to make him hard.

Eyes on Rig he grabbed another one and pushed it between Rig's lips as well. He decided then and there, even if he never tasted them himself, that fried cheese was one of his favorite things on the menu.

Rig licked his lips and Rock groaned softly. "Shit, I'm not going to make it if you eat that whole plate of them."

"You better try one. They're good." Rig licked his own lips clean, that tongue flashing out, tempting him.

"You going to feed me?" Rock asked. He wanted nothing more than to lean over and take a taste right out of Rig's mouth, but that wasn't to be.

He grabbed another couple bites, pushing one into Rig's mouth and then popping the other into his own. "Oh, this *is* good."

"Uh-huh." Rig held up one of the beers in a toast. "To road trips."

He nodded and clinked his glass with Rig's. "Yeah, I can drink to that."

He took a chug, just grinning away at Rig, those grey eyes smiling back.

"Amen, Marine. A-fucking-men."

Their food came and Rock dug in, more hungry than he'd realized. Once he'd hoovered his way through about half of it, he slowed down and watched Rig eat, loving the way Rig savored everything.

Rig ended up giving up some of his chicken, laughing and chasing slick noodles over the plate. He handed over the little pile of carrots that the restaurant somehow felt was necessary to plop on every plate, but was otherwise quite happy with his meal.

Done, he pushed his plate away and sat back, letting his foot hook around Rig's leg and rub the back of his calf.

"Mmm. That was good, man. I'm full as a tick." Rig stretched, just rubbing his belly.

"You're gonna have dessert though, right? It would be a shame to miss out on their cannoli..." And he'd hate to miss that show.

"You know it." Rig's lip quirked up in a smirk. "I bet I can have you wanting in no time."

He snorted. That was a sucker bet. Of course, he'd take it anyway. "You think so?" he asked, legs spreading a little as his cock already was perking up just at the thought.

"I know so." Rig waved the waitress over. "We'd like dessert, please."

"What'll you have, honey?"

"I'll have the tiramisu and he'll have a couple of the cannoli, please." Rock hardly even looked up at her, intent on Rig.

"Oh, good choices. You want coffee with that."

Rock nodded. "Please."

She left again and he grinned over at Rig. "I bet you'll be just as turned on by the time you're done with your dessert."

"Me? Turned on?" Butter wouldn't melt in that mouth. "I'm cold as a fish."

"I'm not fond of fish." Rig though? He was very fond. And there was nothing cold about that man.

Rig's laugh rang out, his Rabbit's smile warming him through.

They were still smiling when their dessert arrived, the cannolis on Rig's plate about the biggest he'd ever seen. Oh man. Rig so was going to have him squirming.

Rig was a fucker, but goddamn, that tongue. Shit. He hadn't gone three bites before his cock was throbbing, aching. Rig licked out the pastry, tongue snaking in and around the cannoli. Rock could feel each lick in his balls. He barely tasted his own dessert, he was so intent on watching Rig.

Those grey eyes were just fastened on him, making all sorts of promises. Well, wasn't he just fucked? This would teach him to stop for dinner a couple hours from home. The drive was going to kill him.

And Rig had that second pastry to finish. Jesus fuck.

"I want you." The words were muttered, low, serious.

"I know it."

He licked his lips. They had to go home tonight, no question as they both had work. Still, hotels might have check-in times, but as long as you were out before noon, they didn't care how much before that you checked out. "There's bound to be a motel 'round here."

"Yeah. We only need an hour or so..." Rig shifted in his seat, a flush just visible at Rig's open collar.

It was a damned shame paying money for a whole night when you only intended to stay an hour. On the other hand, that sweet as fuck mouth and those needy, grey eyes were more than worth it.

Rock raised his hand to get the waitress' attention, motioning for her to bring them the bill. "Finish your dessert and coffee, Rig. We've got places to be."

"You sure you want to waste the cash, Rock? I can keep you warm all the way home."

He leaned in and waited for Rig to do the same and then spoke real quiet. "You think spending time with you where no one can see us is a waste of cash, Rig?"

Oh. Oh, look at that. Rig's eyes flashed, the look hot enough to burn him to ash. "Jim."

"I know." If that chick didn't show up with their bill soon he was going to throw some money at the table and hope it was enough to cover dinner and her tip. He pulled out his wallet.

The check showed up and Rig stood, damn near vibrating. He managed to get the right bills out of his wallet and stuffed them into the waitress' hand, not even checking to see if the total was right. Frankly, he didn't really care. He gave her a tight smile and a nod. "Sorry, we're in a bit of a hurry."

"Oh, you should have said so when you came and I would have..." He didn't hear whatever else she had to say, he was already halfway out the door, following Rig's sweet ass as it made a beeline for the car.

Rig slid into the car, eyes burning holes right into him. "I need. Hurry."

"Yeah, I can smell how much you need." It wasn't helping him drive any either, but luck was with them and there was a Motel 6 two blocks past the restaurant. "I'll get a room," he growled, leaving the motor running by the office.

He made short work of registering for the room, handing the cash over without even a thought for how much it was costing. He had his own personal hungry redneck waiting on that room.

Climbing back into the car, he tossed the room key at Rig. "We're down at the end."

Rig nodded, hand rubbing that pretty cock through his jeans. "Good. Good. I'm ready for you."

Rock nodded. They were both pretty fucking ready. "We'll have a two-fer."

He pulled up into the last parking spot and they climbed out. He didn't even try for casual as he headed for the door, staying right on Rig's ass the whole way. As soon as they were inside, he slammed Rig up against the door, taking that mouth and rubbing against the long, lean body. They were making a habit of this.

Rig pushed him right back this time, though, spun his ass as sweet as you please and dropped down, mouth hot on his balls. Even through the denim of his jeans, Rig could make his knees buckle. His head hit the door hard. Fuck.

He was a lucky fucking bastard. Bracing his back against the door, he dropped his hands to pop the top button of his jeans, his prick hard enough to hurt.

"Mine." Rig moaned, tongue fucking the tip of his prick.

Jesus fuck.

"You fucking know it." No one made him feel like Rig did. No one knew how to work a cock like his Rabbit. He tugged the zipper down, getting his cock completely free for that amazing mouth.

Rig's hands splayed out over his hips, holding him tight as Rig swallowed his prick down. Hungry. Fuck. So goddamn hungry for him. He made a loud noise, half growl, half yell, the sound just tugged out of him by Rig's mouth. "Good. Fuck."

Rig nodded, groaning around his prick, the sound enough to vibrate down through his balls. He made another noise, hips making jerking little movements because he couldn't stop them -- he *had* to move. He could feel his blood rushing through his body, feel it throb in his cock, Rig's mouth making it all feel huge.

Rig's nose was buried in his pubes, throat working hard around the head of his prick. He grabbed at Rig's head, fingers clutching those blond curls as he shot hard. "Rig!"

That pretty mouth never stopped moving; it just worked him and worked him, insisting he stay hard.

"How do you want it?" he asked, fingers sliding through Rig's curls over and over. He could give it to Rig hard or soft, fast or slow. Up against the wall, on the bed, the floor. Anything Rig fucking wanted.

"Now." Rig leaned back, ass rocking on those boot heels as his Rabbit licked those swollen lips. "Right fucking now."

"You got it." He grabbed Rig under the arms, tugging him up and almost tossing him over onto the bed. "Get naked, Rig."

The shirt went flying, then Rig started working his boots off. "You, too. Now."

"Don't worry, it's naked central here." Rock toed off his Kodiaks and pulled his T-shirt over his head.

"Uh-huh..." Rig stopped and stared, lips parted and swollen, hands still at his waistband.

Rock dropped his own hands to his waist, his cock hard and proud, surrounded by denim. Grinning, he turned and slowly tugged the jeans down off his ass, giving it a shake to get them to drop right down to his ankles.

"Beautiful motherfucking Marine." Rig groaned, the sound of the man's zipper loud. When Rock turned around Rig was jacking that prick, watching him.

He flexed for Rig, showing off a little. Nothing made him feel like a bigger stud than the way Rig looked at him.

"You make sure you save some of that for me," he warned, grabbing the bottom of Rig's jeans and tugging them the rest of the way down.

Rig's ass slid across the bed, that long, lean body spread out for him. He groaned and climbed on up, settling between Rig's legs, heat pouring off Rig's body, that hard prick.

"Hey," he growled, looking right into grey eyes.

"Hey." Arching up, Rig's cock painted his belly with lines of heat. There was a patch of skin right where Rig's waist dipped into hip where his own cock nestled.

He rumbled, lips dropping slowly onto Rig's. His Rabbit tasted like him, like fucking and need and whiskey and cream. Rock was fucking addicted. He fucked Rig's mouth with his tongue, their hips grinding together to the same rhythm. He wanted that ass, though, wanted that tight heat that felt like sliding fucking home.

Rig was slick against him, sliding and sweating, grunting into his lips as they moved. He needed in that tight, little hole, needed it bad. And wasn't the fucking lube in the goddamned car. Growling, he backed off and flipped Rig over onto his stomach. He spread Rig's cheeks and dug in, tongue working that little hole.

"Fuck! Fuck, Blue!" Rig went crazy under him, hips bucking and slapping back against him.

"You wait for me, Rig. No coming until I'm in that ass." Then he went back to making Rig as nuts as possible, taking long licks from Rig's balls up along that fine, hot patch of skin and over Rig's hole. Then into it, then another long swipe. Fuck, yes.

"Need it. Fuck. Jim. Now. NOW." Rig was demanding, begging, growling and threatening him.

Fuck, he loved that.

He took one last taste of Rig's ass and then he flipped Rig over again, just manhandling the lean body.

"Gonna watch your face when you come," he told Rig, pushing in slowly.

Rig's eyes rolled up, the expression on his Rabbit's face pure fucking bliss. Fuck, yeah. That's what he was talking about. He kept moving as slowly as he could stand it, Rig's body just clinging to his cock, trying to keep him buried deep. The drag felt so fucking good. That amazing fucking mouth kept moving, lips opening and closing like Rig was talking, but nothing was coming out.

He moved faster by increments, making it last as long as fucking possible. He'd do it all fucking night if he could. All fucking night.

"Left... left Texas for you. For you." Rig pushed up on his elbows, their mouths crashing together. The words had him moving faster, harder, just pounding into Rig now, making it as good as he could for his Rabbit, as their tongues tangled.

He could feel Rig's orgasm rippling around his cock, the heat ratcheting up to something close to unbearable. His fingers dug into the sheets, his hips snapping hard as he tried to push Rig over. Heat splashed over his belly, Rig's cry enough to just send him to Heaven.

Two more thrusts and he couldn't hold back any longer, didn't want to. Groaning, he pushed in hard and froze, spunk spraying deep into Rig.

"Yes..." Rig groaned, squeezed him tight. "Fuck, yes."

"Uh-huh." It was about all he could manage at the moment, a shudder going through him as Rig's body worked his cock.

Rig kept squeezing and shaking, muscles fluttering around him, damn near milking him. He managed another half thrust or two, the sensations just too much as several more heavy shudders rocked him.

Finally, he collapsed down onto Rig, groaning. "Fuck."

"Yeah." Rig nodded, lips on his temple. "Fuck."

He was breathing hard, breath puffing against Rig's neck, the smell of them filling the air. He petted Rig's hip, still buried deep.

"We got time to nap and do it again?"

"We got time." Whether they did or not, they were taking it.

Groaning, he slid from Rig's body.

Rig moaned, grabbing a few tissues from the bedside table to clean them up before octopussing around him, holding on tight.

Oh yeah, for this? They had time.

All the time in the world.

# Chapter Nineteen

Rock sat on the bed and bent to tug off his socks, still debating whether he was going to shower or just change into a pair of sweats. He didn't like it when Rig worked evenings -- had to fend for himself in the kitchen and usually wound up ordering something. After four days of it, he was fairly sick of pizza.

A white envelope sitting on his side-table caught his eye. It had his name on the front. James South. No rank, no address, just his name. The return address in the corner was for that damned law firm that was handling his grandmother's will. The envelope was a little beat up, wrinkled, and he suddenly remembered getting a letter from grandma from the lawyer and shoving it into his pocket before he could read it thanks to all hell breaking lose when his father realised grandma'd actually left her fag grandson some money.

He'd forgotten all about it. Rig must have found it in his good pants pocket or something.

He took the letter out of the envelope and smoothed it out, the writing on it that old lady squiggle he could still remember from birthday checks when he was a teenager.

*Dear James,*

*I maybe should have found you and told you to your face, but enough years have passed, I wasn't comfortable doing that.*

*I thought you should know. I am proud of you.*

*Don't change who you are for anyone. I'm sure you're a fine Marine and a good man.*

*You always reminded me a lot of myself, James. I would have liked to have gotten to know the man you became.*

*Love,*

*Granny*

Rock smoothed the letter out again and read it a second time. He'd never wanted any of Grandma South's money, but this... this was maybe the inheritance he'd been hoping for.

Rock carefully folded the letter up and slipped it back into its envelope. He stuck it at the bottom of his underwear drawer and stripped off his clothes -- he'd have a shower and order himself a pizza.

He did hate it when Rig worked evenings.

# Chapter Twenty

Rock grabbed himself another beer and a bag of peanuts, settling down on the couch and hitting the clicker on the TV. Fucking news everywhere, even the damned movie channel was between films. He glanced at his watch. Yeah, just past fucking six o'clock. Where the fuck was Rig?

It had been a long fucking week. Hell, they were all feeling long lately, but they both had a three-day and he was ready for it to start right now.

He'd been ready an hour ago.

The beer went down smooth and the peanuts kept him from ordering a pizza. Eventually Predator started and he settled in with a third beer.

He heard Rig pull up, or at least he thought he did, but Rig didn't come in. Hell, he didn't even hear the door slam. He waited with half an ear cocked, but when there wasn't any other noise, he got up and headed for the front door.

Rig was in the front seat of the Jeep, sound asleep, keys still in the ignition.

Jesus fucking Christ.

Rock rolled his eyes and headed for the driver's side of the Jeep. He opened the door, hand on Rig's shoulder, shaking. "You're not home until you actually get in the door, Rig."

Those bright eyes popped open, Rig blinking over at him. "Shit. Blue. I just. Damn. Hey."

He snorted and leaned over to undo Rig's seatbelt. "Come on, sleeping beauty. I'll buy you pizza."

"Oh, I could handle that." Rig grabbed his keys, slid out of the Jeep. "Christ, I feel like I've been beat."

"Bad day?" He followed that ass back up the stairs.

"Long. Bad jump."

"You were jumping today?" He growled a little. Rig was a fucking nurse, not in the damned forces.

"Yeah. Landed on my canteen, bruised the shit out of my ass. Got a muscle relaxant to ease the tight, you know?" Rig slumped up the stairs, sighing. "Home, sweet home."

His growl got distinctly louder, but he waited until they'd cleared the door. "That's my fucking ass that got injured."

"Mmmhmm." Rig nodded, heading straight for the sofa. "All yours."

"You know it." He admired the lean form as he grabbed the phone and called up Pizza Hut, ordering one meatlovers and a vegetarian. He knew how to coddle Rig when it was needed. Of course a little personal TLC was also on the books, and given it was going to be over an hour for their food to get there according to the kid on the phone, he was about to let Rig have it.

Rig stretched out, legs sprawled, boots still on.

"You want to watch something else?" he asked as Arnie fought his invisible foe.

"Nah. I like this one." Rig scooted over a little, giving him room.

He took the offered seat and tugged on Rig's leg until it swung up across his knees and he could slowly work off that sexy boot.

"Mmm. Thank you." He liked that smile; it made him hot.

The boot dropped onto the floor and he leaned over to tap Rig's thigh. "Come on, give me the other one." His hand stayed on Rig's leg, stroking.

"You'll spoil me, Marine." Rig groaned, muscles shivering under his touch.

He chuckled. "Don't get used to it. Tomorrow'll be business as usual." He squeezed again and then tugged off the other boot.

"Uh-huh. Tomorrow." Rig nodded, humming low.

He slid his hands over Rig's feet, staying with one and massaging, thumbs digging into the sole.

"Oh, God..." Rig whimpered, toes curling, legs spreading at his touch.

"At your service." He winked and chuckled. Rig usually made noises like that during sex.

He kept massaging, slowly moving along Rig's foot and then ankle. Rig just sort of melted. Man, he could do anything he wanted right now and Rig would just nod.

He worked his way up along Rig's calves. "Three days, Rig. Nothing but you and me."

"Sounds like fucking bliss, Blue Eyes."

150

"You know it." He moved on to Rig's thighs, moaning a little at the feeling of the lean muscles beneath his fingertips.

The damned dog started barking at the back door and Rock rolled his eyes. He'd forgotten he'd let Grimmy out into the backyard. "I'll let him in."

"Thanks, man."

Rig had rolled over by the time he got back, had stripped down to his jeans.

"Well since you asked so nicely," he murmured, straddling Rig's ass, settling on it as his fingers dug into Rig's shoulders.

"Oh..." Rig whimpered, ass clenching against his thighs. Yeah. Somebody liked that.

With Arnie kicking alien ass in the background, he gave Rig the best massage he could, working from shoulder to shoulder, from neck to ass. When he got to Rig's waist, Rig reached down, unfastened the fly. He grinned, moving down a bit to sit on the backs of Rig's thighs, tugging the jeans off that amazing ass to check out the damage.

The bruise was ugly as fuck, black and blue, about the size of his palm, but it wasn't anywhere that would damage his Rabbit. Bending, he gently kissed the edge of the bruise, and then went to work on the undamaged portion of Rig's ass.

"Oh, man. I needed that." Yeah. Yeah, he could see that. Hell, he could understand needing Rig's ass.

He rubbed his jeans covered prick against the backs of Rig's thighs, groaning. "You need anything else, Rig?"

"You." Rig spread a little wider, offer clear.

Rock didn't need Rig to say more, didn't need to ask if Rig was sure -- Rig knew what he could take, what he couldn't. Climbing off the couch, Rock knelt next to it, thumbs spreading Rig's cheeks wide as he licked at that sweet, little hole.

"Oh..." Rig pulled his legs up, giving him a better angle.

Groaning, he licked and teased, no more than the very tip of his tongue going into Rig's body as he wet the outside of that little hole but good.

"Blue. Jim. Rock. 'S so fucking *good*."

He knew it. Grinning, he kept licking and licking. And then he started fucking that sweet, little hole with his tongue, pushing it deep.

Rig groaned low, rocking back against him, riding him with intent. Those thin thighs were spread, balls swinging as Rig moved.

He slid his hand along Rig's thighs, fingers teasing the soft skin. Then he cupped those balls, hefting them, rolling them as he drove Rig wild with his tongue.

"Please. Please..." Oh, hell yes. Rig was shaking, hips rolling like the waves in the ocean.

He could make Rig come just from this. He pushed his face up tight against Rig's ass, tongue going in deeper, wiggling inside. Rig's balls drew up tight as stones, the words fading into rough cries as Rig lost it, the scent of spunk sudden and sharp.

Oh, yeah, that was it.

He slowed his tongue, still licking, making it last, making Rig shudder. Making sure that beautiful cock stayed good and hard for him.

"Oh, sweet fuck..." The words were gasped, broken. Raw.

He slowly rose up over Rig's body. "Not a sweet fuck yet, but it's coming. It's coming right now." He slid his cock between Rig's legs a few times, the soft inner thighs moving to grip him.

"Fuck, yes. Please. In me." Oh, yeah. He got off on that, on how Rig needed.

Rock slid his cock along Rig's crack, anticipation riding his spine, settling hard in his balls. Groaning, he pushed the very tip into Rig's body, that sweet hole just opening up for him. He pulled back and pushed in again. Then again. Teasing Rig. Teasing himself. So fucking hot -- there was nothing else like this.

He pushed in a little deeper, stilled, panting as Rig's body squeezed him tight. Rig groaned, moving back against him, taking him in just a little deeper, then a little more.

"Slow and easy, Rig. Gonna make this last all night long." His hands settled on Rig's hips, guiding their movements, keeping things from going too far too fast.

"Oh... Rocketman." Rig sat up, settled against him, ass hot on his thighs. The moan as he sank deep was sweet, the way Rig rippled around him even sweeter.

"Fuck. Fuck." He groaned, arms wrapping around Rig's middle, holding on as he fucked up into that perfect ass.

"Uh-huh. Yours. So fucking good." Rig's head fell back, throat working.

"You know it. The fucking best." He slid his fingers over Rig's belly, one hand moving up to find those sensitive, little titties, playing them. He felt it in Rig's ass when he pinched them. The muscles jerked and tightened, throbbing around him. Pinching and twisting them, he slid his other hand down to cup Rig's balls, squeezing gently as he pushed in harder.

"Don't stop." Rig's head fell forward, the moan he got almost pained.

He laughed, the sound more a rumble. "I'm not going to stop. Not anytime soon." Not until they'd both come until their brains came out their ears.

"Good..." Rig moaned, shivered around him. "Keep talking. Your fucking voice..."

"Turns you on, does it? Makes you fucking ache for me?" Each word was punctuated by a thrust.

"Yeah..." A flush climbed up Rig's spine, his cowboy nodded, bucking on his cock.

"That's my sweet slut." He let go of Rig's balls, slid his hand around the long, hard cock instead.

"Yours. Fucking left Texas for you." Rig groaned, body moving faster, fucking him harder.

He jacked Rig to the same rhythm, closing his eyes and groaning, trying to hold on as long as he could, make it last.

"Jim. Jim. Blue..." Rig's ass clenched him tight as a fist, squeezing him, rippling around him.

"Right fucking here, Rabbit." His mouth slid over Rig's neck, finding that bundle of nerves that made Rig wild.

"Yes!" Rig shot hard, cock pulsing spunk over his hand.

Hips jerking, he pushed Rig through his orgasm, and then let go, let himself come, shooting deep into Rig. Rig slumped against him, panting, nearly asleep again. Shit, Rock didn't think Rig would make it to the pizza.

He turned Rig's face, took a nice, long kiss. He got a hum, Rig's kiss lazy, slow. When the kiss broke, he gently pushed Rig back down onto the couch, prick sliding out of that perfect ass. "Nice and loose now," he murmured, fingers sliding over Rig's warm, damp skin.

"Uh-huh." Rig nodded, moaning sweet and soft.

He gave Rig a kiss. "I'll be right back."

It only took a moment to grab a blanket from the bedroom, another to slip into a pair of sweats, and then he was back, tucking the blanket in around Rig. His rabbit was sound asleep, smiling.

Grinning himself, he grabbed the remote and settled in his chair, watching the last few minutes of the movie while he waited for supper to show.

# Chapter Twenty One

"You sure your friend won't mind me coming for supper?"

Rock glanced over at the baby green, the kid's brown eyes huge under his high and tight. Lord, Rig was going to love this one, that drawl giving him away as a cowboy as sure as Rig's did.

"He won't mind. And if you're lucky it's chili and cornbread tonight -- you know, a taste of home."

"How did you know?"

Rock just laughed. This one was almost too sweet to do anything more than feed and send home.

He pulled up in the driveway next to Rig's Jeep and nodded at the house. "Just relax, Teddy. Rigger's good people."

He led Teddy up to the house, pushing Grim out of the way. He'd called Rig on the way home, warned him they were having a special guest tonight. A young man in need of a taste of home. "Come on in, the mutt might drool you to death, but he's friendly enough."

"Hey, y'all!" Rig came out of the kitchen looking like sex on boots -- skin-tight jeans, shirtless, dish towel in his waistband. Rock's cock started pointing north, just like that.

"Teddy Matthers, this is Alex Roberts, but we call him Rigger. Rig, this here is Teddy."

Teddy shot out his hand. "Nice to meet you, sir."

"Rig. Hey Teddy. Where're you from?" Rig shook Teddy's hand, turning that grin on the kid.

"A... Abilene, sir."

Rock cuffed the kid on the shoulder. "Call him Rigger." He winked at Rig. "Smells good in here."

Rig grinned at him, eyes shining. "Brisket and potato salad and chocolate pie."

Teddy moaned, a look of bliss on his face, and Rock laughed. Rig made this easy, smooth for the baby greens who needed a hand on the rules on their side of the street. "Sound good to you, Teddy?"

"Yes! Sounds amazing."

Rig's arm snaked around Teddy's waist, leading them into the kitchen. "You want a beer? I tell you what, last time I was in Abilene we went to a big-assed cattle auction. Best burger I ever had."

"Beer? Okay, yeah. You've been to Abilene? Cool. I bet you ate at that little diner near the auction, yeah? With the spicy fries? My Daddy used to take me there all the time."

Rock shook his head and snagged a beer for himself, leaning against the counter.

"Mmm. Spicy fries." Rig's eyes were just dancing.

"Supper gonna be awhile, Rig?" As long as they needed it to, he imagined. Get Teddy mellow and happy, feed him, fuck him through the floor and send him on his way, satisfied and knowing the ropes.

"It's all in the crock pot and fridge. You want to go have a sit?"

"You know it. What do you say, Teddy? Ready to go sit with that sexy motherfucker there?"

Teddy swallowed, eyes going wide again. "Yeah?"

"You don't have to. We don't bite; I promise." No. No, biting would be a fucking waste of that mouth.

"You don't have to, but you'd be crazy to turn it down." Rock winked and slid his hand over Teddy's ass.

The kid jumped and laughed a little nervously, so Rock leaned in, nuzzled beneath Teddy's ear. "Remember what I said? Just relax."

Rig nodded, drew them both into the living room, down on the sofa. "No stress, Teddy. I swear."

He put his arm around Teddy's shoulders, fingers reaching to stroke Rig's arm. "You ever been kissed, Teddy?"

The kid snorted. "Yeah."

"No, Teddy -- by a guy."

"Yeah, sorta. Once."

"You want to try it again? Or you want to watch the news and have supper?"

"Try it again." Damn, the cherries always had that look of amazement about them, like they couldn't believe it was happening.

"Rock's one hell of a kisser, kid. Honest. He's all man."

"Yeah, I can see that."

Rock chuckled, grinning. "I see you don't need any help with the flattery portion of the evening."

He tilted Teddy's chin and brought their mouths together. The kid was tentative, shy, but there was an eager need there. Rock deepened the kiss, sliding his tongue between Teddy's lips. He swept through Teddy's mouth, making sure the kid knew he was there.

Then he backed off and grinned. "Different than kissing a girl, isn't it?"

Teddy laughed, cheeks flushed, eyes a touch glazed. "Oh, yeah. Yeah."

"You think that was good? Let Rig show you what a kiss really is."

Rig leaned over, almost crawling into the kid's lap, framing Teddy's face with those long fingers. "You wanna?"

Teddy's eyes were huge. "I do."

Grinning, Rock took hold of Teddy's hand and put it on Rig's ass. "Don't be afraid to touch."

"'Kay." Teddy didn't take his eyes off Rig though. Not that Rock could blame him. Rig was one sexy motherfucker.

"Just breathe. This shit is easy." Then Rig winked, kissed the kid like the state of the union depended on it.

Jesus fuck, his cock was hard as nails as he watched Rig blow the kid's mind. Mmm... blowing. Teddy's hands opened and closed on Rig's ass, those wide eyes rolling back in his head. He could almost feel that kiss, feel the way Rig made you the center of the universe, made you melt.

His hand slid along Rig's back, fingers tracing the knobby spine. Teddy he teased through the T-shirt, rubbing across the kid's nipple. The kid bucked up, humping up against Rig. "Oh, now, wait up, Teddy. You don't want to go off while you're still in your BDUs." He slid his hand down between Rig and Teddy, the back of his hand rubbing against Rig's prick as he undid buttons.

"Such a thoughtful Marine..." Rig grinned, tugging Teddy's bottom lip, just a little.

"Yep, that's me." He winked and leaned in to nibble at Rig's neck as he tugged Teddy's prick out. It was good sized, not as big as he was, but Teddy would do well for himself with it.

Teddy groaned, bucking into his touch. "That's it, kid. Just ride it."

Rig's fingers joined his, stroking Teddy nice and steady.

"Cute, isn't he?" he murmured into Rig's ear. "Not as cute as you..."

He licked at that sweet spot on Rig's neck and then shifted to see if he could find any on Teddy's. Teddy's jaw was sensitive, the kid shivering for him. He hummed, sticking with it, nosing and licking, while his and Rig's hands worked Teddy's cock. He could tell it wouldn't be long. Hell, the first time never was.

Rig dove back into a kiss, making sure that it was all over but the crying. No cherry could resist Rig's kisses for long. Teddy's cry was muffled in Rig's mouth, heat fountaining up over his and Rig's hands.

"Yeah, that's it." He nodded and kept stroking, making Teddy shudder.

"Mmmhmm. Pretty cherry." Rig chuckled, sucking Teddy's bottom lip, fingers working to keep the kid hard.

"What do you want to do next, Teddy?" Rock asked, voice low, helping in the keeping the kid hard department. He licked that sensitive jaw. "You want that mouth around your cock? You want to feel mine up your ass?"

Teddy shuddered, grabbing Rig and jerking. "I. Oh, God. I."

"Shh. You're good, honey. Breathe. We've got you." Rig's eyes twinkled, meeting his head-on.

He grinned right back, leaned in to kiss Rig hard. His prick was fucking aching and he needed that mouth. "How about we show Teddy here what a blowjob is all about, Rig?"

"We? You gonna blow the kid with me?"

He chuckled. "I was thinking more along the lines of you blowing me. Kid can either watch your technique or help."

"Now that makes much more sense." Rig laughed, pushing right into a kiss with him, those lips soft and swollen and hot.

He wrapped one arm around Rig, the other staying on Teddy's thigh, making sure they had the kid's full attention. Rig rubbed right up against him, cock hard, belly tight as a board. His fingers curled hard around Teddy's thigh, his groan pushing into Rig's lips. So fucking sexy.

He broke the kiss and glanced over at the kid. "Good?"

Teddy nodded, licking his lips. "Real good."

"You know it. Fucking is... better than almost anything."

"Almost anything?" He was hard pressed to think of anything better than fucking. He put his hand on Rig's shoulder, encouraged his own personal cowboy to go down.

"Mmm..." Rig eased down onto the floor, cheek nuzzling the bulge in his BDUs.

His hand slid to cup Rig's other cheek, thumb dragging over that swollen lower lip. "Rig's a master, kid. Watch and learn."

"Can I touch?"

Rock laughed -- this one was going to be just fine. "Hell, yeah."

Rig nodded. "I'm a fan. Touch away and, Marine, give me your cock."

"It's yours," muttered Rock, opening his BDUs, pushing down his regulation underwear and letting his prick push its way out toward Rig's mouth.

Teddy gasped and Rock grinned. "You like what you see, kid?"

"You're huge!"

Rock wrapped his arm around Teddy's shoulder and tugged him close for a kiss. "Good of you to notice."

Rig just laughed, tongue sliding up along his shaft. "You just made his day, kid."

He grinned, legs spreading to give Rig more room. "Teddy's just got good eyes on him." He grinned over at the kid, whose cheeks were more than a little red, eyes riveted on the action going on in his lap.

"Good eyes..." murmured Teddy. "Uh-huh."

It wasn't going to take long for Rig to have him moaning, not the way the man was giving him all the best moves. He watched, knowing Teddy was seeing the same thing, and yet not. Rig wasn't Teddy's Rig. "Watch and learn, kid." His voice was low, husky, his fingers sliding into Rig's curls.

Rig moaned, tongue flicking around the ridge of his cockhead, the heat and tingle just perfect. "Fucking amazing mouth, Rig."

"That's gotta feel incredible," breathed Teddy.

"It does, kid. It fucking does."

"He tastes incredible. So fucking hot." And that was no bullshit.

"All for you," murmured Rock, tilting Rig's head just a touch, looking down into the grey eyes.

Oh, shit. So fucking hot. All fucking his.

"Yeah."

Then his cock was taken all the way in to the root.

Teddy's gasp was swallowed by his own cry. His head went back, his thighs going tight as he resisted the urge to fuck Rig's mouth. Teddy's fingers slid along Rig's cheeks, the base of his cock. Rock could feel Rig's tongue licking and lapping at Teddy's fingers, his shaft, teasing them both.

"Soon," he grunted, hips starting to move. No way he couldn't, he never could resist that mouth.

Rig didn't answer, didn't have to, just kept sucking, pulling, taking him in. He wrapped an arm around Teddy's shoulders and tugged the kid in for a kiss, hips jerking as he came, spunk pouring into Rig. Rig sucked him dry, then cleaned him off, hands sliding along his thighs.

He tugged Rig up for a kiss, the flavor of Rig and him together like a fucking aphrodisiac, getting him hard again.

"Mmm. Marine." Rig rubbed against him, cock hard as nails against his thigh.

"Yep. And you got two Marines tonight." He gave Teddy a wink. "Rigger here's still needing, what do you say we help him out with that?"

"Are you going to suck him?" Teddy asked.

"I was thinking more I'd fuck him -- but you could suck him."

At Teddy's wide eyes, he stroked the baby green's cheek and added, "If you want. Sex is about having fun and feeling good -- if you don't want to do something you don't do it."

Rig nodded, lips just brushing the cherry's. "This should all be easy."

"You looked like you were really enjoying doing it," Teddy said to Rig. "It doesn't... taste bad?"

"Not with the right person, man. Some guys? Yeah. It's bitter as hell. Still, you want a rubber, huh? Just to be on the safe side."

"Yeah, kid. Always play safe. No sucking or fucking without a condom. That's like the number one rule -- and not just between guys."

"But Rigger sucked you without one."

Rock nodded. "Yeah, but we used protection until we got tested and if there's anyone else involved, it's rubbers all the way. I mean it now -- you hear me on that even if you get nothing else out of this." He took breaking the cherries in very seriously, especially shooting home this particular aspect. "Got it?"

Teddy nodded. "I got it. So can I have a condom for Rigger so I can try the sucking thing?"

Rig laughed, clapping the kid across the back. "Eager. I like it. Hell, yes, you can."

"Good boy," murmured Rock. He got up, stripping off his T-shirt and shucking his jeans as he went, searching through the little desk drawer for the condoms they kept for just this kind of occasion.

He grabbed a line of six, figuring that should do them -- enough for the kid to suck off Rig, for him and Rig to fuck the kid if they wanted, and for Rig to suck the kid off, too. Depending how late Teddy stayed and what all they got up to after supper.

He liked to be prepared.

Rig was helping the kid to get undressed, hands smoothing over tanned skin. Kid was pretty; with a little work and dose of self-confidence, he'd be a real stud. A few years and he'd be breaking hearts.

Grinning, he tore one of the condoms off the row. "Heads up," he called out, tossing it at Teddy.

Good thing he aimed it at Teddy's chest, the kid was too distracted by Rig's attentions to have actually caught the mini-missile. Of course, he could sort of get that. Damn. Rig went down on his knees, helping the kid with his boots, letting Rock see that fine ass.

His prick jerked and he grunted. Shit, he wasn't careful he'd be all over Rig again and forget his cherry Marine was even there. "You want to suck him while I take his ass?" Rock asked. He could sit Rig right on his prick and watch the whole blowjob lesson.

"Uh-huh. I want." The kid nodded, lips open and wet like he could just drop over Rig's cock right now.

"We need to get him ready first, then, yeah? Make sure his ass is nice and open for my cock. If you're used to it, you can be a little more hasty, but it feels better if you take your time. Besides..." He sat, legs spread, hand sliding over Rig's ass. "You've got no idea how good it feels inside."

He reached under the cushions and came up with the lube. "Slick a couple fingers up -- we'll do it together."

Rig was finally naked and grinning, ass wiggling a little. "Where do you want me, Marine?"

"Why don't you lie over my lap while we get you ready? Once you're done, you're sitting right here." He pointed at his cock, licked his lips as he imagined that ass planted right there.

Teddy whimpered a little, the kid's cock looking hard enough to hammer nails. Rock made a side bet with himself that sucking Rig would get Teddy off.

Of course, he had Rig draped over his thighs, legs spread, cock rubbing him, leaving wet kisses. His fucking sexy slut.

160

He slid his hands over Rig's back, sliding toward that pretty ass. He spread Rig's ass cheeks. "Look at that, Teddy. Pretty, isn't it?"

Teddy whimpered again, hands shaking as he splooched lube all over one hand.

Chuckling again, Rock gave the kid a hard kiss. "Just relax and enjoy it, 'k?"

Then he guided the kids' fingers to Rig's hole. "Just one to start." He knew how that felt, the way Rig felt alive and needy when you pushed right in, the way those muscles rippled for you.

Teddy gasped, finger jerking back out. "Wow. Oh, wow. It doesn't hurt?"

He guided Teddy's finger back to Rig's hole. "Does he look like he's hurting?"

"The answer to that is no, cherry." Rig shifted, begging for more.

"And that tone of voice? Means if you don't hurry and get another on in there he's gonna start begging and calling you a tease."

He encouraged Teddy to get two fingers in, moving the kid's hand back and forth, making sure Teddy was pushing deep. Then he added one of his own fingers to the mix. Rig grunted, legs spreading. He knew just where to touch, how to do this.

"That's unbelievable," murmured Teddy, voice breathless, cheeks flushed bright and eyes shinning.

Grinning, Rock shook his head. "It's not unbelievable at all -- it's happening."

A soft, almost giggle of a noise came from Teddy. "Yeah. It's... Yeah."

"You ready, Rig?" Rock asked, slowing the movement of his and Teddy's fingers.

"Mmmhmm. It's fucking good, man." Rig was all relaxed and melted for him. Perfect for Teddy to see.

"Time to ride the Rocketman."

He eased his finger out, Teddy following suit, and then he helped Rig move, those long legs straddling his thighs, Rig's back to his chest. Groaning, he rubbed his prick along Rig's crack.

"'Mere kid. Let me hold your shoulders while I get in the saddle."

Teddy stood in front of Rig, Rig leaning over and holding on, that tight ass right there. Rock groaned as Rig started taking him in, that amazing ass squeezing him tight.

"You like it," Teddy murmured, looking at Rig.

"You fucking know it." Rig stretched, rippling around him.

He placed his hands on Rig's hips, thumbs rubbing the prominent bones that framed the long cock.

"Anytime you're ready, Teddy. Put on the glove and take a mouthful."

Just like that the kid sank to his knees between Rock's legs, hands shaking again as he ripped open the condom package.

"It's okay. All good." Rig was settled against him, stretched up tall.

"Take a minute, kid, give his nipples a lick and see what happens."

Teddy met his eyes over Rig's shoulder and then went to it, leaning in to lick.

"Oh... That's it, cherry. Just a little harder. Just a... yeah."

Yeah, fuck. Just like that -- Teddy's licking and nibbling had Rig squeezing his cock. He tightened his hold on Rig's hips, encouraging him to move.

"Just smooth that rubber on now, Teddy. I know you've taken the lectures with the banana." All baby greens got the STD lectures. Hell, they all did.

"Yeah. I have. I just didn't think..." No, they never did think.

Teddy got the condom down over Rig's cock, that sweet ass responding, Rig tightening around him again. Rock started to thrust, slow and lazy, watching as Teddy bent and licked the tip of Rig's prick.

Rig nodded, hummed nice and low. "I like that, cherry. Like it when you work the tip."

"Rubber tastes funny," murmured Teddy, but he kept working Rig.

Rock slid a hand to pet his head, and then wrapped it back around Rig's waist, started bouncing Rig's ass up and down on his cock. Rig groaned, head falling back on his shoulder, lips open, throat working.

"Yeah, that's it. Take the head in your mouth now, suck him lightly. Let our movements push him in."

Teddy's mouth closed over the tip, cheeks hollowing. Rock kept them moving nice and easy.

"Oh, shit, Rock. So fucking sweet." Rig turned, mouth finding his jaw, his ear.

He rumbled, head tilting to give Rig more skin to work with. "Looks fucking sweet."

One of Teddy's fingers pushed up to feel around where his cock slid into Rig's ass over and over again, the kid whimpering and those cheeks hollowing in harder. That was Rock's cue and he started moving them faster, thrusting hard into Rig's ass, which pushed that hard cock deeper into Teddy's mouth.

"Fuck yes. Rock. Right there." Rig started bucking, hands wrapping around his neck.

He slid one of his own hands up, pinching those little titties as he drove his cock up deep and hard, Teddy's head bobbing with each of his thrusts.

"Give it up, Rig. Come on my cock. Show the kid how good it is."

"Yeah. Yeah. Fuck." He felt it all around his cock, Rig's entire body shaking.

Teddy pulled off, eyes wide as he jerked, the scent of the kid's spunk overpowering the smell of the condom.

"Yeah," groaned Rock, bringing Rig down hard again and again until his balls drew up and he shot deep.

"Uh-huh." Rig sort of melted, just letting him hold on.

Teddy was watching them with big eyes, and Rock patted his arm and then the couch next to himself. "Come on up and sit, Teddy."

The kid did, sort of flopping onto the couch next to him, head lolling.

Rock chuckled lazily. "Two melted for the price of one."

"Mmmhmm. You're a stud, Rocketman." Rig looked like the cat who got the cream.

Teddy nodded his agreement and Rock flexed happily, his cock moving inside Rig's body, making him groan. He was more than happy to go with that assessment. "I am."

He was, and after supper, he'd prove it again.

And again.

And again, if necessary.

# Chapter Twenty Two

The steaks were on the grill.

The beer was in the cooler.

He leaned in the hammock, swinging nice and slow, baking in the sun.

Life was fucking fine.

Of course, when Alan Jackson came onto the radio, Rig thought he might be able to die happy. Until about three-quarters of the way through the song when the radio suddenly went to static before settling on a new station, this one in the middle of Steppenwolf's 'Born to be Wild'.

He lifted his head, looking over at his own personal Marine. "Hey! I was listening to that, man."

Rock's head was banging along to the new music, two beers dangling from the man's hand. "And now we're listening to this." One of the longnecks was held out to him.

"Jackass." He took the beer, gulped it down.

"I'm sure you've been listening to that twangy shit for ages." Rock sat on the ground next to him, grinning over at him.

"Like you haven't been listening to that caterwauling since God was a boy."

Rock's grin faded, that blue gaze going sharp. "Are you calling me old?"

He arched an eyebrow, grinned. "Would I do that?" That was a great big yes. He would. But usually only if he could run.

Rock growled, the sound going straight to his cock. "You would."

Rock drained his beer and carefully set the bottle down. It was likely the only warning he was going to get. He slid to the edge of the hammock, feet just barely brushing the ground. One good push and he could do it.

Rock rose up and pounced in one fluid movement, and the hammock flipped under the sudden extra weight at the edge, sending them both to the ground. He scrambled, heading for the door, laughing hard enough he couldn't breathe. Rock was right behind him, pushing him in through the door, the screen shutting as he was slammed up against the wall, Rock's cock hard against his ass.

"Someone's cruising," growled Rock, hips making a circle, grinding that hard cock against him.

"You going to leave a bruise, big guy?" Rock's hands had his hips, held on tight.

"I'm gonna make sure you remember I was here." Mouth sliding on his neck, Rock growled against his skin, vibrating his sweet spot just like that.

"Fuck." Hell, yeah. More. "Not bad for an old man." More, Blue.

Rock stilled, and then that growl was there again, Rock's hands tugging at his T-shirt, pulling it out of his jeans and skinning it up and over his head. "Show you fucking old."

Yeah. Show away. "I'm right here, Blue Eyes."

"Uh-huh." Rock's hands grabbed either side of his cut-offs and tore 'em right off. Son of a bitch, his Blue was strong.

"Jesus." His skin stung something fierce, cock slapping up against his belly. "I liked those."

"I like you better like this," murmured Rock, hands sliding over his skin, touch firm, not hard enough to bruise, not quite. Rock got himself a double handful of ass and squeezed.

"Grabby bastard." He fucking loved this. Playing. Needing. Fucking.

Rock snorted. "Not a gay man on earth would blame me -- look what I get to grab."

Rock squeezed again, fingers trailing along his crack, mouth dropping over his shoulder and wetting it with a hot tongue. Oh, that felt. Uh-huh. He spread a little, hips rolling back toward that touch, those fingers.

"Someone's wanting." Fuck, Rock could sound smug.

"Who?" He'd take Rock smug. Hell, he'd take Rock any way the man wanted to be.

"You," growled Rock, thumbs spreading his ass, rubbing at his hole. Rock's mouth latched onto his spine, tongue sliding over the bumps for a few inches worth of skin.

"Uh. Uh-huh." He stuttered forward a couple steps, hands landing on the counter.

"Gonna fuck you, Rig. Gonna fuck you until you scream." Rock's teeth scraped down along his spine.

"Prom... promises, promises." His thighs went tight and Rig went up on tip-toe, electricity shooting down his spine.

"I haven't gone back on one on you yet." Teeth turned into tongue, the sensations going soft, then hard again, then soft. Rock's hands settled back on his hips, hard cock rubbing against his ass through Rock's BDUs.

"Oh, fuck. So fucking *sweet*, Rock." Rig'd forgotten what the hell they were talking about, oh, a lick and a half ago.

"You know it. Gonna be even better in a moment." Rock's heavy weight disappeared, the sound of cloth on skin loud.

He bent farther, getting ready, bracing himself and spreading wide. Come on. Come on, now. The cupboard they kept an emergency tube of lube in was opened, closed, and then there was Rock, two fingers slick and sure, pushing right into him.

His toes curled, trying to push right into the tile, the skin almost squeaking. "More."

"Demanding." He got more though, didn't he? A third finger joined the first two, pushing in hard and fast.

"Mmmhmm." He spread, pushing back, begging for more.

Faster and harder, those fingers pushed and slid, curling to find -- oh fuck, right there. He would have told Rock, but he was busy jerking, crying out, riding those fingers.

"Yeah, I know what you like." Rock kept it up until he thought he would weep, and then suddenly they disappeared.

"Blue!" He half turned, staring. Goddamn it. Don't stop now.

Rock laughed -- the bastard actually laughed. "I can't get my cock *and* my fingers up there at the same time."

"Bitch." He took a deep breath, calming himself down. "You get me all riled up."

"I thought that was a good thing." Rock's fingers closed around his hips again, fingers gripping him nice and tight.

"You are. It is. Fuck me."

Jesus.

"Whatever you want, Rabbit." With that, Rock's thick cock pushed into him, spreading him wide and going deep.

"Yes..." His head fell back. Oh. That. He needed. Yeah.

Rock rumbled for him, the sound getting under his skin. "Now," murmured Rock, hips starting to push.

"Now." That fat prick spread him, stretched him and gave him what he needed.

Fingers tight on his hips, Rock moved him, pulled him into each thrust so they worked together to get Rock just as deep as that cock could go. Oh, now. Just like that. Rig groaned, hips rolling as he worked to get Rock's prick in just the right spot.

Rock growled a little and shifted him, pushing in at a different angle and just nailing him right where he wanted.

"Rock!" His eyes flew open, fingers curling. Fuck. There. Yes.

"I've got you." And Rock sure did, nailing his gland over and over, hands hard and sure on his hips. The fucking world stopped still, Rig's eyes rolling back in his head as he just felt. They moved like one person, bodies coming together over and over again. "Good, Rig. Fuck."

"Yes. Yes." Fuck, he. Uh. Yeah. Just. Damn.

"Show me," growled Rock. "You fucking show me." Harder, faster, Rock just plowed into him.

He shot so hard his knees went weak, entire body shaking like a leaf in a storm. Rock's growl was nearly a shout, thick cock pounding into him again and again until heat shot into him, Rock's body blanketing him as his Blue collapsed onto him.

"Good." He nodded, pushing back against Rock's weight. "So fucking good."

Rock's mouth latched onto the top of his spine again, tongue sliding on his skin. One of those big hands slid over his belly and his chest, warm, wonderful.

"Fuck." He hummed and sort of melted, fingers opening and closing lazily. "You blow my fucking mind."

"That wasn't your mind that blew spunk all over the couch."

"Ew." He started chuckling, tickled deep down.

Rock was quiet a moment and then started laughing. "Oh, fuck, I didn't even think of *that*. You are one sick puppy."

They laughed together, loud and long, Rock's belly rolling against his back. "Come shower with me."

"I can do that."

Rock licked his neck. "Or I could give you a tongue bath."

"Mmm. Tempter." He stretched, loving it.

"Nah, just greedy. You taste fucking good, Rig." That tongue slid and licked.

"Feels fucking sweet." He squeezed tight, loving the moan it got him.

"You're not convincing me to go shower."

"No? You're sure?" He squeezed again, laughing good and low.

"Christ, Rigger, I'm fucking dead sure." Rock's hips circled a little, the cock inside him shifting and rubbing.

"I like it when you're sure, Marine."

That low rumble vibrated against his back, hips still moving, pushing, threatening to get it all going again. "Good."

Rig closed his eyes, focused on squeezing and clenching, rippling around Rock's cock. Rock's hand slid over his arm, along it, moving slowly, the touch deep. When their hands met, Rock's fingers twined with his and their movements became a little more intense.

Everything else went away -- the whole world faded as they made love.

It went on forever, or maybe it was over in seconds. It didn't matter. The pleasure grew and grew, waves of it rushing over and through him until Rock's voice whispered inside him. "Now, Rabbit."

"Now." He came without taking another breath, just as easy as breathing.

Rock's heat filled him again, the hard body coming to a rest on top of him. Just right.

He settled down, floating. Lord, this was.

Yeah.

Perfect.

# Chapter Twenty Three

Rock fucking loved Saturdays. He got to sleep in until noon before Rig would come in to give him his morning wake-up call. Hell, some Saturdays he'd just roll over after and go right back to sleep. Rig usually had all the cleaning done by the time he got up, sometimes even the errands were taken care of and they got to be lazy for the rest of the day.

Today had been a good one -- he'd had his blowjob and a coffee in bed with Rig. There'd been fresh fucking donuts when he'd finally hit the kitchen for a second cup of coffee and the place smelled awesome, something cooking up in the slow cooker, and a chocolate pie in the fridge.

The game on TV was a damned good one, and Rig had outdone himself on munchies.

Life was good.

Rig was stretched out on the sofa, reading some scary book, one leg swinging lazily over the back.

He grinned, making plans for that long body just as soon as the last few minutes of the game played themselves out. He had plenty of time before the next game started. He debated going for a surprise pounce to take advantage of the scary book read, or starting to build up the anticipation now.

Of course, the fucking phone rang about three seconds before he pounced, Rig rolling up and heading into the kitchen to answer.

Grumbling, he had a few more chips and guac, finishing off his beer as he watched the damned recap. He'd seen the damned game, he'd have been much happier playing hide the salami on the couch with Rig.

It took Rig fucking forever before the man came back, and he didn't stop at the sofa or even the living room. He just headed back down the hall without a word.

Weird.

Rock gave it a few minutes and then got up to get himself another beer. He headed down the hall instead though -- if Rig had been called in to work he was going to fucking bitch. And have a quickie before he let Rig go.

There was a suitcase on the bed, clothes piled in, along with Rig's shaving kit.

"What the fuck? What the hell is going on here?" God fucking damn it, two fucking days a week that they didn't belong to the fucking hospital or base and they didn't always fall together. Was it really to much to ask for their weekends to not be cut short?

"I have to go home. I have a flight in two hours." Rig sounded...

Not like Rig.

Not fucking at all.

That was no answer either, not really. He grabbed the jeans out of Rig's hands, tossed them at the bed, and gave Rig an even look. "What's going on?"

"Daddy's in ICU. They say if I'm going to get a chance to say goodbye, I have to hurry." There was a pure panic in those eyes, a dull-edged horror that he'd only really seen in combat. Fuck.

"Jeremy? Christ." He pushed Rig to sit down on the bed and shoved the jeans in the suitcase, making a quick check to see what else was missing. Socks and underwear. He went over to the dresser for them. "What happened?"

"His heart." Rig stood up, grabbed an address book and some bolo ties from a little, wooden box. "He was on the roof, nailing shingles. Can you feed Grimmy or should I call Reed?"

"I'll take care of the damned dog, Rig. I'll take care of all the shit that needs taking care of. You want me to call the hospital?" He couldn't quite wrap his head around it -- Jeremy was full of life and had a heart as big as the state he lived in and loved so much. Christ, Charlene had to be beside herself.

"I called. I'll talk to Krippen in the morning from Dallas." The suitcase closed with a click; Rig grabbing his hat and plopping it on his head. "I have to go. I'll call."

Rock started changing out of his sweats and into a pair of jeans. "I'll drive you to the damned airport, Rig."

Rig looked at him a second, like the man had just realized he was standing there, was real. Then Rig nodded. "Thanks."

He pulled Rig into his arms and kissed him as hard as he could. Then he looked into those grey eyes. "I'm sorry, Rig. Jeremy's a real good man."

And not dead yet, maybe there was a chance... the look on Rig's face said there wasn't though, so he kept his mouth shut. When it came to hospital shit, Rig knew the score.

"Yeah. Yeah. I. I gotta go. Momma needs me."

"I know." He grabbed the suitcase with one hand, and Rig with the other, heading down the hall and wishing like hell he could change this, make it not be happening.

He was a fucking Marine for Christ's sake, but there wasn't one goddamned thing he could do but drive Rig to the airport.

Life was a goddamned fucking bitch.

# Chapter Twenty Four

Rig didn't bother calling Rock to pick him up from the airport. There were cabs and, after his four beers at DFW, two shots on the plane, and three more shots in the Fayetteville Airport, he wasn't up to anything more than pouring himself in a cab and going home.

Hell, the temptation to just stop at a bar before he made it home was fucking enormous.

Still, he got home around three and headed in, Grimmy scratching and barking and whining at the front door.

"Shh. Hush, mutt. Outside, huh? Rock'll be home in a couple hours." The house looked like it had when he left. Like nothing'd changed.

It ought to look like the whole world had, damn it.

He poured himself another drink and went to sit on the back porch, tapping his Marlboros down and lighting one up.

He'd downed a few more drinks and most of his pack of Marlboros before the front door opened, Rock calling out. "Rig? You're home?"

"Yeah." His body was, anyway. He thought maybe the rest of him was still sitting at home looking for Daddy.

He shouldn't have left Momma there all alone. He shouldn't have.

Rock came into the kitchen, grunting and making a detour at the fridge when he saw Rig. Two beers, tops popped, and Rock joined him on the back porch, sitting next to him and offering the beer.

Those blue eyes took a long look. "You look like shit."

"Been a long week." He hadn't gotten there in time. Daddy'd died before he ever left North Carolina.

"Yeah." Rock took a long drink, inched over just a little, just enough their shoulders were touching. "How's Charlene?"

"Tired." She hadn't cried, not for the longest time. Not until they put Daddy into the ground and everybody left and he took her home to that empty house.

Jesus.

He shouldn't have left her.

"Sissy and Bobby taking time off to help her?"

"Sissy went back home for a couple of weeks, but she'll be back soon."

Rock nodded. "What about work -- when do you need to go back?"

"Monday." He had tomorrow and the weekend to get his shit together. Maybe he'd just stay drunk 'til Sunday. "How're you?"

"Same old, same old." Rock's knee nudged his. "Been thinking of you."

"Yeah." He hadn't really been thinking of Rock. He hadn't really been thinking. He'd been doing.

Talking to the preacher.

Talking to folks.

Making arrangements.

It was pure fucking hell and he wasn't ever gonna die.

Rock's arm went around his shoulders. "I'm sorry."

"Yeah. Me, too." He leaned in for a second, listening to Rock's heartbeat. "I guess I ought to start supper."

"I was gonna order a pizza or something. You just tell me what you want and I'll make it happen." Rock's hand squeezed his shoulder.

"Pizza's fine. Just no more mac and cheese. Ever." He'd smelled more fucking mac and cheese in the last few days...

"That won't be a problem."

They sat for a few more minutes, Grimmy coming over now and then to sniff them before settling at their feet, head on his front paws.

"You need anything?"

Yeah. He needed it to be two weeks ago. He needed things to be normal. He needed his daddy back.

Right now.

Please, God.

"I'll take one more beer, if you're gonna get you one."

"Yeah, I can do beer. I'll order the pizza, too. Meatlovers, okay?"

"Works for me." He wasn't hungry, but he'd nibble. He needed to unpack, do laundry. Shower.

Rock grunted and stood, going into the kitchen to make his call. Grimmy barked as the screen door shut noisily.

All so fucking normal.

All so fucking wrong.

Rig stood up and headed for the storage building. He just needed to get the yard mowed, then he could do something else.

# Chapter Twenty Five

Rock thought he might grab his weapon, head out to the range, and shoot every fucking thing in sight. Or he could go down to the ring on the base and taken on any comers, wipe the floor with them.

Hell, he was halfway sure volunteering for fucking latrine duty had to beat watching Rig pace the fucking floor and chain smoke one vile cigarette after another.

It had been going on for days, ever since Rig'd gotten back from Texas. From Jeremy's funeral.

The man went to work, came home, went through the motions of cleaning and doing laundry and cooking and mowing the fucking yard, pale and quiet as a goddamned ghost the entire time.

And there wasn't a goddamned thing Rock could do to help.

He'd tried taking over the mowing that first day and Rig'd just stopped and nearly dropped him where he stood with that look. Rock wasn't sure if it was helping to have stuff to do or not, but him not doing anything sure as shit wasn't helping Rig any either.

He'd asked if Rig'd cried yet, if he'd said goodbye, and Rig had just shaken his head, said he didn't want to talk about it.

Any attempt at conversation ended in heavy, awkward silence. A comforting hand or arm was soon shaken off, Rig suddenly coming up with something that had to be done.

So Rock watched.

He watched Rigger grow paler and skinnier, watched that cloud of smoke become permanent around Rig's head.

He fucking hated this. He hated that Rig's Daddy'd died. He hated that there wasn't anything he could do.

Finally, he just went to bed, leaving Rig in the garage working on some power tool or something.

Goddamn it.

It was fucking late when he heard the water start in the bathroom, Rig slipping into the shower.

Awake anyway, he decided he might as well join Rig. No doubt he'd just get barked at for his trouble, but damn it, if he couldn't *fix* it, the least he could do was be there.

He made some noise once he was in the bathroom, just enough that he didn't startle the fuck out of Rig as he climbed into the shower. The bathroom was dark as pitch, but he could just see the outline of Rig's shoulders shaking.

"Christ." He muttered and wrapped his arms around Rig from behind, pulling the lean body back against him.

Rig was stiff for just about a heartbeat, then Rig relaxed, melted against him. "Jim."

He'd never heard his name like that -- like Rig was broken and he was the one thing left to fix things.

"Right here." His voice was thick, but steady and he got Rig turned around, head against his chest and just held on.

Rig didn't say a fucking word, didn't wail or carry on. No. His Rabbit wasn't going to pull that shit. Rig just let him do his job, let him support that skinny body. It was the best he could do.

The water poured over them, and they let it; they let it shut the world and everything out. Just him and Rig and the hot, wet quiet.

His hand slid over Rig's spine, just moving up and down slowly, saying "I'm here" and "I've got you".

Finally Rig nodded, lips on his jaw. "Take me to bed."

"Anything you want, Rig."

He leaned over and turned off the water before manhandling Rig out of the tub and into a towel. He didn't linger, didn't try to start anything, just got them both dry and then hoisted Rig up over his shoulder. That Rig didn't complain, didn't fuss, told him more than anything that his cowboy needed him, needed his strength.

He carried Rig into the bedroom, placed the lean body down on the bed, climbing in himself. He touched Rig, hands exploring the familiar face, neck, shoulders, relearning the contours, giving Rig something to focus on. Rig sighed and it sounded good to him, good to hear a noise that wasn't frustrated or wrong, but just peaceful. Rig's hands landed on him, smoothing over his skin, matching his motions stroke for stroke.

His fingers slid into Rig's pits, touching hard enough not to tickle, before traveling down Rig's sides and up over the too skinny belly. He touched Rig's pecs next, thumbs brushing across the sensitive, little titties. The flesh tightened, just a bit, enough to show him Rig was there, feeling this.

He brushed them again and then moved back down Rig's body, finding those prominent hip bones that seemed even more so now. Rig needed to stop fucking smoking and start eating again. He rubbed the soft skin in the little dip right below Rig's waist and next to his hips, smooth and sweet, he loved these little dips.

"Mmmm..." He hadn't heard that sound in too fucking long.

Encouraged, he leaned in and found one of Rig's nipples, teasing just the tip with his tongue as his fingers carded through the blond curls that crowned Rig's cock. Rig pressed a little closer, cock just starting to fill for him.

Yeah, that was it -- time to heal, to feel.

He slid one hand between Rig's legs, stroking the soft skin inside his thighs, thumb rubbing against Rig's balls. Rig chuckled, thighs spreading just a bit for him. Rig smelled good, smelled like sex and need and pleasure.

He let a rumble build in his chest, let it out as his mouth closed over one of Rig's little titties, licking and sucking on the small bit of flesh as his fingers slid over the smooth, hot skin beyond Rig's balls.

"Don't stop, Blue. Need this." This whisper seemed loud as thunder in the dark.

Like he was going to stop.

He shook his head, brought their mouths together to whisper against Rig's lips. "I won't stop."

Rig's tongue slid over his lips, welcoming him right in. With a long, heartfelt groan, he kissed Rig, everything else fading beneath the taste of his Rabbit on his lips, around his tongue as he pushed it into Rig's mouth. He explored Rig's mouth with slow strokes, tasting and relearning.

Oh, fuck yes. That's right. Come *home*, Rabbit.

His hands kept moving, touching that fine skin. Nipples, navel, Rig's balls and the fine skin beyond them, he touched everywhere he could reach.

"Want you," he told Rig, pressing kisses to Rig's cheeks, eyelids, nose, chin.

"Left..." Rig's breath hitched, those bloodshot, grey eyes meeting his own. "Left Texas for you."

"I know. I'm one lucky son of a bitch." He kissed Rig again, this kiss less about taste and exploration and more about need, want.

He reached up beneath the pillow, finding the neglected tube of lube. One of Rig's legs hooked around his hip, hands sliding down over his shoulders. Rumbling, he pressed one kiss after another on Rig, slick fingers pushing between Rig's legs, circling and pressing against that tight, little hole.

Deep sounds started bubbling up out of Rig, the man's lips parted. Those lean hips rolled, taking him in, letting him in. He pushed one finger in and slid it out, then another finger and then another, switching them up and pushing each one deep on its own, before he pushed two in together.

"Fuck, yeah." Yeah, that was what he wanted, Rig focused, watching him, thinking about nothing but feeling. He pushed a third finger in, stretching and spreading, curling his fingers to hit that spot inside Rig.

"There." Rig's entire body rippled, the cry pushed right out.

He nailed that spot again and again, that cry making him harder than nails.

"Rock. Blue." Rig's fingers dug into his shoulders, the grip surprisingly fucking strong.

He pushed his little finger in with the other three, circling them. Fuck, he wanted in there, wanted that hot, little hole tight around his cock.

"Yours." Rig spread, hips jerking, muscles fluttering around him.

"You know it." Rig fucking knew it.

He let his fingers slide away and shifted, moving to lie between Rig's spread legs. "All mine." He started pushing in.

Rig nodded, let out a soft sob and arched toward him, taking him in deep. Moaning, he dropped his head, licking at Rig's lips as he moved slowly, pushing in and out of Rig's body. Rig moaned into his kiss, undulating under him, fucking him right back. Oh, he'd needed this, needed it bad.

And so did Rig.

They moved hard together, faster, mouths fucking as surely as the rest of their bodies. Rig's legs wrapped around his waist, pulled him in tighter, harder, deeper. Yeah, this was what he'd been needing, what Rig had been needing. To find this place where nothing else fucking mattered.

His breath pushed into Rig's mouth, his cock into Rig's body, over and over, and he just rode it. He could feel Rig getting tight all around him, muscles fluttering and squeezing, working his cock. It wasn't going to be long, his balls drawing up tight, his cock head throbbing.

"Blue..." Rig jerked, one hand reaching down to stroke that needy cock.

He knocked Rig's hand away, growling. "Mine." Wrapping his own hand around Rig's prick, he started jacking in time to his thrusts.

"Yeah. Yeah. Gonna." Rig nodded, throat working. "Soon."

"Do it. Fucking show me, Rig." He tightened his grip on Rig's cock, his hips starting to jerk as his orgasm barreled down on him.

"Yes. Yesyesyes." Rig groaned, heat spraying between them.

Moaning, jerking, he shot deep into Rig, tight ass milking him.

Rig's body held him tight, kept him inside. "Blue."

"Right fucking here, Rabbit." He nuzzled into Rig's neck, breathing in the scent of come and sweat.

Rig nodded, wrapping around him and holding on tight. "It damn near killed me to leave there, but I. I just. It was time to come home."

"You have to live your life Rig."

"I know." Rig just kept holding on. "It's late."

"Then sleep." Christ knew the man hadn't done more than catnap since coming back.

"'Kay. You, too."

"I will." Once he was sure Rig was out.

Rig's hand splayed out over his belly, fingers wide. He kissed Rig's shoulder and tugged the covers on up over them both. Come on, Rabbit. Sleep.

It didn't take more than a minute, Rig's breathing evening out. The hold on him never eased, even a little.

It sure beat watching Rig pace.

Beat it all to hell.

# Chapter Twenty Six

"Momma?" He lit a cigarette, legs swinging over the edge of the porch.

"What's up, baby?" God, she sounded good. Right as rain. Almost normal.

"Nothin'." He just. Rig's heart hurt. It hurt bad. "I got all unpacked and stuff. 'M fixin' to go out in the field for a week."

"Well, you be careful. I'll still call on Sunday, just in case you're there."

"Rock will be. You can talk at him."

Momma stayed quiet a minute, then she sighed. "It's not the same."

Rig took a long, long drag, holding the smoke in until it burned him deep. "No. Nothin' is."

"No. Nothin's gonna be, but that's okay. That's how the good Lord intends it. Things change."

He nodded, stubbed out his smoke. "I miss him."

"I know."

And that was that, wasn't it? They missed him. He was waiting on them. And things were going to keep on going, whether anybody wanted them to.

"I gotta get to packing, Momma."

"Okay, son. I love you. If you don't quit smoking, I'm going to beat your ass."

"Yeah, Momma? I'd like to see you try."

Their laughter was still echoing as he headed in to get some shit done.

# Chapter Twenty Seven

"Grimmy! Quit your fucking barking, would you?" Rig shouldered into the house, hands full of dog food, beer, and fried chicken. "Marine? You home? I could use a hand."

"Door was unlocked, wasn't it?"

Grimmy was pulled away and Rock grabbed the beer and chicken from his hands. "Chicken smells good. I could eat a horse."

"Horse meat is real popular in Japan, I hear." He dropped the dog food, kicked the door shut.

Rock snorted. "Yeah, and dog meat in China. I'll stick with the chicken. Tastes better with beer." Rock was wearing his jeans and nothing else, padding ahead of him into the kitchen.

There was a big assed box on the table, his name in Momma's handwriting on the top.

Rock opened a couple of beers and passed one over to him. "It showed up just after I got home."

"Yeah?" He drank deep, sat down to pull his boots off. "You ought to open it, see if Momma sent you cookies."

"You want me to? It's addressed to you." Still, Rock got out a knife and slit the ends open and then the flap up the center. "You think she might've made those ones I like the best?"

"Maybe." He didn't know why, but he just didn't want to see what all she'd sent. Not really.

Rock gave him a long look and then grunted and opened the flaps. "There's a card on top."

"Yeah? What does it say?"

"It's addressed to you, Rig." Rock took the envelope out and held it out to him.

He took it, fingers sliding over the envelope. Momma'd just written, "Son" on the front.

One of Rock's hands landed on his shoulder, squeezing, massaging just a little.

Rig sighed and opened it, chewing on his bottom lip as he read.

"Son, Just wanted to send y'all some odds and ends. I found a Halloween Marine at the Wal-Mart for Jim and a clown hat for the dog. Get your Christmas plane tickets early. I'm thinking on coming to see you this Thanksgiving. I put your daddy's pocket watch in for you and his spurs from back when he was riding. He'd've wanted you to have them. The cookies are Jim's. The cherry candies and Ranch Style beans are for you. Love you, baby. Momma."

Goddamn.

Rock grunted, squeezed his shoulder again, and then started emptying the box, carefully putting the pocket watch and the spurs down in front of him. "Hey, there's something in here she didn't mention."

Rock pulled out Daddy's Bowie knife in its leather holder, a note taped to it. "Jim, Jeremy would have wanted you to have this, Momma."

Rig's throat got all caught up, but he nodded. Yeah. Daddy would've wanted Rock to have it. Rock would take good care of it.

"I'm going to go take a shower." He gathered up the little watch box and the spurs, headed back down the hall.

Rock took awhile to follow him, joining him in the bedroom and sitting on the bed, not saying a word, just sitting next to him.

Rig took a deep, deep breath, then leaned over, let Rock support his skinny ass. "Momma wants to come for Thanksgiving. You'll get homemade pecan pie."

"Yours is good, but hers is better." Rock's voice was a little rougher than usual. "You tell her to come stay as long as she wants. I'll pick her up at the airport."

"'Kay." He reached out, squeezed Rock's hand. He'd never had a Thanksgiving without Daddy.

Rock squeezed back and for a long time they just sat there together, not talking, not doing anything, just sitting.

Finally Rock grunted. "That shower sounds good about now."

"Yeah. It does." He nodded, leaned down to tug off his boots. "You have a decent day, Rocketman?"

Rock shrugged, standing and working off his BDUs.

"It was a day. How about you?"

"It was a day. Glad to be home." As he said the words, he realized he meant them.

"Yeah?" Rock gave him a smile, moving to stand between his legs, hands on his shoulders, rubbing. They both chuckled as that fat prick started to rise, slapping him on the chin.

"Yeah." He leaned forward, kissed Rock's belly, the tip of Rock's cock.

Rock made a soft sound, fingers moving slowly, massaging. "Your mouth's something else, Rig. Always was. Still is."

Oh, man. That made him smile. He leaned a little harder, eyes closing as he focused on the musk and heat and salt of his Blue. He got another one of those sounds, this one deeper, coming from Rock's belly.

It wasn't even passion, right now. This was more comfort and good and...

Yeah.

Not having to think.

He was a fucking fan.

Rig kept kissing and exploring, tongue dragging over Rock's slit, slipping around the crown. Rock's fingers kept massaging his shoulders, rubbing up and down along the back of his neck and up over his skull, relaxing and warm, making him feel good all over.

It was so easy to sigh and open, let Rock in deeper and deeper, let that cock fill him up. The low moan slid over him like one of Rock's hands, caressing him as surely as any touch.

"So good," murmured Rock, hips making tiny, little movements that slid the fat prick along his tongue.

Rig just nodded. Yeah. Yeah, Blue. So fucking good.

Rock's movements grew a little bigger, hips rocking a little harder. The thick fingers slid through his hair and traced his face. His own fingers found Rock's balls, cradled and stroked the velvet soft skin there.

A soft gasp sounded, a shiver going through Rock. "Oh, fuck, Rig. Yes."

This was it. Just this. Just what he needed. Rig started bobbing his head, sucking and pulling, throat tight around Rock's flesh. Rock kept moaning, babbling now and then, almost incoherent.

His fingers slid back, tapping the sensitive strip of skin behind Rock's balls. Several drops of liquid slid out of Rock's slit, landing hot and bittersalty on his tongue. "Gonna make me come, Rig. Gonna make me shoot down your throat."

Fuck, yes. Come for me. I need...

"Fuck..." Rock jerked hard, pushing deep and shooting hard, spunk going down his throat, filling his mouth. Rig drank Rock down, moaning, swallowing, loving on his Marine for all he was worth.

Rock's hands patted him, sort of slid over him in lazy, sated motions. He could see Rock locking his knees to keep from going down. Rig pulled back, lips sliding on the tip of that heavy cock.

Groaning, Rock slid a finger over his eyebrows. "You gonna keep me hard?"

"Gonna try." He grinned, tongue pressing in, just a little.

"Oh, fuck." Rock growled, fingers curling into fists against his head. "Yeah, you do that. I'm gonna fuck you through the mattress."

"Promise?" He could handle that. He so could.

"You know it. You won't walk straight for a week."

"I'm in." He ducked his head, licking at Rock's nuts.

"And I'll be in you," groaned Rock, cock sliding along the side of his face.

"Mmmhmm." Rock smelled like... Like right where he belonged.

Rock's legs spread a little, giving him more room, letting him get to the skin just behind those heavy balls.

"Hot motherfucker." Rig groaned, pushing in, surrounding himself with his Marine.

"You fucking know it. Pretty fucking sexy yourself."

His mouth was too busy for any more of an answer than 'mmmhmm', but Rock heard well enough. Rock spread a little further for him, not hurrying him at all, just letting him do what he wanted, letting him take what he needed. Finally he had to lean back, just to catch a breath, rest his jaw. Rock was a fucking addiction.

Rock grinned down at him, cupping his cheek. "Slut," murmured Rock, blue eyes just shining down at him.

"Yeah. Yours." Asshole.

Beautiful fucking asshole.

"Why don't you stretch on out and let me run the rest of this show." His Blue did like to drive.

Rig flopped back on the bed, cock bumping his belly. Rumbling happily, Rock climbed up onto the bed, bending to kiss the sole of his right foot. His toes curled in response, leg muscles trembling.

Rock's chuckle blew air over his foot, and then another kiss was placed on his big toe, one on his ankle. Meanwhile, Rock's fingers slid up along his shin. Rig relaxed, spread, just let Rock have it all. Let Rock have *him*.

One soft kiss followed another, Rock spending time on both his feet and up along his legs. Each kiss built on the last, sending sensation and goosepimples along his skin.

"'S so good. So fucking good." Rig reached for his cock, stroking it nice and easy.

"Uh-huh." Rock kept kissing, fingers sliding on him, too, but it was those lips that were making magic. His legs were nudged further apart by Rock's nose, his inner thighs licked and sucked.

He pulled his legs up and back, offering about as baldly as he could. Rock hummed, the sound tickling against his skin. Those hot lips moved to the crease where his thighs met his torso, sucking hard enough Rock had to be bringing up a mark.

"Blue..." Oh. Oh, fuck. That was hot as hell.

The only answer was harder suction, Rock's fingers playing over his balls. Rock finally moved on, licking his balls, taking one in. Rig went still, focusing on the pleasure, on the sensation and heat. Tongue working his ball, Rock hummed, making the whole thing kind of vibrate, the sensation shooting up inside him.

His moan just rang out, echoed through the air. Goddamn. Yes. Fuck.

Releasing the one ball, Rock gave the other one the same treatment, hands sliding beneath his ass. Then Rock let his ball go and tilted him, spreading him wide so Rock could lick from behind his balls to his hole, tongue just dancing over his skin.

"Fuck. Rock..." He grabbed hold of the sheets, fingers twisting in.

Rock chuckled, breath huffing over his wet skin, making him goosepimple.

"More. More. Please." He'd beg. He would. That felt so good.

"More of what? This?" Rock blew across his hole, making him clench. His Blue chuckled again, and then that tongue slid over his skin again, teased his hole. Better, but not nearly enough.

"Yes..." Yes, more of that.

"Yeah. Fuck, yeah." Rock's face pushed against his ass, stubble dragging against his ass cheeks as Rock's tongue slid back and forth and back and forth across his hole. He just started moving, rocking and begging, needing Rock with all he was.

Eventually that back and forth tongue finally started to push in, just the tip to start, but soon Rock let his motions pull that tongue deeper and deeper until Rock was fucking him good and hard with that tongue.

Fuck, yes. He spread wider, rocking up and up into that touch. One of Rock's hands moved up over his cock, fingers sliding over his slit and dragging the slick drops up over his belly, rubbed it into his navel. "Gonna make me come..."

"Wait for me, Rig." Rock turned, biting his inner thigh gently.

"Make me so fucking hard, Blue."

"I try." Rock looked up at him, winked. Two fingers slipped into him, circling inside him.

"Uh-huh..." His shoulders left the mattress, hips jerking and rolling as he rode.

"Sexy fucker," muttered Rock, bending to lick at one of his nipples.

"Yours. Fuck me."

Rock laughed, the sound happy. "My pleasure, Rabbit."

Fingers slid away, were replaced with the blunt, thick heat of Rock's cock, the heat slowly pushing into him. A deep, raw sound came out of him, his body stretching and burning over Rock's prick.

"Fuck. Yes." Rock groaned, kept pushing until he was seated deep. "Just like that."

"Yeah. Just like..." He couldn't stop grinning, smiling for real for the first time in days. "Need this, huh?"

"Uh-huh. I know what you need." Rock thrust, nice and hard, slipping away and then filling him up with that single push. "I've got what you need."

"Yeah." No shit. Rock had what he needed in spades.

Rock nodded, those blue eyes just staring down at him, sharp as a razor. Over and over again Rock pushed into him, filling him up and giving him everything. They groaned and shifted, their skin slapping together, his cock caught between them.

Rock bent to kiss him, cock shifting inside him, sliding across his gland. He cried out into the kiss, fingers grabbing Rock's hips. Rock's tongue fucked his lips, hips pistoning, like a fucking machine.

So close. So fucking close. Jesus. Rig jerked and bit, moaned low and came.

"Rig. Yes." Rock groaned, hips jerking faster and then stilling as heat pumped into him.

He couldn't do a fucking thing more than nod and hold on.

Rock pulled out and rolled over. "That gets better every fucking time."

"Uh-huh." Better. Hotter. Whatever.

Rock's arm pushed under his shoulders and he was tugged into Rock's side.

"Shower can wait on a nap."

"Yeah." Rig nodded, already half asleep.

Rock grunted and tugged him a little closer, one hand solid and warm on his hip.

Just like it should be.

# Chapter Twenty Eight

Rock grabbed the mail on his way in. He gave the mutt a couple of pats and toed off his boots before heading to the back door to let Grimmy out into the yard. "The old biddy next door's been nosy lately, Grim. Go bark up a storm."

Grim gave him a single bark and took off across the yard.

A beer, the last piece of chocolate pie, and Rock settled at the kitchen table. Bills went into a pile for Rig to deal with, junk mail he tossed in the general direction of the garbage. Most of it made it.

There was a letter for Rig from Charlene. She'd written a couple times a week since Jeremy'd passed.

He put that next to the bills.

The last envelope was addressed to James South and had the name of the lawyer's office in the corner. He looked at for a long while, debating whether or not he actually wanted to open it. There was nothing stopping him from tossing it in the garbage with the flyers.

Rig wandered in, arms full of laundry. "Hey, Marine."

"Hey, I didn't realize you were home." He put the letter aside and started in on the pie. Damn, he loved this pie.

"I was fucking around in the back room."

"Fucking around? You were doing that without me?" He gave Rig a wink.

"Yep. Me and the storage boxes are having a wild affair."

He chuckled. "They discovered your mouth, huh?"

Rig's laugh just rang out. "You know it."

He leaned over and wrapped an arm around Rig's waist, tugging him in. "Good day?"

"Not bad, Marine. Not bad at all. Did some good work." Rig leaned in, kissed him hard enough to steal his breath. "You?"

"The usual. It's looking up though." His cock throbbed in agreement. "Way up."

"Perv." Rig grinned against his lips. "You ate the last of the pie."

"It was chocolate pie." Rig knew better than to leave that in the fridge if he wanted it.

"It was." Rig's laugh was fucking sweet.

He grinned and let his hand slide on Rig's ass. "I got a letter."

"Yeah? Who from?"

"That lawyer's office." He growled a little. Oh, the lawyer'd been neutral, not taking sides one way or the other. But it got his hackles up, thinking of that meeting.

"Well, you'd best read it. Then we can put it behind us."

He nodded. Yeah. Long as he didn't have to go back and see those fuckers again.

He opened the envelope, eyebrows rising as a letter and a check fluttered out. A check for twenty-five thousand dollars from his grandma's estate. He passed the check over to Rig and opened the letter. It was short and to the point. The case against the estate had been dropped.

"Huh." He'd seen the look in his father's eyes when the man had railed and claimed he'd never see a penny. He'd believed that, hadn't cared really. He had his letter from Granny.

He passed the lawyer's letter over to Rig as well.

"Well, there you go." Rig nodded, lips set firm. "You don't ever have to deal with those nasty Yankees again."

"Yeah." He wondered for a half a moment why things had changed, and then decided that he didn't give a shit. Those 'nasty Yankees' had written him off years ago.

Rig folded the check up, handed it over. "Here. You keep this safe."

"Might need it some day," he agreed, pulling out his wallet and sticking the check in it. He'd take it to the bank in the morning.

"That's that then."

"Yessir." Rig nodded, tossed the letter in the trash. "All done."

"We oughta celebrate. You feel like steak? I'm feeling a little flush right now."

"Hell, yeah. You buying the beer, too? I'll wear my good boots."

"You know it." He leaned a bit, checking out Rig's ass. "You need help getting them on?"

He got this grin -- wide and happy and horny and just all fucking right. "I might could. Yeah."

"Excellent. Boot changing's a specialty of mine." He got up, started slowly walking toward Rig.

Rig stepped backward, licked those fine fucking lips. "Yeah? You gonna demonstrate."

He grinned, feeling his cock perk right up, start to fill out the front of his BDUs. "You know it." He took a few more steps, letting Rig keep just ahead of him.

"You're a hot son of a bitch, Rocketman." Rig's look was frank, admiring.

Damn, but his own personal cowboy made him feel like a million bucks, every damned day.

"You know it, Rig." He pulled off his shirt, giving Rig more to admire. Rig groaned, fingers clenching. "Tit for tat, Rig. Take yours off." He wanted that skinny body naked. The sooner the better.

"Tits? Where?" The t-shirt was stripped off, showing off that taut, little belly.

He hummed, his cock pushing hard against his pants. "I see a pair. Well... little man ones. You think I can make the owner of them beg?"

"Not a chance."

He chuckled and started undoing his BDUs, still moving forward. They'd be in the bedroom in a few more steps and then that ass was his. "I don't believe you."

"Nope? You're damn sure of yourself."

He chuckled. "No, I'm sure of you." He sped up, reaching for Rig.

"You're a smart man." Rig moved right into his arms, cock hard and pressed against his thigh.

"Yep."

He took a kiss, moaning into Rig's mouth as his hand slid into the man's jeans and felt up that amazing ass. Rig opened right up, the kiss enough to erase everything away. Goddamn. He rubbed their fronts together, bumping their cocks, their hips as he sucked on Rig's tongue.

Rig whimpered, bucking up toward him. He worked his hands back out of Rig's jeans and started undoing them, fingertips brushing the tip of Rig's cock as it strained to get out.

"Tease. Oh, fuck. Good." Rig's head rolled, eyes just burning.

"I'm no tease, Rig. You know that." He pushed a finger against Rig's slit, moved it back and forth, and then went back to peeling Rig out of those jeans so he could get a proper hold of the long cock.

The tight denim fought him, but he managed. Hell, he was a Marine, wasn't he? He finally got them peeled off, growling softly at the sight of his cowboy, naked and wanting him.

"What do you want?" That pretty cock was full and bobbing, hard and wet-tipped.

"You. Mouth, ass, I want it all, Rig. And then I want it all again. We might do steak in between, though." He pushed Rig gently back toward the bed.

"Hell of a plan." Rig went, nice and easy. "One hell of a plan."

He let Rig get himself settled on the bed as he stripped his own clothes off, eyes on the lean body, watching each muscle move, shift, twitch. Then he climbed up after Rig, slowly moving upward, letting his cock drag over Rig's stomach, chest.

"Fucking fine..." Rig leaned up, licking and kissing each inch of skin.

Groaning, he gave Rig some extra time at his nipples, that mouth licking and sucking as he rubbed his cock over Rig's abs. That fucking mouth was so fucking hungry, so fucking needy. Rig sucked and pulled, teeth scraping against his skin.

"Greedy," he muttered. It wasn't a complaint; not for a fucking second. He moved up a little higher, torn between wanting that mouth on his cock and wanting everywhere else. Rig's tongue slid over his ribs, tickling him. The shivers got him, his skin going all goosepimply. His elbows locked to keep himself from dropping down onto Rig, his moan coming from deep in his belly. "Fuck, Rig."

"Uh-huh. Good plan. Fuck Rig."

"You know it. Gonna do you right." He moved up until his cock bumped into Rig's chin, rubbing the tip against the day's stubble. Fuck, that was hot. Rig rubbed his cheek all along Rock's shaft, all the way down to the base.

Groaning, he reached for the headboard, knees settling in Rig's pits, his cock sliding across Rig's lips. He got a grin, then Rig started sucking the very tip of his cock, pulling hard enough that his eyes rolled back into his head. Yeah. That mouth. It was something else. Something special.

A shudder moved through him as Rig's tongue pushed into his slit. At his groan, Rig pushed harder, fucking his cock. His fingers curled around the headboard, eyes glued to where his cock disappeared between Rig's lips. He wanted to fuck that mouth in the worst way. He wanted to let Rig have him however Rig wanted him even more.

Rig gave it up so pretty, lips sliding on his shaft, just brushing his skin on the way down, pulling hard on the way up.

"Fuck. Fuck." Another shudder went through him, his nerves just singing.

The blowjob was enough to drive him out of his fucking mind, suction and pulling and need and fuck. Finally, he couldn't hold back any longer, and he started pushing, thrusting into Rig's mouth, watching his cock spread those lips wide. Rig just took him in, opening up, letting him in deep. Those long fingers wrapped around his hips, pulling him closer.

He fucking loved that, how he could give it to Rig and his cowboy just wanted more. He moved faster, headboard creaking under his hands. Fuck, he was close. Rig started swallowing, tongue licking and lapping.

"Rig!" He cried out, hips jerking his cock deep as he came, spunk shooting down Rig's throat.

Rig took him down, hands opening and closing in time to the body underneath him. He groaned, hips working more gently now, shuddering as his tongue slid over that agile tongue, Rig making sure he got every single bit of pleasure out of his climax.

"Best fucking mouth in the country, Rig."

Fuck, those eyes... Rig smiled, humming low around his prick. It sent another shudder through him and his cock jerked, and any thought of going soft disappeared just like that. He fucked Rig's mouth a moment longer, knew how much Rig loved having his prick between those swollen lips. Almost as much as he liked having it there himself.

With a groan, he pulled all the way out; time to turn the tables a little.

Rig moaned, almost protesting as he pulled free. "Sweet fuck."

"Sweet suck," he corrected, giving Rig a wink. He threw himself down next to Rig, arms stretching up over his head. "You gonna come ride?"

He got a chuckle and a nip, Rig's teeth sharp on his bicep. "You know it."

Then that tight ass settled against his cock, Rig straddling him. He moaned happily, hands sliding along Rig's thighs, over Rig's hips.

"Hey." Rig leaned down, gave him a deep, slow fucking kiss that tasted like him.

Rock slid his hands up over Rig's back, fingers trailing up that spine, as he opened wide, let Rig take that kiss wherever he wanted to. Rig moaned for him, arching under his touch like a great big cat.

So fucking sexy. All fucking his.

"Gonna help me get you ready?" he asked, one hand leaving that warm skin to wander beneath the pillows until he came up with the lube.

"Mmmhmm." Rock chuckled as Rig licked and kissed all along his jaw. His own personal slut wasn't listening. Hell, he could suggest anything and Rig would hum and keep rubbing.

"Gonna suck me again?" he teased, humping up so his cock rubbed along that ass.

"You need it again?" Rig pushed back, cock leaking between them.

He grinned and shook his head. "I was just making sure you were paying attention -- I want your ass."

"Thank God. My balls ache."

Laughing, he grabbed one of Rig's hands, spurting some of the slick stuff onto it. "Time to get ready then."

"Man, you want me to do *all* the work." Rig's laugh rang out, fingers slicking his cock up with a few quick pumps before disappearing around to that tight hole.

"You know it." He groaned as he watched Rig start to dance on his own fingers. "Sex on a fucking stick, Rig."

"Uh..." Rig groaned, head on his shoulder as Rig rode.

He reached down and around, feeling where Rig's fingers were sliding in and out of that sweet fucking ass. He teased one of his own in there with them, pushing it in, then going back to just feeling Rig's ass up again.

"T...tease." Rig bit his chest, groaning against his skin.

He jerked, grunted softly. "Only if I don't actually fuck you, and believe me. I'm going to fuck you."

"Good. Want it, deep and hard. Want to feel you all through supper."

Good and hard. He could so deliver on that. "Soon as you get those fingers out of there, it's all yours."

Rig grinned, those fingers wrapping around his cock, rubbing the tip against that slick, puckered hole.

"Fuck. Rig. And you called me a tease." He bucked a little, hoping to move them forward.

"Uh-huh. Fuck Rig." That little ring of muscles squeezed the tip of his prick, almost kissing it.

"More," he growled, grabbing Rig's hips and tugging Rig down hard as he bucked up into that perfect heat.

"Yes!" Rig groaned, head falling back, throat working. "Fuck. More."

"Lots more." He thrust up again, using his hands to guide Rig, keep his Rabbit moving up and down and meeting his hips. He got a great look, Rig's belly tight, sweat sheening the long body.

They moved together like they were made for this, not missing a beat, bodies slapping together with loud, dirty sounds. Rig kept muttering at him, the filthy words making him as crazy as the smell of sex and men and sweat.

"Sexy motherfucking slut." He growled, one hand leaving Rig's hip to wrap around that long, hard cock.

"Yours. Yours, Blue. Fuck, don't stop."

He shook his head. Rig always told him not to stop and he never did. Never would. He was going to fuck his motherfucking sexy slut until they put him in the goddamned ground. Rig's leg slipped and he pushed in deep, making Rig cry out, jerk.

"Oh, right fucking there." He nodded and pushed harder on his next thrust.

Those eyes rolled, Rig's lips open, wet. Parted. He grabbed the back of Rig's neck, bringing that beautiful mouth down to his for a no holds barred kiss.

Rig shot, ass squeezing him, spunk spraying over his belly.

"Yes..." He nodded, thrust up again and again, making Rig jerk and cry out, making that sweet body shudder and keep squeezing his cock.

Rig's hands were on his shoulders, keeping them going, staying right there with him. He held out as long as he could, thrusting and loving every fucking second, every squeeze and slide of their bodies together.

All of a sudden he was coming, shouting out and pushing deep as the spunk sprayed out of him.

"Mmm." That was a satisfied goddamn sound.

"Uh-huh." He grunted the word out, arms wrapping around Rig's body, holding onto his Rabbit.

Rig settled, face in his throat. "It'll all settle out, Blue, huh?"

"You know it."

He stroked that long back, fingers finding Rig's spine and rubbing over it. "You fucking know it."

Rig nodded. "Yessir. I surely do."

"Good."

Yeah, it was good -- him and Rig, it was all good.

**Personal Leave**

Printed in the United States
119732LV00006B/252/A

9 781934 166376